HUGO HAMILTON is the author of five novels, two memoirs and a collection of short stories. He was born and lives in Dublin.

From the reviews of *Disguise*:

'An eloquent and haunting book about identity and the construction of a self under duress. . . . Though much of the historic and personal material here is cruel and brutal, the tone of the book is oddly consoling. He does tenderness very well'   HERMIONE LEE, *Guardian*

'Subtle . . . a narrative that moves elegantly between past and present'   *Sunday Times*

'This novel is about identity, both personal and national, the vicissitudes of memory, the impossibility and necessity of love. The opening is thrilling but Hamilton knows the real story is in the repercussions. And the final chapter is almost unbearably moving, wonderfully understated, damn near perfect'
RACHEL SEIFFERT (author of *Afterwards*), *Financial Times*

'Stirringly honest and engaging'   *Scotsman*

'An exquisitely gifted writer'
JOSEPH O'CONNOR (author of *Star of the Sea*)

'Quite simply, this is one of the best books of the year . . . A tale of brilliance'   *Irish Examiner*

'Hugo Hamilton has fashioned a monumental theme. He brings the reader through a whole series of microcosms, dancing flash pictures of different societies, different times. They all contribute to an overwhelming sense of unease, an unsettling shrine to emotional fear. The book and its skill are the reality'   *Irish Sunday Independent*

'This is an intriguing and beautifully layered new novel by one of my favourite Irish authors. Hamilton writes with intelligence, grace and remarkable beauty. He's one of those novelists whose work never really leaves you'   *Gloss* magazine

'*Disguise* is not one to keep to yourself; it is a book that raises questions about the personal and collective identity from a man in the know'   *Image* magazine

---

By the same author

The Sailor in the Wardrobe
The Speckled People
Sad Bastard
Headbanger
Dublin Where the Palm Trees Grow
The Love Test
The Last Shot
Surrogate City

HUGO HAMILTON

Disguise

FOURTH ESTATE • London

Fourth Estate
An imprint of HarperCollins*Publishers*
77–85 Fulham Palace Road, Hammersmith, London W6 8JB

www.4thestate.co.uk
Visit our authors' blog at www.fifthestate.co.uk
Love this book? www.bookarmy.com

This Fourth Estate edition published 2009

I

First published in Great Britain by Fourth Estate in 2008

Copyright © Hugo Hamilton 2008

Hugo Hamilton asserts the moral right to be identified as the author of this work

A catalogue record for this book is available from the British Library

ISBN 978-0-00-731470-6

Printed and bound in Great Britain by Clays Ltd, St Ives plc

This novel is entirely a work of fiction. The names, characters and incidents
portrayed in it are the work of the author's imagination. Any resemblance to
actual persons, living or dead, events or localities is entirely coincidental.

For Coman and Theresa

125921

(detail from 'Szene aus der Hirschjagd/Scene from the Staghunt' by Joseph Beuys)

One

They must have been out of their minds with fear. They ran down to the basement holding hands, shouting, still half asleep, crashing into each other in the blackout. The children could feel the adults shaking. They could hear the panic in their voices. They could hear the sirens howling through the apartment blocks and the deep hum of organ music around the city as the planes arrived overhead.

When the first of the bombs came whistling down through the air, they huddled together praying. 'Now it's our turn, God help us.' They were so frightened that they lost their personalities. Some of them marked the nights of bombing in chalk on cellar walls. Defenceless creatures clustered together underground, holding their hands over their ears, while above them the black formation of planes crossed the night sky. Wave upon wave of them with deathly silences in between. They followed the descent of each bomb, trying to guess how close it was. They felt the earth jump each time and felt the force of the blast in their hair, along the scalp. It blew out the windows and sucked the slates off the roof. It cut through buildings and opened them up like the cross section of a doll's house, showing how people lived inside with their neat interiors, beds, dressers, tables and tea sets. Some of them perished in their apartments, either too late to flee into the basement or else deciding to stay and ignore their fear, comforting themselves with the last of the wine and their doomed black humour while the sky lit up with dropping candles, like a Christmas tree. The phosphor came spilling down the stairs, into the living rooms, gleaming white luminous fire trickling along the bedroom walls until everything was in flames.

Gregor Liedmann was asleep in his bed and never even woke up. He was almost three years old and went straight from his dream into death, surrounded by his pencils and his writing pad and the wooden ship that his grandfather Emil had made for him. His mother said he was very good with words. He was an early speaker and was already counting and writing the alphabet. Large letters sloping down the page at an angle. That's how he went to sleep every night, with the writing pad under his pillow and the sharp pencils around him which his mother then had to remove very carefully like a patient game of Mikado sticks to make sure he didn't wake up again. He was dreaming about spitting. He used to watch the two older boys across the landing holding on to the banisters and spitting down into the stairwell. He observed the spit falling silently, swaying on its way down and eventually hitting the polished floor below with a click. He got into trouble one day when the old woman with all the hats suddenly looked up and saw him. The older boys had disappeared by the time she came up the stairs to make a complaint, so he had to listen to her saying what a disgusting child he was, spitting down on people's heads. And though his mother told the woman that it was not the worst thing she could be hit by in these times, she was cross with Gregor afterwards and said she would take the pencils off him if he ever spat down the stairwell again.

2

Now it was one of the big blockbusters coming for him. Four thousand pounds of black steel packed with high explosives like a hard chocolate cake. His mother came running through the hallway, but she was thrown back by the blast and landed on the far side of the house with the ceiling on top of her. They found her in a bed of plaster, under a blanket of entwined batons and criss-crossed joists. When she woke up, they had to hold her back because she wanted to continue running into Gregor's bedroom which no longer existed. The back of the house was missing entirely. The boy gone. No sign of him left, or his room. Nothing but a shell of unfamiliar walls, rooms cut in half, missing doors and flaming architraves. If it wasn't for the brightness of the fires all around and the smoke and the neighbours holding her back, she would have walked straight out over the cliff, down into that emptiness left behind by her son.

They were still putting out the fires the next day, clearing the debris from the streets to make way for transport. The trees were raining cinders. People were lost and disoriented, walking in a daze. Everyone coughing, searching in the rubble, rescue workers picking up beams of blackened wood to see who might be underneath. The day was dark. And cold. There was a terrible silence and clouds of smoke hung over the city, keeping back the sun. Some of them got the idea of wearing bathing goggles against the dust. People were being carried away on pieces of wood, in barrows, on children's prams. Bodies covered in grey dust, naked, unrecognisable, red and black and pink, shrunken with no features left. Some of them fused together in the very position in which they had died so they had to be carried out in a charred embrace. In some places they found nothing more than a trace of life left behind, a liquid, a piece of grease, wax remains around a cup or a bent spoon. A melted button. Many of the basements were connected in a warren so they could escape from one house to the next all the way down the street. In one corridor underground, they found dead people huddled on both sides of a steel door, all hoping it would lead to air. The injured could be heard crying and moaning. A young girl standing on the street in a state of delusion with her head wrapped in a scarf, asking for an apple. Does anyone have an apple for me? she kept trying to say, even though most of her jaw was missing and she could hardly enunciate the words. And everywhere the names being called. Names echoing along the blackened hulls of apartment blocks, deep in the backyards where walls were still collapsing without notice in a profound rumble, making people run away in every direction all over again.

Gregor. Gregor, my pet.

She wandered through the streets, searching and calling for him as if he was playing outside with the other children. She returned to the ruin of her apartment block throughout the day and was comforted by neighbours. They had their own losses to deal with, but they took her in and shared their food with her. At night she would wake them all up calling for her son, believing that she had heard his voice. They knew the doctors had told her she could not have any more children. So she clung to the hope of finding her boy alive, searching for him every day, finding nothing after seven days but a shard of a pencil. She stopped to pick it up. The lead was missing, but she could clearly see the rounded imprint of a tiny black tube running through the wood. She held it in her hand for a while, knowing that it must have belonged to Gregor, then walked to the park where they were burying the dead. There she dug a small hole in the earth with a stick in order to bury this piece of a pencil, kneeling down for some time and praying for him.

She could no longer sense cold or hunger, only the loss of her child.

'What will I tell my husband?' she kept asking, which some took as a sign of extraordinary love and optimism. The more cynical and grief-hardened spoke with brutal clarity and told her she would be lucky if her husband ever came back. She cried openly when they said that. Spoke his name softly as if he was in the next room and would come out any minute to stand by her side. She spent her days wandering about, isolated in her grief, with nothing more to lose, and maybe that is what separated her from the others who were still focused with such vehemence on survival. While she increasingly lost interest in living, unable even to nourish herself, they continued their instinctive hunt for opportunities, searching for little deals and bargains that would help to keep them alive. They spoke with inspired doom and joked about their own fate, a sign that they understood the value of life all the more. They developed extraordinary faculties for suppressing their grief and concentrated on sniffing out food and warmth, chocolate, coffee, cigarettes, clinging on to the little luxuries that gave dignity and status to their lives. She had lost all these survival skills. She lost her sense of direction and could not recognise the streets any more. All the familiarity had been taken away. In some places the street names still stood on the corner, giving the numbers of the houses, though the street itself had disappeared and the whole district began to look like open country.

They could not understand a woman who no longer cared for herself. They feared the contagion in her grief. There was worse to come when the city fell into enemy hands and they made it clear they could not look after her indefinitely. She had gone from being a mother back to being a child, so they urged her to get out of the city. It's what she should have done long ago, they said, before the bombing started. She was more of a country girl, from outside Nuremberg. So they helped her write letters home to her father and mother. A neighbour managed to get her a train ticket south, halfway home as far as Jena.

So she fled the unforgettable smell of damp charred wood that still stuck in the back of everyone's throat, walked through more and more collapsed streets, took shelter from another wave of bombing in an underground station along the way, until she got to the southern cross where she waited for days to be allowed on a train. Everything was in chaos. A journey that took only three to four hours before the war now took her almost five days. People were fleeing everywhere, soldiers making their way to the front in the opposite direction. Luggage left behind. Children separated from their parents. Lawless boys roaming around, fighting and stealing food, anything they could get from vulnerable people on the move. Even more distressing, an adult taking a piece of bread off a child.

She stayed with some elderly people in Jena who had lost two sons in the war. After weeks and weeks, when it was already spring, her father finally came to collect her. As it turned out, her mother was already dead and her older brother was missing in action on the front. So her father seemed more and more determined to rescue what was left of the family and came to take her down south to safety. He came in his truck and perhaps it was one of the miracles of war, that he found his daughter despite all the odds. They watched as he embraced her and held her for a long time against his big round stomach before they left again, heading south, away from the Russian front.

Her father had avoided conscription for the early part of the war because of illness. Overweight and unable to walk very well, he continued working as a delivery man, groceries and hardware. But as the war was approaching the end and they began calling up old men and young boys, he was called up too, in spite of his poor health. They placed him in a uniform that was too small for him and gave him orders to deliver a squad of new recruits to the front line and to return with a consignment of weapons that were in need of repair. But instead of delivering the faulty weapons, he held on to them in the back of the truck and invented a job for himself that would keep him out of the war. With instructions to that effect on paper, he and his childhood friend Max went from town to town on a bogus mission, collecting defective weapons. An ingenious scheme at a time when every weapon counted. As the war began to be fought village by village, farm by farm, this phantom mission seemed more and more credible. He had turned shirking into a heroic piece of patriotism. The back of his truck had a collection of old rifles with tags indicating their origins and what was wrong with the firing mechanism or with the barrel. He never took them anywhere to be repaired, just drove around with the same weapons, adding one or two here and there, or merely changing the date on the tags. It was a risky enterprise, a flagrant act of desertion. Even more so now on this rescue mission to bring his daughter home at the very end of the war.

As they drove south, mostly in the early hours of the morning or late at night, she sometimes had to put her head down or travel in the back with the weapons.

Occasionally, she even had to get out and meet him further along the road after a checkpoint. As they got closer to Nuremberg, they stayed with people he knew from his travels. He had a network of connections, mostly women, a trail of girlfriends throughout the countryside, women whose husbands were away at the front, women who loved his stories and his optimism and, above all, his singing. He joked about his job and said it was not only defective weapons he was searching for but also defective women.

As they moved on each time, he kept trying to comfort his daughter with his humour, with all the jokes and stories he had gathered on his elliptical trips around the countryside. She wept constantly and he sang songs to her. But nothing could bring her child back.

The roads were congested. Everybody was on the move, with horses and carts, trolleys and bicycles, some with nothing but the clothes they stood in. Some of them found it hard to know where to go and sat on their suitcases with sad eyes looking into the distance. People were fleeing with terrible stories that caused even more panic along the roads. They were returning from the east in the same cattle trucks on which people were previously sent away. And there in this great drift of people looking for a place to stay and to not have to move ever again, her father left the truck parked at the edge of a small town in order to get some more fuel on the black market and came back instead with a three-year-old boy.

In the middle of the night, half asleep, she waved her hand and turned away. She didn't want somebody else's child. But her father got in with the toddler on his arm, setting him down on the seat between them, speaking with a softness in his voice that tranquillised her. He sang a song to keep the boy happy and to keep her happy at the same

8

time. He explained that he had been given the boy by an old woman who had come all the way from the East, from Danzig, and become very ill along the road. The boy had lost his parents, but now she was unable to look after him any more. He showed her a photograph of his daughter and assured her that the boy would be well taken care of now.

'Look, he's the image of Gregor,' he kept repeating. Perhaps only a few months younger at the most. A beautiful, healthy boy, who would grow up just the same as her own son. He had found his mother now and she had found her missing son. In the ungodly scheme of things, this was a story of double misfortune turned into multiple good luck. A young mother who had lost her only son, matched up with a son whose mother had been taken from him. What an extraordinary reunion this was.

She looked at the boy with revulsion. He was frightened and cold, snivelling and coughing. His eyes were infected. He was holding his ear and sucking a button on the shoulder of his woollen jumper at the same time, staring into the dark outside the windscreen, worried what was keeping his mother and why she was not coming to collect him. There were two barrels of green snot under his nose, which her father tried to wipe off with the sleeve of his uniform, but the boy only flinched and the green lines veered away across his face. He started shaking his head and trying to stand up with the pain in his ear, crying, or whining, a sound that resembled the squeak of a door opening very slowly.

The boy understood little German. God knows where he was from. There were no records, no documents, no indication what had happened to him or how he got here. He had no identity. No name. But none of that mattered any more now, because he would be given a new name and a new identity and a new, ready-made biography.

9

Her father began to call him Gregor, even though she tried to stop him from doing so. He gave the boy a sweet and started the engine. 'What am I to do with him now?' he pleaded. 'Send him to an orphanage, give him away to the Red Cross, or some convent?' As they drove on through the night with the rain falling and the windscreen wipers making everyone drowsy, he let the boy hold the steering wheel and he soon stopped crying and fell asleep with the vibrations of the engine and the hot air in the cab and the warmth of two people beside him on either side.

Along the way, he stopped the truck once more and held her hand. Looked her in the eyes with that persuasive intimacy for which he was so well known and so loved by people everywhere. He placed her arm around the sleeping boy's shoulder and told her in his firm, fatherly way that she would soon learn to love this boy.

'Promise me one thing,' he said to her. 'Promise that you will never, ever tell anyone that this is not your own son. Not even your husband.'

He made her shake hands with him. Then he made her smile and told her that nothing mattered, as long as she called him Gregor. He was her son now, written on her documents. Before long she would forget that she ever lost her baby boy in the bombing. They were not out of trouble yet, but he would bring her to safety. The war would be over very soon. Her husband would come back from the front in time and find her. They would be together again as a family, just as before, eating breakfast around the table and laughing, all three of them. In a big album, she would keep all the funny stories and the photographs of Gregor. He would grow up around her imagination. He would go to school every morning with a big hug and return in the afternoon with his own stories. She would buy him a new writing pad and new pencils so that he could continue learning the alphabet, just as before, kneeling down in the kitchen with the pad open on one chair and his dinner on another chair, so that he could alternate between eating and writing, one word, then a forkful of food, followed by another word.

Nobody could tell the difference.

Two

He has reached the long avenue of trees now. They stand in a guard of honour lining the road on either side, straight and tall. There is one missing on the right, like a soldier fallen over in a faint, while the rest of them remain upright in position. They say these avenues were created all over Europe long ago to shield the horses and the passengers in their carriages from the sun and also to provide shelter from the cutting wind and snowdrifts in winter. Now the sun flashes between the trees, throwing black and white stripes across the tarmac. Somebody switching a light on and off, making it difficult for him to see while driving. There is a warning sign erected for motorists showing a car bashing into a tree with black exclamation marks springing up from the point of impact.

It's a warm day at the end of September. Gregor is driving through the flat landscape south of Berlin, down to the disused farm where his former wife Mara is spending the summer with her stepsister Katia and her husband Thorsten. They have invited him to take part in the fruit gathering over two days. Mara phoned to say it would be great if he could join them. He would not be alone for the weekend.

What did she mean by that? Alone without whom? Even solitude is a communal act, so they say. Gregor and Mara have been separated for years. They still live apart, but lately they have begun to see each other a lot more. And maybe she had invited him in order to prove something, to repair things between them, like a family caretaker, keeping everyone in touch. She explained to him that she had invited a 'heap of people' out to the farm to pick the apples and she wanted him to be there.

'Before your son disappears off to Africa,' she said.

Their son, Daniel, has inherited money and has decided to spend some of it working in the Sudan with his girlfriend Juli.

The farm is situated outside the former East German town of Jüterbog. Daniel got a job as an extra on a film set there a few years back, where the Russian Army had been garrisoned after the war, right up to the nineties. After which everything suddenly seemed to go backwards in time. It must have been quite an event, seeing the soldiers packing up and leaving after such a long time, trucks pulling out and belching fumes for the last time. History receding and the buildings in which they were billeted for all those years through the Cold War torn down and turned into a film set, which ironically made the outskirts of the town look like ruins at the end of the Second World War. For the people living there it was one last glimpse of those terrible years before the town and the landscape finally settled back into a kind of ancient anonymity. It has become quite empty now. Everyone has fled from here into the cities and they say the land is already so deserted in some places that it will eventually be handed back to nature. The forests will grow back one day and the wolves will return, maybe even the bears. Who knows, all the fairy tales that came with them as well?

The mushroom season has begun. It has rained overnight, and Gregor thinks it might be a nice idea to arrive with some fresh wild mushrooms. He's brought wine, but the mushrooms would be really thoughtful. He stops the car at the edge of a forest and steps out. He can smell the familiar morning scent of the earth and the vegetation. It gives him a feeling that is hard to describe. An echo of childhood? Of home? Of long ago?

From the boot of the car he takes a fruit basket which belongs to Mara. He walks off into the forest, carrying it on his arm, the way he used to do with his father and mother. He's good at spotting the dark places where mushrooms grow, those tiny flecks of unusual colour, shades of brown and beige and white along the floor. He's good at making the connection between varieties of trees and what might be expected to grow in the vicinity. He makes instant decisions about frilly aprons and gaudy shapes that are attractive and treacherous at the same time. A skill that he received from his father, one that he rejected for years and has only recently taken up again.

He's good at keeping directions in mind. He has always been quick to memorise his surroundings. Always mapping. Always aware of geography. Another skill he was taught by his father, or is that a faculty which has been sharpened by the nature of his own origins?

While concentrating on the natural signposting along the floor, he comes across a bomb crater in the forest. It disturbs the sediment of his memory. He's always had to manage his past and there were devices, certain skills he developed as a young man, that could filter out the unwanted. Sifting and sorting was a phrase he brought with him from somewhere to describe this mental activity in which each person compiles their own memories in such a way that they can live with themselves.

Here, where he least expected it, he finds himself standing in front of this random piece of evidence from the past. Lots of people would pass it by thinking it was a perfectly natural dip in the earth. There is nothing growing inside the crater, and maybe that is what has caught his eye.

The funny thing is that he instinctively wishes he could show it to Mara. Wait till she sees this, he finds himself saying almost aloud. How long have they been separated now and still he carries on reporting to her internally? They never divorced. She lived with an architect for years in Berlin, but that came to an end because she could not bring herself to divorce Gregor. He lived abroad for years, but still they continued to keep in touch. A distant, proxy sort of relationship in which they went on with their own separate lives, returning to each other from time to time in order to compare information.

He marks the place in his mind, in case he needs to come back here, should he want to show it to her. A turning to the right off the main sand track, after the spot where he saw the wild boar footprints and some bits of thick, wiry fur, where they must come to drink at night and roll around in the mud and maybe fight. Right in the heart of the forest, where the track straightens out and leads through a dark hall of mature trees. He has the impression that he's standing in a church or a great mansion, with the occasional beam of light coming down from a high window. The silence is almost absolute. A place from which all sound has been withdrawn.

If memory has a physical shape, then it must be something like this, Gregor thinks. The interior of the forest with paths leading through vast interconnecting rooms where you can get so easily lost.

He finds himself staring into this large hole in the same way that he would stare at an animal, holding his breath and not moving. It's like being in the presence of some great elk which will be gone again with a burst of movement as soon as he blinks. Not a sound. Not even the soft transfer of indoor air. It seems to be staring back at him, asking him questions, this bomb which has missed its target. He feels the shock of it going through him even sixty years after the event, the wind suck and the earth shower and the violent tremor underfoot. It gives him the sensation that people must get with a near-miss traffic accident, unable to figure out why they have been picked out by this contorted luck, the only person to have escaped unharmed. Standing beside such a vicious bomb crater, he feels like man living in the afterlife.

The crater itself measures about the size of a swimming pool, ten or twelve metres across but shaped like a funnel, perfectly round, almost like something produced by nature itself. There is a thin layer of branches and twigs lying at the centre. The earth has levelled off at the edges over time. There is an old, damaged oak tree standing next to it, but most of the other trees around it are conifers, reaching up straight. Who knows, maybe those trees were all saplings then or maybe didn't even exist and the bomb actually fell in an open field, on a clear and starry night, with only the ragged oak tree to witness the thud and the scattering of soil and the thunder of planes receding into the distance.

All over the city and the region, they still find unexploded bombs from time to time, on building sites, on road-widening projects. It's like a folk memory in the ground. Full of shrapnel. And remains. Lots of remains, buried in shallow earth. The remains of soldiers, men of whom it is hard to tell any more on which side they fought and for what? The remains of people who never belonged to any side. People who have gone beyond pain and grief and hunger and resentment. Beyond memory even.

What the hell? Gregor thinks to himself. It's probably not a bomb crater at all. He spent long enough in forests as a child with his father to know that this might be nothing more than a dumping pit. People used to dig large holes in order to bury their refuse in the forest. And maybe this is the physical shape of memory, ultimately, a common landfill site. A hole in the ground intended for items that once clamoured to be remembered but then turn out to mean nothing after all.

He continues to collect his mushrooms until he feels he has enough. The basket is almost full, and yet so light in comparison to mass. He turns and traces his way back along that instant map he's made for himself in the forest. By the time he comes past the crater again, he has already dismissed it in his mind. He hardly takes any notice of it now and doesn't stop to have another look. Instead, he sees only the exit ahead of him, a small green light at the end of the path where the trees cut off and the fields begin. And when he comes back out into the open at last, he has the feeling of lights coming on again after a power cut.

As he drives on, away from the forest once more, he passes through a farm of wind turbines standing in the fields. Dozens of them spreading right across the flat, open landscape. They stretch out into the distance, all facing in the same direction, gliding across the earth in formation. The ones further away look tiny, but those up close look enormous, casting spectacular shadows across the land around them and towering over the road, making him feel small as he drives right through them. Tall, silent birds on either side, with long white necks, lazily turning their wings. There is very little wind and some of them are hardly moving at all. Some are already completely still while others are settling down as though they've just landed.

Three

What is Gregor Liedmann's first real memory?

A moment at night, in the dark, sitting in the cab of a truck between two people. There is a woman on his right-hand side and a fat man on his left, driving. The woman must be his mother and the fat man must be his grandfather, Emil. There is a pain in his ear, like the point of a sharp knife being pushed right into the eardrum. He wants the pain to stop. It must have been a terrible ear infection, he imagines now, so the fat man smiles and gives him two sweets for the journey, one red one for now, and one green one to keep in his pocket. He has the red sweet in his mouth, a hard-boiled sweet with a special raspberry flavour that he has never had before. He still gets the taste of it when he thinks about that journey, sitting between two warm people, watching the needle jumping on the speedometer. The fat man has two hands on the wheel and sometimes he takes one off to change the gears. He watches the steering wheel spinning free, out of the man's hands, as they make a turn around a corner until the road straightens out and the hands grip the wheel again.

He knows they are talking to each other quietly over the top of his head, but he cannot hear anything or understand what they are saying because it's not his language. He can just about hear the fat man calling the name Gregor from time to time and patting him on the head. His name is Gregor now and he is sitting in a truck going to a new place with a red sweet in his mouth, as red and shining as the tail lights on the truck. The woman has a blanket spread out over her knees and over his own knees to keep warm.

Then the knife is back in his ear again and he throws off the blanket. He tries to stand up in the cab to get away from the pain, but the woman pulls him down again. The fat man allows him to hold the steering wheel. He takes him on his lap and lets him drive the truck with his arms around him. He feels afraid at first, but it feels very warm, sitting on the man's knees with the smooth throbbing of the engine in his hands. The man takes a hold of his hand to place it on the gear lever, under his own hand, while he changes gears. He can hear the cogs catching and the engine sounding deeper. He has worked out how to drive the truck by himself and wants to be a truck driver when he grows up. The pain is gone and the road is straight and flat from there on, but he cannot go to sleep because he has to keep his eyes on the wheel and on the lights shining ahead through the rain and the windscreen wiper swinging from side to side. He never wants to get off the truck again. He wants to keep driving forever. He has to do a pee in his pants and feels the warmth spreading around his legs, but the fat man just keeps talking and laughing.

Gregor is now in his early sixties. He has spent years as a musician living in Toronto and also in Ireland, travelling on a strange, empty sort of journey around the world before he eventually came back to live in this calm suburb of Berlin. His face has become quite familiar here, cycling past the red-brick church with its three spires of differing heights and a set of melancholy bells. He's often seen shuddering along the cobbled streets with his back straight and his trumpet in a case over his shoulder. He makes his living mostly as a music teacher now. For such a tall man, his bike appears to be a little too small, a borrowed child's bike. His long legs forked over the saddle as he waits at the traffic lights. On his way home, he usually stops at the café with the art deco furniture to read the paper. He's known by name in most of the shops. In the bakery with the till inside a glass shrine. In the newsagent with the blues playing all day and the candles lit every afternoon. In the Spanish wine dealer's and in the bar with the stuffed flying seagull hanging from the ceiling.

Perhaps he fits in best here with all the other ageing anarchists and draft dodgers from the late sixties. All those stone throwers with long hair and beards and dirty fingernails who turned their backs on their parents and shook the country by the neck and then settled down eventually to become parents themselves. The true veterans of sixties optimism, the anti-Vietnam War brigade who shook off militarism and authority. Flower-power people who blurred the boundaries forever between men and women during that golden era when craziness became a virtue and things took on an inspired, meaningless beauty of their own.

Many of the people around here have also travelled a lot, collecting cultural idiosyncrasies from around the world before returning to live in this semi-eccentric, semi-chic and ethnically mixed suburb of Berlin. It's a district full of borderline people who never fully gave up their anarchism. Musicians and actors and activists and socialists who altered course at one point or another to become second-hand clothing merchants or furniture dealers or tea specialists or small-time importers of rugs and African art, goods that cannot be had in mainstream shops. People who worked as tour guides all over South America and Indochina for years and then came back to start up quiet businesses which would allow them to stay at home and have a late family, but not look like they surrendered. Anything but orthodox medicine or law or public service. People with a trail of marriages and relationships behind them. Like the man in the organic cheese shop who studied architecture and had two girlfriends at the same time and could not make up his mind between them and ended up losing both. Like the lesbian mother in the hairdresser's with the Virgin Mary in the window who has one child from each of three marriages. Like the owner of the second-hand furniture store who sits at the back of the shop playing his electric guitar all day until a customer comes in and he has to switch off.

Every city has its cultural and ethnic frontiers. Up on the main street, he lines up at the checkout in the Turkish supermarket with women in headscarves. Mothers who are unable to correct their own Berlin-born children in the host language, mothers who cannot tell the difference between hazelnuts and chestnuts until they hear the words in their home language. Turkish men outside on the benches talking and touching each other gently at the elbow to make a point with the same care and affection that they give to aubergines or apples. Families together on benches in summer drinking tea. The edgy tension of young Turkish men and the throbbing Eastern beat blasting out from a car. He hears the impact of their culture taking shape in his own language, a cool kind of slouching, immigrant slang that has taken hold in the city.

He has become part of the older generation, replacing the war generation that went before them, soon to be replaced themselves by new generations of fathers and mothers from all kinds of places, sitting on the little wall watching their children in the sandy playground at the side of the church. They once grew vegetables in this church-yard during the war. Now the children dig in the sand with little spades. Voices of children echoing around the streets. Lots of children everywhere and cool fathers pushing buggies with iPods to mark the progress of generations going forward all the time and everything becoming younger and newer and more modern than anyone ever thought possible.

And maybe this is the right time to start reclaiming his memory. His wife Mara still wants him to search for things that might place his true origins beyond doubt.

Lately, they have been meeting for coffee, setting off on their bikes, sitting in the Greek restaurant with a candle between them. She arrives round at his apartment carrying a basket of fruit or a cake, holding it with a flat hand underneath. She's usually dressed up with earrings, ringing the bell and running her fingers through her hair. Her bicycle has been left outside his apartment frequently, locked up against the railings in the inner courtyard overnight. She appears on his balcony, watering the flowers. All these outward signs of intimacy must mean something. Their lives are far more relaxed now. They have become more accepting. They have reached a point where they can live with contradictions. They can surrender to a cheap pop song, for instance, which they might have switched off when they were younger and more uncom-promising about the kind of things they allowed themselves to be shaped by. Now they can look back at a lifetime without accusation. Perhaps even with fondness, nostalgia. They can now calmly go back and sift through everything again.

Why does Gregor remember that moment in the truck so well, more than any other? Why is everything else such a blur, before and after? Sometimes he cannot distinguish between his memory and what he has been told, between what he experienced and what he has read in books. He is made up of all those things that he has heard about and read about. All the things he rejected as much as the things he accepted, what he believed as much as what he didn't believe.

This journey in the truck remains a real memory. A concrete recollection. No question about that. Gregor recalls the pictures of his grandfather at home when he grew up. The innocent appearance of Grandfather Emil in uniform just after he enlisted in the First World War, that boyish idealism before battle. He remembers the photographs of the bloated, beer-drinking grandfather, much later at the start of the Second World War, that mischievous smile for which he was so well liked.

He can remember him singing, or humming, as he drove the truck. Even though Gregor must have been half deaf with the ear infection, he could feel the vibrations broadcasting through his chest. He will never forget the warmth of this man behind him, letting him drive the truck. And maybe it's so vivid in his memory now because that journey came to an end. In the middle of the night, the truck stopped and they had to get out, with the blanket over their heads now to hold off the rain. Is that the reason why he remembers it so well, because he wanted to get back on the truck and never get off again?

He cannot remember when he ate the second sweet, because he has no memory of a green sweet, only the red one. He thinks he lost it, because he searched for it in his pocket. He doesn't know how it went missing.

Are the happiest memories always overshadowed by loss? Just as the bad memories must be counterweighted by good times? Maybe this missing boiled sweet is somehow caught up with the larger loss which cannot be accessed any more. It replaces all the missing people and places and events that he has forgotten. Even as an adult, he still has the recurring dream of finding the green sweet in a place where he never looked before. Some inside pocket he forgot to check.

He can recall very little else from that night. He must have fallen asleep in the truck, because the fat man woke him up, calling, 'Gregor, Gregor.' Again and again he heard his soft, singing voice, two descending notes that will forever be associated with the journey being over, the cruelty of waking up with a pain in his ear and the time in the truck coming to an end.

The fat man opened the door and the cold morning air came in. He lifted him down and helped the woman out. He had to stay with the woman, because the fat man had to go elsewhere. He promised to be back soon, that much he could understand from his gestures alone. The fat man smiled and held up a fuel canister, shook it to show that it was empty and pointed down the street. He saw him getting on the truck and driving away. There was a house on fire at the end of the road, he remembers. The rain was falling and the flames were going up into the sky at the same time. The sky was orange. The fire brigade was standing in front of the house spraying water through the windows. The woman took him into the train station, where they waited, wrapped in the blanket, with lots of other people in the same room and steam rising from their wet clothes. They waited and waited and waited, but the fat man never came back.

Four

He is glad to see the shape of the house where Mara is staying. The low roof surrounded by trees and open farmlands. He has been here before, but it's some time ago now, in the spring. This time there is a tight blonde stubble left behind in the fields by the machines and rectangular bales of hay placed at intervals. He has switched off the music in the car so he can hear the crows in the nearby woods. Nobody comes out to greet him, so he remains sitting in the car for a moment with the window open, listening. He's not accustomed to the lack of formality in the country, with no doorbell. He wonders if he should go to the front of the house or whether it's best to go round the back. He thinks of calling them on his mobile phone, but that seems a little absurd, a real city thing to do.

He takes the bag with the bottles of wine and the basket of mushrooms from the boot of the car. The main door of the farmhouse is facing out towards an ancient cast-iron pump in the middle of the yard. The yard is deserted, surrounded by farm buildings. The porch over the main door is half covered in creeper and some of the windows, too, are overgrown with wild roses. The place looks uninhabited, but then he sees Mara's car parked at the other end and hears voices round the back. A child laughing somewhere. And Mara coming towards him with her arms out.

'Gregor. We didn't hear you coming,' she says.

'I thought I was in the wrong place,' Gregor says.

He gives her the bag with the wine. Then he holds out the basket of wild mushrooms.

'Mushrooms,' Mara exclaims.

She seems surprised, but her smile is quick to come back. She doesn't expect him to explain. She knows the story of mushrooms in his family.

Gregor's father was a hunting fanatic, shaped by war, a man who wanted his son to stay close to the earth and develop heightened survival instincts. So he taught him how to collect mushrooms and berries and plants which could be cooked and eaten in times of decline. On his birthday, Gregor was often given a survival manual. He was brought up to prepare himself for catastrophe. Ready for things that had already happened and for even worse to come. He grew up with all that Boy Scout knowledge of how to light fires without matches, how to preserve food, how to live in freezing conditions. By the time he was nine, he was ready to spend his first night out in the forest alone. His father wanted him to be able to survive long after the rest of civilisation had been extinguished, though he never explained what he should do if he was the last person left on earth.

As a boy, he loved this challenge. It was a great game. His father was as tough and uncompromising as the elements. He preferred the laws of nature to the conventions of society. He trusted nobody and made comparisons between animals and human behaviour. He wanted Gregor to understand the world as a contest, to respect nature as the only guide to what was genuine and what was false. To stay alive he had to become an expert on poison, on treachery. So his father set tests for him in the forest.

Contrived a family game of Russian roulette with deadly mushrooms in which Gregor would stand in front of three varieties in separate containers, all of them looking very much the same. One of them fatal. The others safe to eat.

His mother would stand looking on from the hunting lodge that his father bought for half-nothing after the war, the one place in the world where he felt his rule was absolute, this brutal contest with the environment in which he triumphed over everything.

'Have you gone mad?' she would say. 'Klaus, is this really necessary? Have we not had enough of this in the war?'

But that was precisely the point of it all. His father never got past the rules of war. Those split-second judgements, those warrior instincts which people had adapted so successfully into sporting activities, were still regarded by him as the ground rules of life and death. You had to be ready to return to the wild, to the most basic forms of life. Perhaps all this was an oblique way of describing what his father went through for years in Russian captivity but never wished to speak about directly. Gregor stood there in the first glorious moment of peacetime in Europe and held his family's life in his hands. It was his choice. And whatever he picked out would be put into the meal. 'Are you sure?' His father would ask him once more with a sceptical expression, because you could not guess. Guessing was defeat.

With his nervous mother looking on, he would pick the variety he thought was safe. She was a martyr, maybe half hoping they would all be poisoned one day so that she could then say to her husband, 'Look, I told you so.' She was also profoundly shaped by war and hunger and hated any game with food. She hated seeing food wasted and constantly made people eat up, long after they had no appetite, which is possibly why Gregor never feels hungry, even now.

It was she who cooked the mushrooms and Gregor remembers the smell exploding in the forest air. They would eat the meal and his father would smile to himself. Only he knew for sure whether they were eating the lethal substance or not. They could all be found dead weeks later, lying around the mountain shack in various poses of agony, holding their stomachs, tongues swollen, dehydrated, bowels running, a delusional scrawl made with fingernails along the earth as they dragged themselves away in search of water.

Gregor never knew the conclusive result of his decision until much later. He knew the mildly poisonous mushrooms would manifest themselves within hours, but the deadly ones would only show up after twenty-four hours, or after a few days, even weeks later, by which time there was very little that could be done. The best mycologist in the world could not save them. He knew that some mushrooms were very deceptive. After all the vomiting and cramps, there would follow a strange kind of remission where you felt much better and even started laughing at the idea of being poisoned, just before you died. There are some varieties that have only recently been declared poisonous, varieties that people have been eating for years and which have only now begun to kill. In Poland, just across the border from where they stand now, a mother and daughter were recently killed by repeated ingestion of a milky green mushroom that was always safe and that he remembers choosing himself many times in the test.

One day he failed to make the right choice. He must have been about thirteen or fourteen, a time of innocence, before the truth was revealed to him about many things. One fine day in autumn, just like this one, he suddenly realised he had made the wrong decision. Within an hour or two of eating, Gregor began to see the world in blue. They were out along the trail, with his father ahead, holding the gun on his arm, pointed downwards, half cocked. His mother had stayed behind at the lodge, reclining in the hammock with a magazine on her lap and the portable radio playing the local American Army station. Country songs fading into the distance behind them as they walked further and further into the trees until the music was only a faint memory, far away on the other side of the mountain.

Everything turned monochrome, as though he was looking through a shard of blue glass. His father had become a giant blue insect ahead of him. The tree trunks turned navy. The grass and the weeds, a mat of blue fur along the ground. He thought of his mother's fashion magazines, with all the blue handbags and sunglasses and lotions with the prices written underneath. Blue women in brassieres and corsets. Women in tweed suits half sitting on the bonnet of sports cars.

He began to feel the nausea. He went on for a while without saying a word, afraid to stop and tell his father that they were all going to die. Afraid of his father's disappointment at finding out that his family would be extinguished and the rest of civilisation would go on as before. His father kept striding away to his death without a word. Maybe he could endure much more. In the war he ate maggots. He ate gruel that would have killed a wild boar. He ate insects and bits of fungus and kept it all down with the kind of formidable mental discipline and a stomach as indestructible as an enamel bucket.

Did his father get it wrong? Did he really allow the family to consume the poisonous food as part of the lesson? Did he deliberately place three poisonous varieties in the bowls, like a double bind, or was it a genuine mistake? He thought of his mother already writhing in her hammock, tearing out photographs of women in brassieres, reaching for the glass of iced blue wine on the porch of the hunting lodge.

Gregor staggered on his feet, his blue father swaying ahead of him along the path. The earth swirling, the same way that it did when he used to spin himself around as a child, his first experience of narcotics. He wanted to call his father back and explain what was happening, but then he collapsed.

He woke up running, half carried by his father. Minutes later, they were driving through the blue landscape, down into the nearest town where all the people were blue in the streets. But then, as soon as he got to the hospital, all the colours became normal once more. Just as suddenly as the blue wash had covered his eyes, it disappeared. The nurses measuring his pulse did not have blue faces. 'It's gone,' he told them. 'The blue colour is gone.' He heard his father speaking in a low voice to the doctors, giving the name of the mushroom they had eaten, saying it was absolutely impossible that the boy was poisoned. He swore with his hand on his heart that he would never leave something like that to chance. Luck was not something he would want his son to base his life on. So the only explanation left was that Gregor must have had an allergy. Or more than likely, his father said, that he made it all up. Gregor's pulse and breathing were fine. So were the blood tests and the urine tests. He told his mother that he never wanted to eat mushrooms again. He said he was finished with the forest, but his father said that was all nonsense, more like falling off the bike. The only thing to be done was to get back up.

Mara has put the mushrooms inside the house in the shade. She comes out and pulls Gregor by the arm, over to a table set under a tree where the rest are sitting under the shade.

'We're just having second breakfast,' she says.

He approaches the table and goes around shaking hands with everyone. Thorsten, Mara's brother-in-law, rushes around to get him a chair, finding an even spot on the flagstones. Katia is there with her five-year-old boy, Johannes. She is pregnant and sits with the sunshine coming through the tree, landing directly onto her belly. The skin is so taut that her naval protrudes like an embossed symbol. Martin, Gregor's best friend, gets up to give him a big embrace, slapping him on the back.

'What kept you?' he asks in a friendly way. 'We've been working here for hours.'

'Sure. I believe you,' Gregor returns.

'Gregor has collected all these wild mushrooms for the dinner,' Mara says. She whips away some of the crumbs from the table and sets out a new place, pours coffee. There is a basket of fresh bread in the middle. One or two wasps hover around the jam.

'You haven't really started already?' Gregor asks.

'They were up at six in the morning,' Mara says, nodding towards Thorsten and Katia.

'We were delayed,' Thorsten says. 'There was a young deer lost in the orchard when we came to start in the morning. Running in every direction, completely frantic. We had to leave the ladders for a while and disappear until it found its way back out through the gate. Otherwise, it would have run itself against the fence all the time.'

Beyond the orchard wall, Gregor can see the outline of a tall ladder leaning into one of the trees. He wants to tell them about the bomb crater in the forest, but instead he tells them how the forests are full of mushrooms. Mara seems happy that he has arrived. She tells him that Daniel is on his way, with his girlfriend.

He finds himself wondering if he would ever manage alone in the wild without other people. What if the new catastrophe really does come? All those survival skills taught to him by his father seem to be of little use now, sitting here around the table. And how long could you survive mentally, that was the question? Living alone in the city is sometimes a struggle in itself, but there is a comfort in the anonymity and belonging that he finds there. He needs the reassurance of the streets, the clustering of people, the quiet feeling of support provided by their numbers. Even those moments of aggression experienced in the city bring some kind of odd confirmation of life. He needs to be able to sit in a bar, without speaking, just knowing that other people are around him. He is afraid of emptiness. After all that training by his father, he thinks he may be useless in situations of great calamity. When the next great disaster approaches and people are running in all directions again, Gregor feels he might end up being a coward. Who knows, he may not even realise how bad things are and keep going on in some naive delusion that everything is fine. In distress, he might make all the wrong decisions, pick the wrong mushrooms. Ultimately, he may have ended up exactly the same as all the other hopelessly interdependent people living in the city, unable to live without cups and spoons and takeaway coffee. Helpless without newspapers and the Internet and public transport and places to congregate. Helpless without the city's memory coming up everywhere through the streets. Helpless without the shelter of history.

Five

Gregor Liedmann grew up thinking that he had been preserved, like a dead animal. He had reasons to suspect that he was not the biological son of his parents. There were certain discoveries he had made which convinced him that he was, in fact, an orphan and that he was Jewish. At some point he decided to run away from home and eventually ended up in Berlin in the late sixties, a city full of peeling facades and people on the run from something or another. Whenever he was asked, he would explain that he had been found as a three-year-old boy among refugees during the last days of the war and that he had replaced a child of the same age who had been lost in the bombing. In other words, he had stepped into the shoes of a dead German boy. He had taken on his identity, his name, his date of birth, his religion, his entire existence. He had grown up in the south of Germany, in the suburbs of Nuremberg, the only son in a Catholic family. His parents had revealed nothing to him, but he had come across some evidence which suggested that he was a changeling, an impostor living a surrogate life inside the persona of a deceased German. Every time he looked at himself in the mirror, it strengthened his conviction that he was not one bit like them. His mother was an anxious woman who spent her life making lists to pass the time. His father was an obsessive hunter who filled the house to bursting with antlers and stuffed animals. And maybe it was no wonder that Gregor felt a bit like an exhibit in a natural history museum. It was only when he started a new life in Berlin that he could be himself again. He felt a huge weight lifting off his shoulders being able to tell people that he was originally from the East, that he was a Jewish survivor and that he had no relatives left alive.

There was no proof, however, no document, no testament, no reliable witness, no primary memory to substantiate any of this because he was so small when it all happened. Only the word of his uncle Max, the man with one eye who came to visit and once revealed something unintentionally and whose memory remained contested. Gregor can remember seeing him at the end of the war. Another clear recollection of standing outside a building with his mother and seeing a sick man being carried out by the soldiers. The soldiers are American, he knows that now. And the sick man is Uncle Max. But then his mother stopped him from looking, buried his face in her coat.

There are other flash memories which he still tries to place in order. He recalls seeing people lying on the ground in the street. He recalls planes flying low overhead. The sight of a town being bombed and houses collapsing right behind him. He is always in the company of his mother in these situations, though he cannot be sure if it is the same woman in each scene, only the feeling of holding hands and being taken care of. He has no idea of chronology and finds it difficult to place these recollections in any single line, to verify them or separate them from what he has read or received since then. These memories fit the pattern of flight from the East. They are all associated with being in a hurry, with people running, with great fear all around him.

He remembers waiting in a room. Maybe it was not just one room, but several rooms, one after the other. Long hours sitting on a bench with his mother constantly looking up to see who was coming in the door. He must have read everything in her face, looked at her eyes to try and understand what was going on.

And that one solid memory remains of standing in the street with soldiers all around. Unable to understand what anyone was saying to him, he refused to take anything from them, didn't want the black stone they put into his hand and only later understood that that this must have been chocolate. The soldier smiled and bit off a bit and chewed it in his mouth. But he still didn't want a piece of this black thing, only the sweets which the fat man on the truck gave him. The soldiers and the people in the street were waiting for somebody, and then the sick man was brought out on the stretcher with blood around his eyes and nose. But then he was not allowed to see any more.

These memories were never fully explained by his mother and when he eventually ran away from home, he was in a state of confusion. He had made his own attempts to figure out the mystery of his origins and felt there was something being kept from him. He was only a young boy, not even eighteen, full of doubt and anger and fear. He had not yet found a way of explaining himself or telling his own story.

He never even waited to do his final exam in school. Just packed his bag with the minimum of clothes one day after a terrible argument at home. He got his guitar, rolled up his sleeping bag and took his passport from the glass cabinet. Went to the post office to withdraw all the money he had saved up. He sent his mother a note later on, giving a list of reasons for leaving. He said he could no longer sleep in a house full of antlers and dead creatures. His whole life had been a preparation for catastrophe, being able to live on nothing, surviving on roots and eating ants. He gave his parents no right to reply. It had all gone beyond that point of no return. He knew what they would be saying as they stood in the living room, reading the note over and over again. 'Let him see what it's like' or 'See how long he survives out there in the big world, paying his own bills.' He knew that his mother would be worried about him and maybe he wanted to prove to himself that she had nothing more to worry about.

And then he was off. Right from the start he had a clear idea where he was going. Scotland. There was something he had read about the place. He had seen a film about the Battle of Culloden and had an old Scottish tune in his head. In his mind, the Scottish people were like himself, people who had things done to them. When he arrived in Glasgow he didn't understand a word. His English had all come from the American radio stations, phrases such as 'give 'em hell' which sounded funny to people in Scotland. They thought he was a German comedian. He moved on up through the Highlands and slept in barns to save money. He was hoping to stretch his savings out so that he could stay away forever. The survival instincts that his father instilled in him were coming in handy now.

As the light began to fade every evening, he would walk the road searching for a barn or a shed situated away from dwelling houses, away from people. Once or twice he had trouble with dogs, but he was able to get around them. He would bed down and make a mattress for himself on the hay. He was amazed how warm it was to lie on straw. He was sleeping rough and proud of it. Sometimes he was scared of the dark and stayed awake, listening to the sounds, imagining people creeping up towards him, but then he would fall asleep, and by morning, he would find himself laughing at his own fear. One night he heard a terrible scream nearby, almost human. He scrambled further back along the hay. He had no knife with him for protection. His father had once ceremoniously given him a hunting knife with a handle made from a deer's foot. But he wanted none of those things to come on this journey. He wanted to be able to trust the world. In the morning, when he moved on, he found out the reason for the scream in the night. A dead deer, caught in a wire fence, hanging from his hind leg.

He wanted to get out of the museum of the dead and travelled as far as he could, all the way up to Inverness. He had no trouble getting into pubs because even though he was only seventeen, he was quite tall. The only trouble he had was getting through the narrow doors with his rucksack and his guitar. In Inverness he ran into a group of young people who invited him to stay. He thought they were out to rob him. When they found that he could play the guitar, they insisted on taking him home to one of their small council houses.

'You big lanky fucking German bastard,' they kept calling him. They slapped him on the back affectionately and forced him to have another whisky. He sang his heart out and they sang along. They told him he could stay as long as he liked, though he could hardly make out what they were saying because of the Scottish accent. He found himself saying 'yes' very frequently when he was asked a question. They asked him if he had any sisters. They said he didn't sound like a German when he sang. They told jokes that he didn't understand, so he laughed, pretending that he got it. And next morning over breakfast, he did get one of their jokes. A fly landed on somebody's cornflakes. The boy chased the fly away with his hand and then examined his cornflakes for a long time before he said: 'I do-nae think he ate any of it.' The others grunted, but Gregor laughed out loud. He kept on repeating it like somebody with learning difficulties.

'I do nae think he ate any of it,' he said slowly. They stared at him as he learned the joke off by heart.

He had trained himself to live on nothing. His father would have been proud of him. When he started running out of money, he lived on tea and toast, and jam. He did not allow himself to phone home or ask them to send money. He was determined not to fall into that trap, so he made his way down to London to try and get a job.

He found London dreary. He could not afford accommodation, so he slept in Victoria Station. He started looking for work, knowing that he could go back to Germany any time to work there. But he wanted to live in a foreign place, without support. It was a mission of survival, sleeping in one of the alcoves of the station every night, and in the morning, putting his stuff in a locker to continue looking for work. He managed to get a job on a building site, but he got fired at the end of the day because he was so thirsty and kept going away to the tap for water. He was not really a worker like that. If only he could play music, but nobody wanted to hear his songs.

He saw a rat once or twice, but that didn't bother him. He slept in his clothes with his empty wallet and his passport in his trousers where he would feel it most if somebody touched him while he was asleep. He trained himself to detect the proximity of another human being, even in sleep. If somebody stared at him for a moment too long, he would open his eyes. The presence of a person nearby would wake him up. If there was no danger, he would go back to sleep again in an instant. He lived the way that his father had imagined for him, ready for the worst. And one night, curled up in his sleeping bag on the floor, monitoring the sound of trains echoing in his head and the sound of London voices drifting past, he woke up with a man standing right next to him. A well-dressed man, carrying a briefcase.

'You seem like a respectable lad,' the man said. 'Why are you sleeping rough like this?'

Gregor told him that he was looking for work. The man smiled and asked more questions. Where was he from? Why were his parents not helping him out? Gregor told him that he was on his own now and had no parents. So the man offered to help him get on his feet in London. He said he could give him a place to stay until he got settled.

'Look, I've got two sons of my own, travelling off somewhere in Australia at the moment. I'd hate to think of them lying around in railway stations.'

Gregor told him he was fine. But then he took up the offer when the man insisted. He had a politeness in his voice which Gregor felt he could trust. So he got into the man's car, a Jaguar, Gregor remembers, and they drove to the suburbs where he lived in a large detached house, with well-kept gardens and Alsatian dogs patrolling the grounds. There was something welcoming about this wealth and he gave in to the luxury for once.

It was only when the man served him a meal in the middle of the night that Gregor realised how hungry he was and how fed up he was of toast and jam. He was given beer and the man drank whisky. Gregor was soon drunk and elated. He told some of the stories about Scotland, about the fly in the cornflakes.

'I do nae think he ate any of it,' he said, and the man laughed heartily.

Then everything went wrong. Gregor was tired, knocked out by the rush of luxury and kindness. It was warm in the house and he fell asleep in the chair. Maybe it was the feeling of being at home. He never suspected anything until he woke up lying on a bed, with most of his clothes off, down to his underpants. The whole thing was a trick. The man was on the bed beside him in his silk dressing gown, stroking Gregor's chest.

'Fuck off,' Gregor shouted, pulling away. In his German accent, it was comical, not even remotely hostile.

'Relax,' the man said, smiling. 'You've got nothing to worry about. You're a tired little monkey, I'm going to put you to bed now.'

Gregor got into bed, but then he found the man getting in beside him.

'I'm not like that,' Gregor said.

'Nonsense,' the man said. 'Every boy is like that, only you have been denying it.'

The man was right. Gregor had had some encounters with other boys at school, on long weekends in the country. They sometimes ganged up to pull each other's trousers down. And once or twice it led to things that would have counted as homosexual, though it was only experimental. A test to see which direction was right for him.

The man must have sensed hesitation. He slid his hand down to his groin and Gregor leaped away from the bed, though he didn't get far because the man came after him and forced him back on the bed, face down, pulling off his underpants. The politeness was gone. Gregor could feel his erect penis and his balls behind him, like a soft, wiry brush or cleaning utensil from the kitchen, stroking across his buttocks.

'My lovely German boy,' the man said.

'Fuck off,' Gregor shouted. 'I'm Jewish.'

The man stalled and backed off, allowing Gregor room enough to move away at last and pull up his underpants again. He stood there with the words echoing inside his head. He was transformed by them, untouchable, unafraid.

'You're lying,' the man said. 'You're not even circumcised. Look.'

Gregor found himself having to back it up. He explained that he was an orphan. He told the story of how he had been brought from the East as a refugee. He explained that no Jewish boys would have been circumcised during the war. It would have meant certain death.

That calmed the situation down. Gregor continued his story, as much as he knew of it. And where the facts failed him, he began to make it up. He said he had no parents at all now, that his adoptive parents were dead. For a moment he wondered if it was a mistake to portray himself as a victim, inviting people to prey on him. Would it not have been better to say that he was a prize-winning boxer, to make up a story of how violent he could be? But he had said the right thing after all.

'I thought you knew,' the man said. 'I thought that's why you came here with me.'

'No,' Gregor said.

'Then you're very naive,' the man said.

It was true. Gregor had ignored all the questions he should have asked himself. He had been preparing himself for living on wild mushrooms and dealing with wild animals. He was ready to rough it in the wild and knew how to trap a rabbit without weapons. Knew how to shoot and how to use a knife. But here in the city of London, he was a lost child. Alone, at the mercy of other people.

Gregor felt guilty and stupid to allow himself into this situation.

'I'm sorry,' he said.

And then the man became very polite again. He offered to take him back to the station. They got dressed and the night unravelled in the opposite direction again, back into the plush Jaguar with the wooden dashboard, back along the same route into the city. At Victoria Station, he offered Gregor money. Gregor refused, but he forced a few notes into his rucksack. Then he was gone again.

He was embarrassed using the money, but he continued travelling, this time around the west coast of Ireland. When the money ran out again, he made his way back to Germany and worked for a while in a car plant near Frankfurt. After six months he was off again travelling around Greece. Each time the money ran out he went back to Germany to work in one of the cities again, anywhere but Nuremberg, until he had accumulated enough to travel again. He was in Turkey when the Berlin Wall went up. He was back in Munich when the Cuban Missile Crisis blew up. Drifting back and forth for a number of years like this, meeting people, in and out of relationships, discovering as many countries as possible including Morocco and Spain, until he eventually decided to make his way up to Berlin in the late summer of 1967.

He had heard that things were happening up there and on the train to Berlin he met some young people in the same carriage who were excited about going there also. He drank beer with them and they gave him an address where he could stay in the city. Tell them you're a friend of Lutz

von Blessing Doehm, they told him. He thought it was a
joke, but then he arrived at the apartment and was given a
place to stay on the floor of a commune that later became
quite famous because the apartment was owned by a
well-known writer. A young man who introduced himself
as Fritz came down the stairs to tell him he could stay as
long as he liked. There was music playing all day and all
night. It was hard to sleep. Everybody was stoned. He
never met anyone called Lutz. Instead, he met Martin who
had also run away from home under a cloud of anger and
resentment.

'I'm not German really,' Gregor told him. 'I'm Jewish,
from Poland originally.'

'Welcome to the club,' Martin answered. 'I'm half-
Russian myself. My father was an officer in the Russian
Army.'

Berlin was the place for everyone to begin afresh.

Six

He feels at home here, in this orchard. Is there some distant memory of starting his life in a place like this? Or does everyone get that when they pick apples on a warm day when the summer has spilled over into extra time? That feeling of being connected to the earth in an unbroken chain going all the way back in time, doing what people have done here in this same place for hundreds of years.

The trees are old. Planted long before the war. They must have seen a few things, when this landscape was a battle zone and the farm became a last line of defence. The Russians in the nearby woods and the Germans holding out in the farmhouses. The trees would have witnessed the barn at the far end burning down with the young horses inside. They would have heard their screams. They say the apples from these trees have a unique flavour. Some of the trees are so gnarled that it's a wonder how they can still deliver the sap to all those distant branches. They are too old to be pruned. And this year has been so dry, the branches are so frail and laden down with fruit that they crack at the touch. Even with no wind, the larger beams sometimes break off overnight.

The orchard was planned to ripen in phases through the summer – cherries, red berries, gooseberries, plum trees, apple trees and pear trees. Isn't that what mystified the

Russians most when they finally conquered these farms one by one, how well designed and logical everything was in comparison to their own? How insane it must have appeared to them that anyone would want to invade any other land when they already had such manicured farms, designed with the vegetable gardens terraced in neat rows, and the orchard facing south and west to maximise the sunlight. And those strong, brick-built farm buildings to provide shelter from the bitter winds coming from the north and the east.

Each variety of apple was chosen to blossom in staggered succession, but in the great heat this year, everything has been ripening together, more or less. Even in spring, the blossoms were all out at the same time, virtually. The birds got most of the cherries, and the berries, stripping them like strings of pearls. The apple trees have produced such a great crop this year.

When Gregor came to visit the farm in spring, they took him for a walk over to the lake, to hear the frogs. It was late afternoon, with the clouds low overhead and the hint of thunder in the air. They invited him to stay for dinner, and afterwards, when he drove home, he found himself returning to the lake to hear the muddy chorus of frogs once more in the dark. Stayed there for almost an hour listening to the sheer volume of sound around him. Frogs close by going silent for a while, making it possible to hear the ones further away, arguing back and forth. Thousands of invisible voices elaborating at once, like some enormous talk show going all the way round the rim of the lake. Flashes of sheet lightning across the water and a delayed rumble in the air. Quite deafening, he remembers. He could not see any of the frogs and that made them seem larger, more human, more unafraid of the elements out here. A brash thunderclap right above him made him jump, but the frogs were not bothered and kept on talking. He hardly noticed that he was being savaged by the mosquitoes, alone in the dark with his T-shirt over his head like an old woman. In school some days later, he got the children in class to imitate the sounds, giving each child a random word to utter in exchange for a croak, a glorious dictionary of babbling classroom frogs.

He feels the affection of this gathering in the orchard. Mara says she expected more people to come, but they will probably arrive tomorrow. There will be a huge crowd here for Sunday, she says, and maybe it's good that they have today for themselves, just the family and their close friend Martin.

Everybody is working now in small groups, talking among themselves, telling stories and joking, discussing local events and world events. Some of them bending over, collecting the apples off the ground after the fall of the past few days. Others high on stepladders picking by hand or catching the fruit with nets on long poles. They treat the apples with great care, grasping them with an upward movement, stem and all, so as not to damage next year's growth. Johannes, the little boy, is advising them, telling them not to mix up the good apples with the bad apples, speaking to everyone with an authority that he has heard in the voices of the adults.

'Does that make sense to you?' he asks, and the adults smile at the sound of their language filtered through the child's mind.

The rotten apples are thrown onto the wheelbarrows. Those with bruises, those with too many black marks and those that appear to be damaged by worms or by wasps go into boxes and buckets to make apple juice. Thorsten maintains that you know that an apple is ripe when you see maggots inside. It seems to be timed by nature to fall at the same point. Some of the apples will be cold-pressed on the farm, but the majority will be pressed in a local factory and sterilised before being put into cartons. At Christmas, they will drink hot apple juice with cinnamon. Some of the pears seem almost comically deformed, but still very good to eat. The cooking apples go into separate boxes along with the bruised apples which will go into making cakes or stewed apple while the perfect, edible ones go into small sacks. Thorsten has got the sacks from friends in the Oder region, not far away on the Polish border. One summer when the river burst its banks and caused great flooding, the army was called out and distributed thousands of sandbags to local people so they could create dykes. Strange that time, seeing the German Army going back across the Oder River into Poland with sandbags. This year, the sacks are being put to even better use for storing apples. Over a dozen of them marked with the letters THW are already lined up at the side of the garden, ready to be carried away and stored inside the farm buildings.

Those on ladders can see out beyond the boundary wall across the fields and over to the lake. On the other side, they can see the small forest two hundred metres away where the Russians hid when the farm became the front line. They can imagine the shots being fired across the field between the farm and the forest. There is a car driving along the road, clinging on to the edge of the horizon, and above the field, a kestrel hovering. Every now and again, an apple falls to the ground with a bony kind of thud, such as the sound of a hoof on the earth. The discovery of gravity each time. The grass underneath has been cut so that the fallen apples are easier to find. There is a wide rake leaning against a tree. At the centre of the orchard, a small table set up with glasses and a jug of water which catches the sunlight. A white cloth is spread over the jug to stop the insects from landing in it and drowning. There is a general hum in the air of wasps and bees and flies and more silent fruit flies. A robin comes to stand on the handles of the wheelbarrow from time to time. The little mechanical chirp he gives is an imitation of the squeak of a wheelbarrow.

Gregor reaches up for one of the high apples. A small sack attached to a long pole catches the apple after he shakes the branch a little. In the blinding sunshine the apple seems to float in the sky and he is afraid it will miss the sack and fall straight down on him instead. He has to look away into the shadows for a moment to regain his sight. A pleasant sunblindness.

Mara has not changed. She sits on an upturned crate, wearing gardening gloves, in charge of the sorting. Katia beside her, sometimes holding her belly for a moment with a heaving kick inside. Mara is very healthy, except for some trouble with her back from time to time, and a cancer scare some years ago. She's not one for health updates. Her long, bare suntanned arms reach over to pick more apples from a basket and there is a small, powdery thumbprint bruise midway between her right elbow and the shoulder. She's wearing a loose white top and a skirt with slightly faded colours. She lifts her skirt to carry a bunch of apples in her lap, showing her legs for a moment. She wears bashed-up tennis shoes on her feet, no socks. In the light coming through the trees it would be difficult to say what age she is now. Her hair has flashes of grey, tied up at the back, more wavy.

Martin is standing some distance away, talking to Thorsten. Thorsten is a doctor in the local town and his wife Katia is a schoolteacher. He has inherited this farm from his aunt who fought for it at the end of the Second World War, then had the farm turned over to the state and fought for the right to live there on her own farm during the GDR years, only finally getting possession of the farm back again in her eighties at the end of the Communist years. Then she passed it on to Thorsten because she was too old to live alone.

Gregor is talking to Johannes. He asks the boy what he would like most at this moment in time. Johannes thinks for a while with his hand on his chin and says he would like an elephant to come into the orchard. Gregor agrees this would be wonderful.

'I would like an elephant to come into the orchard, too,' Gregor replies to the boy, 'and an orchestra behind it.'

Johannes goes around asking everybody else in turn, what they would like best. An idle conversation in which the adults have been turned into children. His father wants a group of elves to come and pick all the apples overnight and put them into the store and turn them into apple juice, but that seems not to be so far from reality. Martin says that his greatest wish at that very moment would be to see an enormous chocolate cake appear on a table with a white tablecloth and a bowl of sweet cream.

'You'll just have to wait,' Mara shouts.

'But I need something sweet,' Martin says.

Martin has always been able to declare his appetite. He has not changed much either, only become more rounded in a self-assured way, wearing trousers with red braces over his white shirt. He needs to be near food, and it makes Gregor think of his grandfather Emil who also had to be near food at all times. Maybe that's why they became friends and got on so well in the first place, because Martin in some way replaced his grandfather who went missing when he was very small. Martin is always joking. Always talking about food. And sex. Somebody who is able to keep the conversation going and not talk about serious things always. Mara says he can go a little over the top sometimes. 'You must have stewed apple coming out your ears,' he said earlier on. And when he arrived at the farm, kissing everyone and shaking hands, he leaned down without any shame to listen to Katia's baby, with his ear right beside her belly. In front of her husband Thorsten, he spoke to the foetus inside, saying, 'Hello. Everything all right in there?' Martin gets away with that public intimacy. He's been married twice before, has two children. Now he's living with a young woman from Croatia, though she's at home visiting her parents. He runs a legal practice in Berlin, but he would love to give it all up to concentrate on more enjoyable things, such as taking up a job as a chef. He loves the idea of cooking as a performance.

'Have you tasted one of these?' Mara asks, showing him a perfect Grafensteiner.

'I can't,' Martin says. 'I can only eat shop apples.'

'Are you crazy?'

'I'm allergic to organic. All those minced up worms they put into the apple juice.'

'Look,' Mara says, holding up a perfect apple. 'There's not a single worm in it. It's the most un-damaged, un-spoiled, yet un-eaten piece of fruit ever created.'

'No thanks,' Martin replies. 'I can't eat anything that has not been made safe through commerce.'

As a student living in the commune in Berlin, Martin used to sit down at night with a wooden board, the way people sometimes eat cheese and crackers. He would smoke a joint and then set about cutting up an apple and a bar of chocolate, systematically. It would take ages, while they were listening to music. It was done with relentless technique, resembling an assembly line, cutting everything up first with great care into a series of apple boats and chocolate triangles the way his own mother used to do it for him, then sitting back to look at the arrangement for a moment like a child before he would begin to eat.

Everyone begins to reveal their own chocolate confessions and Thorsten says Katia hides chocolate all around the farm, the same way that alcoholics hide schnapps. A premeditated vice. Every now and again he finds one of the secret places where she has stashed her supplies, and still there are more, he's certain of that.

'You never put on any weight, Mara,' Katia says in a tone of exaggerated envy.

Martin talks about his own 'limited baggage allowance'. And then, before anyone has noticed anything, Thorsten returns from one of the farmhouses with a bar of Swiss chocolate. They hear the rustle of the silver paper. And the little crack of chocolate breaking off at an angle, never neatly along the squares. Martin is the first to get some, and when Gregor is offered a piece, he declines.

'He's never liked chocolate,' Mara says.

Gregor remembers the black stone offered to him as a child by an American soldier.

When Johannes comes around offering the chocolate, Gregor tells him to give his bit to Martin. Then Johannes asks Mara what her wish is, and she says she would like all the clocks and all the watches in the world to stop, right this minute. She is not wearing a watch herself and neither is Katia beside her, so Johannes runs over to his father to find out what time it is.

'It's eleven fifty-five,' he calls out.

'Eleven fifty-five,' Mara says. 'What's keeping Daniel?'

Everyone laughs quietly at this sudden urgency in her voice. She smiles at herself. At that moment, her wish seems to be granted. The insects hover. Everyone is motionless. The sunlight floods in through the branches. She is blinded and lifts her hand up to shield her eyes so she can just about see the outline of Gregor stretching up with his long pole into the top branches. Everything in the orchard stands still.

Seven

When Gregor first arrived in Berlin, he was like a void. They said he was a quiet, sensitive sort of person who didn't talk very much and was interested mostly in music. He was tall and good-looking, and received a lot of sympathy whenever he told people he was an orphan.

'You're a bit of a loner, aren't you?' the girls would say to him. It was meant as a compliment, of course. The dark horse. The mystery man. They looked into his eyes the way a climber would stare across a mountain range. They attempted to conquer that frontier and laughed, calling him the great unknown. He was the kind of person who might go out for a packet of cigarettes and never come back. He left the bathroom door open as if he was the only person left in the world. He disappeared at a party, without explanation, leaving his coat behind. He never phoned back when somebody left a message.

Because he hardly spoke, they would speak for him, guessing what was inside his head. 'I know what you're thinking,' they would say. They would set multiple-choice questions, all he had to do was nod or shake his head. Entire monologues would be put into his mouth while he remained mute. And when he revealed that he was an orphan, they became even more curious, passing the news around like a tabloid confession, as though they wanted to adopt him all over again. And maybe they envied his story. Maybe they were orphans themselves to some degree, disowning their parents, wishing they had no lineage. The freedom of having no family tree.

He placed all of his feelings into his music. He was able to keep a party going with a guitar, but he always sank into a phase of introspection soon afterwards. He was as thin as he was tall. He could 'live on nothing', they used to say.

Martin and Gregor got a job together, working in the warehouse of a publishing house. Martin was studying law and Gregor was attending a course on music composition. In the waiting room of Martin's legal practice in Berlin, there is a framed poster with the word 'Wanted' written over the top. It offers a reward for the return of a small painting of the artist Francis Bacon, which was stolen from an exhibition in Berlin. The portrait was done by Bacon's friend, Lucian Freud, a fellow artist with whom he had a falling-out later on. It shows Bacon with large lips and large eyes turned down, a sad, vulnerable expression in which he appears to be thinking about the nature of friendship and how it never remains static, always increasing or fading. The painting itself has never been recovered. The poster is like a shrine to friendship.

They both wore beards. They often sat on trolleys, holding philosophical debates to pass the time. They kept nix for each other after a hard night so the other person could sleep it off in the bookshelves with a couple of medical dictionaries for a pillow. Gregor still recalls the subsidised dinners in the canteen, pork and red cabbage and salted potatoes, served in a tin tray with tin foil across the top. He refused to eat pork and had to have a special lunch provided. Now and again one of the employees would make remarks about him. There was a residue of fascism left in the arguments of older men who spoke of 'back then', meaning under Hitler. Men who sometimes used Nazi phrases and said weirdos such as Martin and Gregor should be 'taken away'.

Gregor arrived at work every day with his curly hair and a detective hat on his head. He wore white shoes and a tweed jacket, a full contradiction of styles. Martin was equally noisy in colour and style, with long hair and round glasses, carrying a doctor's medical bag. Gregor's beard was very black and he had a bright smile that could disarm people even in the most disastrous circumstances. He was taller than Martin, but he had the habit of hunching over to make up for his height, speaking to people from the side, as though he was uncomfortable with the responsibility that his height gave him and wanted to compensate by giving the impression of being smaller, more crouched, more looked after. Martin had the bigger laugh and could often be heard throughout the warehouse, irritating the hell out of the foreman, while Gregor laughed more in towards himself, a laugh that was shrinking rather than expanding.

Life seemed like one long party at the time, with Gregor playing 'Riders on the Storm' like an anthem on his guitar every night. Everything revolved around music and sex and drugs. The genius of youth. All that glorious time-wasting and useless enterprise. Gregor remembers taking acid and staring for five hours at his luminous hands, seeing right through the skin like thin parchment at the veins inside, wondering whose blood flowed through them.

On the autobahn outside Frankfurt one day, he and Martin were hitchhiking back to Berlin in the middle of winter when they were questioned by the police. It was a time of mistrust and tension in Germany. A time of protest making up for a time of lack of protest. A time of street demonstrations and rioting and potential terrorists.

It was getting dark early and they were both frozen to the bone. Gregor wore a cashmere coat, which he had picked up for nothing but which was far too small for him, and his detective hat. Martin wore a thin anorak and tennis shoes, hopping around from one foot to the other. There were dirty bits of hardened ice left at the side of the road from the last snow and the only thing keeping them warm was their beards. They cursed each other for the idea of hitching in winter, particularly when Martin's father had plenty of money and they could easily have taken the train.

They had a hard time getting a lift. Two eccentric figures, one with his bashed-up doctor's bag and the other with his guitar case, imagining the dreamy heat inside the cars going by. Motorists staring at them with those vacant, alarmist expressions as they passed by. They waited for like-minded people who might take pity on them and kept an eye out for cars like the one-stroke DCV, or the Renault 4, or the Volkswagen; high-mileage, proletarian vehicles that had become a symbol of new, alternative life. They had almost given up hope when a car suddenly pulled up ahead of them. At last, they said, picking up their bags and running towards it. But they stopped short when two men hopped out of the car and confronted them with handguns and badges.

'Drop your bags,' one of the men shouted.

They were ordered to step over the rail into an adjoining field. Within seconds, Gregor and Martin found them-selves walking away down a slope with the men shouting orders, pointing guns at their backs. It seemed like such a calm place, with crows in the trees, the autobahn out of sight, like a river in spate behind them, and the winter sky fading to an icy blue.

'Take off your coats and throw them to the side,' the policemen demanded.

Martin did as he was told and threw his anorak away.

'And that stupid fucking hat,' one of the men bawled at Gregor.

Gregor refused to take off his hat, or his coat.

'What's all this about?' he demanded, turning round towards the policemen.

The policemen directed their weapons at Gregor. He had been turned into a suspect by them, but his refusal took on a moral momentum, contradicting their unspoken accusations. Underneath the hippy clothing, there was a need to assert his identity in public, without any shame, without any doubt. This was the moment for it. He smiled, like a flashlight shining through his black beard, while the officers waved their guns and screamed at him to turn away, using the word 'asshole' in every phrase. Gregor then became serious, withdrew his smile and stared straight at the officer, telling him that he was refusing to take off his coat in the middle of winter.

'You won't get away with this any more,' Gregor said. 'I'm Jewish.'

It was like a grenade going off. He was saying it for the first time with great confidence. Everything changed. It was clear that Martin and Gregor were no terrorists. This was just a routine piece of opportunism, two thug policemen deciding to humiliate two free-living hippy wasters. But now it was all going wrong for them. The officers began to shrink back, looking at each other for reassurance. Out there in this ravine with the sound of civilisation so close by along the autobahn, they were asked to stare into the eyes of history. One of them continued bawling out orders for a moment, but the other began to weaken and said it was OK, all they needed was to see identification. Martin and Gregor showed their student ID cards and the policemen backed off, out of that history lesson as fast as they could.

When they got back to Berlin, Martin laughed and said it was the best one he had ever heard yet. He embraced Gregor again and again and said he had 'saved his ass' out there on the autobahn. Martin had been carrying an almighty knob of hash, enough to land him in jail and disqualify him from ever working in a legal practice if he had been caught in possession. He had told Gregor nothing about it. They had a fierce argument over it, with Gregor asking how Martin thought he could smuggle such a thing all the way through the GDR when people were searched so thoroughly every time that they had to lay out every spoon, every pencil, every item of clothing on a table by the roadside. Women often had to undergo the humiliating ordeal of displaying all their clothes, item by item while the East German border guards examined it all with great fascination. How did Martin think he could get away with carrying hash through that frontier?

'You're my guardian angel,' Martin said.

He kept repeating the story that evening, laughing in irrational bursts. 'Wait till I tell everybody about this,' he said. 'There we are getting searched on the side of the autobahn and Gregor saves the day by saying he's Jewish.'

'But I am Jewish,' Gregor insisted.

'I know,' Martin said. 'But it's such a great story. There's me standing with a fucking massive lump of dope in my pocket, not knowing what the hell to do with it, whether to throw it away into the grass or swallow it or what, and then you tell them you're Jewish. Brilliant.'

'I'm not joking, Martin.'

And then it dawned on Martin for the first time to ask questions.

'How do you know you're Jewish?' he asked.

'I was told by my uncle,' Gregor replied. 'Uncle Max. He's dead now, but he told me the whole story.'

Gregor continued to bring out the facts in small increments, always enough but not any more. Martin absorbed the information, becoming his spokesperson, telling people in advance about Gregor's background.

'Saved by a Jew,' he would say, putting his arm around Gregor and ruffling his hair.

There was no proof that Gregor Liedmann was Jewish, but that didn't stop people from believing him. In the next few weeks, Gregor went to a doctor and asked to be circumcised. The doctor naturally wanted to know why he was doing this, and once again, Gregor boldly explained that it was for his faith. The doctor arranged the operation, and after that, Gregor made further attempts to place his identity on record. He had marked down his religion as Jewish on official documents. Dues were deducted from his pay packet each month which went directly to the Jewish community, but when he approached the rabbi in Berlin, there were difficulties in establishing any Jewish parentage.

He spoke to the rabbi on a number of occasions, explained that in the nature of things during the war, it was impossible for anyone to admit that he was Jewish. He was in hiding, brought from the East under cover as a German refugee. It was understandable that he had not been circumcised as a child, but he had rectified that in the meantime and was now ready to enter the faith fully to make up for lost time.

The rabbi shook his head and said he could not accept him into the community. He understood Gregor's wish to become Jewish, but he was not in a position to take anyone who came in off the street and accept their word for it. He urged Gregor to find some solid evidence of parentage, particularly on the mother's side, then he would welcome him with open arms.

Despite his efforts, Gregor didn't get very far. He had no great wish to attend the synagogue or to go through any religious customs. He merely wanted to belong to the Jewish community in Berlin. And maybe it didn't matter to him all that much ultimately, because everyone already believed him. They never asked too many intrusive questions because it seemed grotesque to demand identity papers from a Jewish survivor. They were in the process of altering their society with new music and new habits and new forms of tolerance that would make up for all that was gone by. They accepted the fact that Gregor was Jewish, simple as that.

But as with everything in Gregor's life, there has always been a question mark floating behind him. Every statement contains a hint of the opposite. Some filament of doubt inside every utterance which calls that very thing into question. They say that every YES contains a NO. Every book title, every line from a song, every clip of dialogue in a movie is always in conflict with itself. Some innate cynicism in the words that shows up the reverse of what was meant. The only strong statement left is the question itself. Who am I? Where do I belong?

Eight

Gregor first met Mara after a street demonstration in Berlin. He and Martin found themselves on the periphery of a protest, observers sitting on top of an advertising hoarding alongside a newspaper photographer when a baton charge came their way. Policemen came and whacked them around the ankles from below, forcing them to get down. This time Gregor had no defence. It was the photographer who called out with great indignation, bawling out the name of the right-wing paper he worked for. So the policemen apologised to the photographer and turned on Gregor with redoubled hysteria. He received two blows, one to the shoulder, one to the side of the head, before he could limp away around the corner. They must have assumed Martin was with the photographer because he got away unscathed.

Mara came across them, crouched beside the wall outside a shop, right underneath a cigarette machine. Gregor was naked from the waist up. He had taken off his T-shirt and Martin was holding it up to his forehead to stem the blood. She took them upstairs to the apartment where she lived, bandaged his head and washed his face and chest. She was a nurse, training to become a physiotherapist. She gave Gregor a clean shirt belonging to her boyfriend who was away at the time. Then she tried to teach them yoga and had them both lying on the floor with their legs in the air to increase the healing power of circulation.

Afterwards, they drank beer and smoked and talked. Each of them had their own protest stories. She told them about the time she was caught shoplifting and tried to argue that she did it because she disapproved of capitalism. Martin told the story of how he was caught without a ticket on the underground and tried to escape, only to run straight into a newspaper stand on the platform. Mara told them that the apartment had once been raided and ransacked by the police. Martin pointed out that it didn't help that everything was painted red. Red doors, red window frames, even a red fridge which Mara told them had been turned upside down, literally, in the middle of the kitchen one day when she returned. Gregor announced with great solemnity that he was retiring from protests. He said he was not very good at getting his head broken by truncheons and would leave that to people with bigger heads, like Martin. She asked Gregor if there was anything he did better than getting his head cracked, and when he said nothing, it was Martin who spoke for him.

'He's a musician,' Martin told her.

'A musician,' she said, staring at Gregor.

'I'm lucky they didn't get my hands,' Gregor said.

'And a composer,' Martin added. 'He's a Jewish composer.'

'Wow,' Mara said. 'And that's the way the bastards treat you.'

Martin then retold the story of the autobahn. Mara clenched her fist and shook it towards the balcony. By then, both sides of the street outside were lined with police vans and policemen dressed in riot gear sitting inside.

It was a time of engagement with society, with history. A time for casting off constraints. A time of truth and self-accusation. And nudity. The naked body had become a provocation and great symbol of freedom in the aftermath of war. There were 'happenings' everywhere and speeches given at the university about the importance of open relationships.

Mara took Gregor's bloodied T-shirt and carried it over to the window, stepped out onto the small balcony and tied it to the railings. She then came back in and sang a song that she had learned in school, an unusual song that one of her revolutionary teachers had heard from a German folk group, a sad marching song that was written by the inmates of a concentration camp in the north of Germany.

'Wir sind die Moorsoldaten, und ziehen mit dem Spaten.'

She then found a guitar in one of the rooms of the apartment and Gregor sang a few songs. Other occupants came back and told more stories of street battles. Martin eventually found himself a place to crash out in a corner for the night and Mara took Gregor by the hand. She pulled him into her room and he felt as though he had been connected to a powerful battery, sending a high voltage surge through his limbs.

With the bandage round his head and his bloodied T-shirt hanging out like a flag of resistance from the balcony, they lay down on the mattress on the floor, surrounded by posters and Trotskyite flyers. There was no wardrobe, only a rail for the clothes. There was a suitcase set up in the corner on two boxes, like an altar, with a mirror and some make-up. Her favourite possessions, a nice pair of shoes, beige and black, with laces and clacking heels. That and a sun hat and a frame full of butterflies with pins stuck into them.

'Is that not a bit cruel?' he asked her.

'Not really,' she answered. 'It's giving them life after life.'

They exchanged more information about themselves. She was from Köln, had three sisters. A conservative father who had remarried and was deeply disappointed not to have a son. She had escaped to Berlin, it turned out, freeing herself from a rigid Catholic, Rhineland upbringing. She asked him plenty of questions and he told his story, how he had grown up not far from the site of the Nuremberg Rallies, in the shadows of where the Nazis staged their great pageant, the triumph of the will. It came as a shock to him when he was taken there on a school trip one day, standing with his school friends on the steps where Hitler held his speeches, a place which had become so iconic in world history.

'What surprised me most of all was how small and insignificant it had become,' he said to her. 'Overgrown with weeds. Not much bigger than the school soccer pitch, really.'

He talked about his adoptive parents. They were people who felt things had been done to them. His mother regarded herself as a helpless victim in life, unable to affect any change, either during the Nazi period or in the aftermath of the war. He spoke about her habit of praying out loud when she heard shocking events on the radio, but always retreating into her private life of anxieties and obsessions, as though her existence had nothing to do with the rest of the world.

'She had the habit of doing the singing yawn,' Gregor said. 'The real doh-re-mi yawn, C, D and F sharp.'

'My mother is the same,' Mara said. 'Only two notes, though.'

She was excited and emotional and wanted to stay awake for a few more hours, listening to him talking, looking at him lying on his back, staring up as though he could see his childhood projected onto the ceiling. She told friends later that he made love as though he was steering a riverboat into the sunset, with his eyes closed, humming. And Gregor said very little about that first encounter, only that she moved like a washing machine, going into spin.

But there was more to this meeting. After a number of other random encounters, Mara moved in with Gregor. She left her boyfriend behind, a medical student from Austria with lots of money, who kept the fridge stocked up with beer and food and followed her everywhere, to her classes, into bars. Even hung around in the distance among the trees when she and Gregor were lying in the grass along the canal together. Gregor had his own entanglements. The commune which Martin had set up had egalitarian, anti-consumer principles, with strict rules about private possessions. Even personal relationships were open to plunder. On the night that Mara moved in, Gregor's guitar was stolen. Days later Mara found it in a junk shop nearby and bought it back again. And when Gregor played it that same evening in the apartment, a young woman burst into tears and admitted that she was the one who had stolen it, out of jealousy. Members of the commune discussed the issue methodically around the table later on, like a revolutionary subcommittee. In principle, the guitar was communal, but she had transgressed the laws by selling it off for private gain.

Not long after that, Gregor and Mara moved into their own apartment. Now and again, she would try to coax childhood recollections from him. His adoptive parents were very strange. His mother was a bit of a martyr, he told her.

His father was obsessed with hunting. The house was full of antlers. He grew up with a stuffed badger standing on a dresser on the landing, snarling with his claws up in the air. The living room was like an assembly hall full of dead creatures staring down at them while they sat watching TV.

Mara became an archaeologist, trying to restore his lost life. While he composed pieces of music on the piano, she pinned the notes up on the walls. Rows of score sheets going all around the room and out into the little corridor of their apartment. The pages fluttered every time they walked by or opened a window. Notes rising and falling. Bursts and bouquets. Chords like solid oak furniture. Lazy notes that dragged their feet and other notes that could not be held back. Together they would work and travel and reinvent the void he had come from. They would reimagine his true origins like a lost piece of music that had been burned in a fire.

When Mara became pregnant some years later, they got married. She took him home to her parents, announcing that she was getting married to a Jewish survivor. They didn't want a big wedding, because Gregor had no relatives.

'The bigger the wedding the smaller the marriage,' he joked. So they had the smallest wedding in history, at a Berlin registry office, with no ceremony and no photographs and no witnesses present, except Martin.

They went to a bar afterwards to have a few drinks, sing a few songs and to break a glass. But the real wedding came some weeks later when Gregor and Mara were travelling around France together. In a railway station in Paris, they met an Irish building worker who had worked on construction sites in Germany and spoke a few phrases in German to them. He was drinking beer early in the morning at Gare Montparnasse and kept quoting the lines of a song he remembered called 'The Lover's Ghost', working himself up to the point where he could sing it to them. All around them in the café, the people with their luggage listened. Even the trains seemed to pause for a moment while he sang.

You are welcome home again, said the young man to his love.
We will never from this moment have to part.

It was the story of a man who dreams that his lover has returned to him, even though she is already dead. While he is in mourning, she has come back to him for one night and is allowed to stay only until morning, until the dawn comes up. They lie in each other's arms once again and the man begs the cock not to crow so that the night will never end and she will never have to leave again.

When it was time for the Irish builder to get his train, he shook hands as though he didn't want to leave, as though he recognised something in them that had disappeared from his own life, some girl he had left behind, some break-up which had conscripted him forever into a lifetime of regret.

'Stay as you are,' he said to them with more than a hint of confession, as he picked up the small shoulder bag containing all his possessions. 'Don't ever fall apart.'

An Irishman on his way around Europe warning young couples in train stations to stay faithful to each other. They dismissed the romance of it. But the steely, calloused grip of his handshake remained imprinted on them. Every nail, every splinter, every frozen piece of scaffolding, an entire cement-bitten biography etched into the palm of his hand. This was their real wedding. The wedding in the railway station. With the noise of trains and loudspeakers and the hiss of a coffee machine, they had sworn a silent, undocumented pact with only the Irish construction worker as a witness. They would never run into him again and he would never know whether they had kept their promises to each other, but there was some binding significance in this railway wedding that was unlike any other marriage contract.

Nine

His mother told him about the journey at the end of the war. She talked about his grandfather, Emil, and how he brought them south in his truck. They stopped in a town and she waited at the train station with Gregor, while Emil went to get some more fuel. It was too risky to get fuel from any army depot, so his best friend Max was busy getting some on the black market.

She must have been in shock at the time because she could never remember the name of the town. Sitting for hours in the waiting room of the railway station as the place filled up with refugees fleeing from the East. She must have stared at the name of the town in front of her for so long that she tried to forget it afterwards. Every time the door opened, she looked up, hoping that it was her father, coming to collect them.

They waited all afternoon and by nightfall, a large crowd had gathered. Most of them had come on foot, hoping for a train to take them further west. They consulted the timetable outside the office, even though it had become an illusion and nobody really believed any of those promises any more. They spoke of delays and expected departure times, staring at the station master's door, waiting for news, clinging like an act of faith to the idea of normality, hallucinating the sound of trains in the distance.

Gregor and his mother had not heard the sound of a train in all the time they sat there. She was asked again and again how long she had been waiting and people repeated her answer among themselves.

'All day,' they whispered. They didn't know if that was a good sign or not. When it grew dark, Gregor slept in her arms, but he kept waking up again, fretting with the pain in his ear. She spoke to him in a calm voice, but he was almost deaf with his infection. She asked people if they had any olive oil but they shook their heads. The only thing that would soothe him was the button on the right shoulder of his jumper, which he kept sucking as he rocked himself back and forth.

The people who came into the station were exhausted. They had left everything behind. They had counted the living and counted the dead. They had been running and walking for weeks, and they had come away with their lives many times over. Their lives were, in fact, the only possession they had left. They had lost most of their belongings and what they had brought with them had often been bartered away, or stolen. They had seen their homes destroyed or taken over. They had seen bridges blown up right behind them. They had seen towns through which they had passed disappearing in a wave of bombing that took no more than five minutes. They had thrown themselves on the ground when low-flying planes came over them, strafing the road. They had picked themselves up each time and moved on. They heard women screaming in barns as they passed by, moving onwards all the time, driven by fear, by the certain knowledge that they could never go back. Clusters of them sticking together to help each other. Others vying with each other, doing business, arguing over the price of things, over the value of an egg. People crouched around a dead horse, cutting sections off a steaming animal from which life had only just departed and which had only moments ago pulled a cart laden with passengers and possessions. Men and women cursing the animal for letting them down in the middle of the journey, having to leave most of their belongings on the road, with only a knapsack full of warm fresh meat, dripping blood on the back of their legs as they walked. They had witnessed hunger and death many times over. They had seen people dying with the cold. Mothers who could not feed their babies because their breasts were frozen. Mothers carrying infants who were already dead. They had seen them huddled by the side of the road and seen the bodies of those who had died, lying like inflated cushions inside their clothes. They had told themselves not to look, but could not avoid the curiosity of a single glance whenever they saw people kneeling in prayer, if only to reassure themselves that they, at least, were still alive and moving on. They had told their children not to look, protecting them from seeing the worst. They had witnessed people who were half dead, covered in blood, dying in the middle of the road with others making a wide arc around them as they passed. People coughing and crying, not knowing whether to stay with the dying or whether to go ahead. Grief that seemed so real at first, until it was seen so often that they became numb. Old people unable to move on. People vomiting. People relieving themselves openly because there was no time to lose and no dignity left. They were all strangers on the road and nobody recognised anyone any more. All kinds of people in mismatched clothes passed on from the living and from the dead, making their way along the road into the unknown. People said the names of towns where they came from, uttering the ordinance of their lives in an attempt to restore their identity, even though the maps were now changed forever and there was no meaning left in those names, only a frail recollection of their place of birth ebbing away as they pressed on. Many of them gone into a kind of voluntary blindness in which they could not accept the realities of the new world into which they had been forced to enter, even when the houses looked similar. The shape of things in front of their eyes only reinforced their loss. They were refugees with nothing, no place in the world, no framework of relatives or friends or neighbours, no landmarks of childhood, steeples, shops and schools. Their orientation was gone. They had lost the grasp of local geography. Nothing was familiar to them any longer and there were things which they could not remember properly because they lacked the known surroundings which might trigger off their memory. There were things they could only remember among their own people, in a place where they were at home. They were on the run, fleeing into a great emptiness, with a deficit of belonging. They had lost the capital of their lives. The entire substance of their identity was nothing more than a story they carried with them in their heads.

Sometimes they would see people going in the wrong direction, unable to carry on because there was somebody they could not live without. Lost expressions on their faces as they went back against the tide, searching for the person left behind, crying as they went, gazing into the eyes of all those on the move in the hope of some recognition. Children calling for their mothers. Everywhere those asking if they had seen or heard of their loved ones, sons, daughters, mothers and fathers, giving the names, giving descriptions of those who had only just missed being there by some strange misfit of fate. Three girls who had failed to make it to the last train in some faraway town and had therefore been separated forever because they were unable to meet their father at an arranged meeting point. A twist of grotesque luck which shaped lives beyond all imagination. People who would never see each other again in this great shift of human settlement, no matter how hard they looked, and would remain forever with an image of someone, held firm in time, not growing any older, just like a photograph standing still in memory, kept alive, just short of being forgotten. Sometimes it was more of a relief to know that somebody was dead, because they, at least, had been absolved from grieving, unlike the living for whom each loss was a double grief, as though the other might as well be dead. Sometimes it was not even the loss of another person that was so painful but the thought of them crying and searching in a panic, the inability to let them know that everything was all right and not to worry.

There were moments of extraordinary luck, too, in which loved ones met each other by some unimaginable coincidence when they had already been given up as lost. Some people even got married along the way, blessed in a hasty ceremony by a priest before they moved on again. There were those who considered themselves lucky and those who considered themselves unlucky. Those who put their loss behind them and those who would never be the same again. Those who prayed and those who cursed and resented. Those who stole and those who gave. Jokers and worriers, optimists and pessimists, opportunists with an eye for gain and suckers who were only waiting to be taken advantage of. Those who had been let down and those who had hope. Those who looked forward and those who looked back.

Their pain and indignation was always overshadowed by the news of worse things elsewhere, by reports of concentration camps.

At some intersections along the road, the military were picking out able conscripts from among the young and the old who might still serve in a desperate defence of their country at the end of its days. Men dressed as women to avoid being detected. Mothers hid their sons in trolleys, turning them back into babies, telling officers with tears in their eyes that their sons were sick and useless and unable even to hold a gun in their hands. Teenage sons who bid farewell to their mothers at the last minute with the belief that they could defend them from the enemy. Other sons going off whimpering like infants, pushed along into the prophecy of death, trying to look back and wave and maybe see their mothers waving one last time. Only the weak and defenceless allowed to carry on, as long as they did not block the vital passage of military vehicles heading in the opposite direction back towards the front.

In the middle of all that, they had also witnessed great kindness. A man giving away all the food he had brought with him to a family with seven children. People helping to put a wheel back on the trolley, giving precious time away to others whom they might never see again in their lives. Doctors and nurses setting up a makeshift surgery, staying behind to look after the sick and injured, patching them up so they could carry on on their way. A roadside operating theatre in which a doctor amputated the leg from a screaming young boy, clutching at the uniform of the nurse with his hand as though it might have the properties of an anaesthetic. People passing only metres away who were locked into their own misfortune and could no longer feel the pain of others. And each time they entered a new town, they were seen by the inhabitants with great suspicion, shown only where the train station was, because this was not a place with any permanence either, only a halfway stop along the endless road of refugees.

In the waiting room of the train station they looked for available spaces to settle themselves for the night, for a few hours of sleep. Because they had lost everything and had no homes to go back to, they had an instinct for finding the best places away from the doors. These were occupied first, as though they had a value. Even if they would inevitably forsake their places in order to move on again, they settled into them with a touch of permanence, laying out their coats, packing a pillow out of some garment, making sure they were out of the draught, as though this could replace the idea of home. There was some pride in having found a place by the wall. Those who came later had to sleep right in the middle of the floor where they were vulnerable, where their belongings were not as safe. Those close to the doors complained about being stepped over as they slept, even though they had the advantage of being the first up and out if a train came.

Some people talked all evening, comparing the journey so far, telling each other the terrible stories they had witnessed or heard along the way. There were rumours of worse to come, at the mercy of the enemy now as much they were at the mercy of their own beliefs. There was a man who had left his house in Silesia with nothing, only his camera and a few rolls of film with which he had preserved every part of the house, every corner, every picture on the wall, every piece of furniture. He had even photographed the contents of the drawers and the storage space under the stairs. Captured the view from each window, even from the attic skylight. Later he would settle down somewhere and recreate his entire life and belongings and family history. No matter what happened to his house, he would have everything intact in an album. He kept his bag firmly by his side, patting it as though it was full of money, or food, things he would fight to the death over.

There was some comfort in numbers. Mostly they talked about their loved ones and about where it might be possible to get some food. Some of them took off their shoes and talked about the terrible state of their feet, asking for nail scissors, asking what should be done with an ingrown toenail. Some began sewing and repairing clothes, looking at what other people wore and exchanging items that were more suitable. They reappraised the value of everything against the background of their chances. Out of despair came ingenuity and invention, self-help and self-analysis. People began to correct each other on tiny details, a brutal trade of criticism and counter-criticism in which they established a code of survival and self-surrender. Rational thought suppressed the emotional. They elevated themselves above their misery with intelligence, with frugality, by being hard on themselves, by biting back pain, by having no sympathy for weakness. It was the start of a new contest of correctness. Some of them argued about the correct time, saying the clock on the platform was slow. Some said it was a mistake to leave your coat on at night. Some blamed themselves for not seeing all this coming.

Gregor's mother did not talk very much about herself. Though they asked her questions, she remained silent, under instruction from her father not to reveal anything.

Some people became worried, weighing up their chances and suddenly deciding to leave, giving up precious space in the corner. Even though they were giving up the best place in the whole station and might never get such a good spot again, it was better to move on and get a bit further west while the roads were less congested. And what if a train came, those who remained behind said, just after they had set out on the road? Then they would be sorry not to have been more patient.

The door squeaked every time it opened. A tiny whistle in the hinges that became so familiar that she could not settle down to sleep. She sat with Gregor on her knees, twisting and turning all night with his bad ear. She imagined her father in the doorway with his great smile, telling her it was time to go. All the envious glances of other people around her who wished they had a father like that coming to rescue them.

By midnight she was in despair. The room was packed and the air was stuffy. The people around her were talking up a storm of fatalism. Some of them tried to remain positive, but they were outnumbered by the others, imagining a terrible outcome to their lives, forecasting obscene and cruel endings for themselves and everyone else. Their skills of pessimism allowed them to form friendships and allegiances, it gave them sympathy, even advantage and power. The more they spoke of doom, the more respect they gained. A talent passed down to them over centuries. They had an eye for disaster. They outdid each other preparing for the worst. Glorious, operatic forms of doom which helped them to overcome their own fear. One woman said she was sure that she would not live through this night. Another woman said it was certain that she would never see her husband again. And maybe this, too, was part of the great skill of emotional survival, to accept the worst of all possible so that something better will emerge.

There was no chance of a train. They knew that. It was too late. Nobody had any faith in the timetable in any case, and they looked out into the rain, knowing what was ahead: another long trek on the roads the next day and maybe nothing more than the shelter of a cold railway station at the end of it all, with a place that was even less comfortable than what they had. Their doomed forecast was the only certainty left.

She tried to get Gregor to sleep with his bad ear down on her lap. The boy was whimpering and sucking on the button of his jumper. She spoke to him, or spoke to herself really, because she was in a confused state, wondering if she should go and search for her father. It was the boy who brought her back to earth and made her think more rationally. She could not watch him suffering any more and began to beg people once more for some oil to put in his ear in order to soothe the pain.

She tried to make him eat some bread. But he refused. He only wanted to suck the button at the top of his jumper. Would not let it go. She could see that the button was hanging on a loose thread, but still she could not get him to let it go.

'Come on, Gregor,' she kept saying to him. 'Give it to me. I'm afraid you might choke on it.'

He was almost deaf with the ear infection and she had no language with which to persuade the boy. In the damp air of the train station that night, she got him to stretch his feet out on the bench and lean his head against her. The button had come off and he had it in his mouth, hiding it at the back of his teeth and refusing to let go. She tried to force him. Tried to take it from him, but the boy put up a huge struggle and screamed with his mouth shut.

'Gregor, if you don't give me that button you'll swallow it in your sleep and then you'll die,' she said.

Older women around her advised her not to try it by force. They told her to let him fall asleep first. And then she sat watching him until his eyes finally closed over in exhaustion, but still resisting sleep. In his mouth, his only possession. When he began to drift off, she tried once more to slip her finger into his mouth and dislodge it, but he woke up every time and shook his head from side to side. His lips held tight.

'Come on, Gregor,' she said, 'please give Mama the button.'

She made all the gestures she could in order to explain it to him. She tried to reassure him with smiles, but he returned a look of suspicion. And it was only when she decided to forget about the button and hum a song in his good ear that she eventually won him over. Or maybe it was the other way round. The boy had won her over. It was the great surrender. He pushed the button forward to the tip of his lips.

'Can I take it now?' she asked him. And this time he allowed her to remove the little red button at last. She said she would put it away safely and sew it back on the jumper as soon as she could. But the boy was already asleep.

Ten

After such a long time in the womb, when an infant is born, it continues to perceive itself as a physical part of the mother, like an arm or a leg. Only very gradually does it begin to understand its own individuality.

When Daniel was a baby, they used to lie in bed for hours watching him. His small fat legs in the air and his hands reaching out to grip one of his own feet without really knowing that it belonged to him. He was still a part of them both that summer, lying naked in the middle of the bed with his eyes open, smiling and making his first sounds. Gregor and Mara naked on either side, with the window wide open and the top branches of the trees in the street swaying in a warm breeze outside. Once, Daniel peed suddenly. His small penis rose up and sent out a fountain of sweet urine, wetting both of them and himself also. They laughed. He became frightened by their sudden laughter and began to cry. So Mara held him close and they all took a bath together.

They were in that timeless zone of early parenthood, enthralled by the reflection in their own baby. They had time to watch every development, every laugh, every burp. The tiny pink pearl that formed on his upper lip after breastfeeding.

Mara was working as a physiotherapist by then. She was able to arrange her appointments so they could be together like this in the mornings. Gregor was giving music lessons and playing with a cover band at night. He was busy composing by day, and some of his more abstract pieces were getting noticed.

They needed nothing from the past. Everything was riding on the future. On their lives and on this little boy who was not even aware enough to notice that he was poking himself in the eye with his own thumb. Mara laughed a lot. Gregor sang a lot. They became babies themselves, barking and buzzing and making baby sounds. Daniel was the shape of their joy, and what more confirmation did they need from life than to hear his tiny sucking noises nearby at night. There was a sweet smell of milk in the bed from breastfeeding. And once or twice, it was milk love between them when her breasts began to leak across his chest. Afterwards, he always paid great attention to some part of her, circling his index finger round and round her kneecap while they whispered late into the night with the milky street light coming in across their bodies, staying awake inside their luck as long as they could. Her head coming to rest on his chest, listening to the resounding hum of his voice in her ear. His singing finally putting her to sleep.

One night, Mara brought up the subject of circumcision.

'We'll have to get him circumcised,' she said.

'I don't think there's any need for that,' Gregor replied.

'But of course we have to do it,' she said.

'It's far too late, Mara. It's meant to be done within eight days of birth,' Gregor said. 'Anyway, it's not that important any more.'

'Why not? I didn't think you would be against it?'

She lifted her head up from his chest to look at him.

'I don't know, Mara. It's very traumatic for the child. Also for the parents,' he said. 'It has to be done without an anaesthetic. It's all very strict. They say that some mothers faint at the sight of it.'

'But it's all forgotten very quickly.'

'I'm not so sure about that,' Gregor thought.

'You don't remember it, do you?'

'No, I suppose not.'

He got himself into a bit of potential trouble then. He had allowed her to assume that it was done as an infant and that he had managed to survive miraculously until the end of the war without being detected. He had allowed her to believe things that were not quite true, without stepping in immediately to correct them. There was so much that remained vague in his life that he was glad sometimes when something was unequivocal. She talked about his penis and said she was glad that it was circumcised. To her it was unique, rough and smooth at the same time on her tongue. She had trapped it inside her mouth until it fused with her palate and finally exploded under pressure.

It was too late to go back now. Too late to say that it would have been virtually impossible, not to mention insane, for any parent to carry that operation out in wartime. He was afraid it would weaken the evidence and he allowed her assumptions to stand.

'They say it makes a man less sensitive,' he argued.

'I haven't noticed,' she said.

'I'd hate to put him through that for nothing,' he continued. 'Doctors don't believe it has a function any more. They don't think it has anything to do with hygiene. Believe me, Mara. We don't want to put little Daniel through that horrific pain. For what?'

'It's your identity,' she argued. 'This is a survivor baby and we want to celebrate all that.'

'The bloodline comes through the mother,' he said. 'You would have to be Jewish.'

In any case, he told her, he had already been to see that rabbi, that it was not that easy to be accepted into the Jewish faith.

'You see, there's no real proof,' he said. 'There's nothing on paper, Mara. They won't accept my word for it. It was only something I was told, by my uncle Max.'

'Why didn't your mother tell you?'

'She didn't know,' Gregor said. 'She wasn't sure. I was brought up as a Catholic and there was never any talk about me being Jewish. You see, she didn't have any proof either.'

'Except the fact that you were circumcised,' she said.

There was a buoyancy in her voice. She wanted to put all that doubt out of his mind about his true origins. She wanted to bring him back to life and to confirm the existence that he had lost. And maybe she wanted to fight for him and his identity, some atonement for what had gone on in the war.

'Why are you not more positive about this?'

But they stopped talking about it and lay awake for a long time, drifting in their own thoughts. They heard the sound of a truck outside, parking on the street below their window. They listened to the driver getting out and closing the door. After a short while the door closed again, so they wondered if the driver had been stretching his legs and got back in to rest a few hours before driving away on some long journey across the Continent.

'Is it one of those big ones, with a separate cab?' she asked him. 'The ones where you can sleep overnight in a bunk?'

83

They described it for themselves, with pin-ups of nude women in straw hats at the back of the cab to keep the driver company. Gregor wanted to get up and have a look for himself, but she would not let him disturb the way they were lying together. They even fell asleep for a while, only to wake up again, wondering if the truck was still there or whether it had moved on. They spoke about the truck that Emil, his grandfather, drove and what it must have looked like. Once again, Gregor wanted to get up and go to the window to check. But she turned him round and lay behind him with her warm, milky breasts against his back. And somehow, that night, he felt that even happiness could sometimes be a lonely thing. They fell asleep and woke up with Daniel's cries in the morning. Gregor got up and brought him to the bed with Mara so that she could breastfeed him. Then he stood at the window and after a while said: 'The truck has gone.'

By morning she had changed her mind. Gregor had managed to put her off with his talk of the scalpel violating her baby boy, cutting into his foreskin. The sound of him crying. The distress in his eyes. A moment of helpless self-awareness in which he felt totally alone in the world, with the pain darting through his entire body. His mouth opening in a silent cry, full of terror, before he found the breath to actually scream. That bright moment of cruelty entering into his memory forever.

But that didn't stop her trying to get Daniel accepted as a Jew. She said there were those who thought nothing of identity, people who felt it was not much of an issue any more, except for those who are dispossessed.

'You have lost something and we must put it back,' she said.

He had nothing but the name given to him by his adoptive parents.

'We're not going to deny your people any more,' she added with a finality in her voice. 'We have a duty to all those relatives of yours who were killed. We want to give them their dignity back.'

He could be sullen sometimes. He could go into himself, a refugee, staying silent for hours, doing nothing but playing his guitar. Alone. An orphan again. Right in the middle of their happiest years, the trapdoor opened up underneath him and he became a loner again. She was concerned about him sometimes. She had a friend whose young husband had killed himself. And Gregor's favourite book was written by Egon Friedell, a man who ended his life during the Nazi years by throwing himself out the window, even shouting a warning into the street beforehand to avoid injuring pedestrians.

Was it hereditary, that faculty of doubt? Or was it something he got from his adoptive parents. They were refugees, too, and had that dreamy gaze into the past, to what might have been, to empty places in memory. Was there some distance in his mother's eyes as he grew up? Some feeling that he would never live up to her dreams? The boy who could never match up to the child lost in the bombing.

Was there some companionship in his depression, some fear of happiness, some overproduction of defensive thoughts? Maybe depression is linked in some way to lack of belonging. Was that the old cure for depression, she wondered, the constant reference to tradition, the rituals, the barmitzvahs, the baptisms, the big weddings, the songs and the ceremonies of transition? Is that why people don't need tradition that much any more because there are other ways of dealing with mental disorder now?

She was all the more determined to restore his sense of belonging. She arranged a meeting with the rabbi, but the same arguments came up again. Lack of proof. No documentation. No evidence in Gregor's favour, only the word of his dead uncle Max.

The rabbi remained polite, but then Mara became angry, with Daniel on her arm.

'I don't believe it,' she said. 'Not that long ago, this baby would have been taken away to Auschwitz on less evidence. Now the evidence is not enough.'

She stormed out into the street with Gregor behind her. And that afternoon, it was she who became gloomy. Until a new idea came to her.

'Go to Warsaw,' she said, lifting herself up. 'Go to Danzig, Gregor. Go and see those places where you might be from.'

He did that. He applied for a visa and went to Warsaw some months later in the hope that he might recover some grain of memory. He read about the Warsaw Ghetto and the uprising. He learned about the conditions there and about the woman who had smuggled children out through the sewers. The city had awakened something inside him. He cried openly on the street, with people staring at him as they passed by, wondering what his story was and what painful memory had suddenly come up through the asphalt.

Stepping onto the streets of some strange city was not evidence. He could tell people that he had been to Warsaw, but he still felt a fake. Though his friends were not asking for proof. They went to his concerts and heard him play with his band at night. They loved his music and believed his talents had been handed down to him through generations, a quiet cultural evolution which reached a peak every time he performed, a human flaw turned into virtue, a hollow place turned into song. All the evidence they needed to hear was in the minimalist fingertip passion of his notes, in those bent and curtailed riffs, in the raw, breathy survivor blast which filled the empty spaces.

They were aware that biography is never a stationary thing, but something that constantly changes shape. They accepted the facts on trust and began to say it was 'very likely' that he came from Warsaw. They were willing to believe him and he only needed to say that it was 'possible' that he was one of the children rescued from the ghetto. All they wanted from him was to say that he 'believed' he was Jewish. The evidence was inside all of them. It screamed at them from the history books. Who would dare deny it? Who would question a man who escaped from this dark corridor of time and came out alive?

Eleven

Gregor's mother also explained to him why his grandfather was fat. When Gregor was growing up, she showed him the pictures of Emil before the First World War. A tall, handsome young man. She also showed him the pictures of his grandfather before the Second World War, a bloated man who had trouble with his health and drank too much. He was sometimes unreliable. He was a deserter in the Second World War, but there were reasons for that, she told him. He was not a criminal, only a man who should never have been called up.

She told him that things happened to Emil as a soldier in the First World War. It was a miracle that he ever married after his experiences on the Russian front.

Later in life, Gregor began to call it the poets' war, not only because there were so many poets on both sides who took part, but because of the great passion with which men threw themselves into that war like lovesick poets. They went to the front in a kind of patriotic haze that was close to being in love. It must have been a time when love was something so much more tragic, more elevated and pernicious, more once in a lifetime. Not something that happened twice. Maybe love has become more transferable now. Back in the time of the First World War love was more apocalyptic, like the love you gave to your country.

His grandfather Emil would have formed the opinion that fighting for his country was the greatest act of love he would ever experience in his lifetime. The act of love to the nation, to the greatness of his people and their noble traditions. And war was the ultimate expression of that love in which he would be embraced by the masses.

When he was given his heavy boots and the itchy uniform as an eighteen-year-old country boy and taught how to hold a rifle in his hand and ordered to spend days practising how to slice his bayonet into straw men lined up in the barracks square, he was convinced how glorious it would be to die in battle. To have an enemy bayonet slice through your own stomach was a wonderful, painless experience to a man who truly loved his nation. The general with the straw moustache who made all these speeches about the manliness of sacrifice described it all as patriotic bliss. Fear was the natural, preliminary rush of excitement that comes with love, and dying in battle was the closest thing you could get to sleeping with a woman.

When Emil got to the front, it was anything but romantic. The men liked him because he brought jokes and songs. Every night, they would ask him to sing his songs about maidens and courtiers, songs about lovers unable to return to each other. But he didn't go out to fight in order to sing about women. He was expecting the place to be full of women and love. He was waiting for women in white flowing clothes to lie down with him in the fields. He had begun to imagine them semi-naked, walking out of the tall fields of wheat or dancing in the woods. He imagined them leaving the milking and dropping their buckets and the warm white milk running through the grass as they came running towards him. Their embrace and their coy giggles and the freedom of their bodies. But there was not a single woman in sight. Instead, it was all men shouting orders. Men with bad tempers, men with bad skin, men with bowel problems, men who seemed lost and held photographs of their loved ones or their mothers, knowing they might never see them again. Men stealing from each other. Men cursing and men telling lies about themselves. Men who got drunk and found prostitutes outside the camp, paying for love even though it was promised in such abundance to all fighting men.

Emil was eager to get into battle, eager to feel the dreamy embrace of war. When he heard the cannons in the distance coming closer, he felt the fear which had been described to him so accurately as a first kiss. When he saw the enemy appearing for the first time on the flat landscape ahead, he wanted to get sick. Some of his comrades soiled their trousers without even knowing it. Many of them fell in the first encounter. He saw men groaning with their intestines in their hands. Men with missing limbs staring up into the sky in a state of blissful exhaustion, comrades he knew by name, dying as though they had just fallen asleep on their backs in the middle of it all.

Emil was not blessed with the sacrifice of love himself. He was in shock at the sight of blood and death all around him. Fear kept coming in waves, like a great emptiness in the pit of his stomach, in his sphincter, in his genitals. He could hardly eat any more. He felt the stings of heat under his uniform. He got baby hands whenever he had to lift his weapon. He sometimes suspected there was something wrong with his heart and that he would just drop dead any moment. What he hated most was the lull where nothing happened. That great absence of women when the men spent hours doing nothing but smoking cigarettes and writing letters and listening to other men rambling about their lovers, real and imaginary. He saw men who could not wait any longer fumble in their trousers. In each other's trousers. Gentle sounds of dying every night in the tent right beside him, men growling in each other's arms as they tried to bring that glorious moment of death to each other.

And then he killed a man. For weeks he had been shooting aimlessly at everything that moved ahead of him. Who knows where all those bullets went to. But he knew at first hand when he had taken the life of another man, because it changed everything. A Russian soldier of his own age appeared from behind a barn one afternoon and stood a moment with his broad, indestructible chest, defying death as though he was protected in some way by the prayers of his family back home. Emil raised his gun and shot into that chest. The other man blinked, but remained standing. He must have been struck by the same paralysing fear, unable to lift the heavy rifle, even though he seemed like a strong farming type himself. When he eventually tried to aim the rifle back at Emil, he fell down dead. He had been praying. There was a brass icon opened on his chest, a triptych of religious figures carved into panels. The white ribbon that normally kept the icon doors closed still wrapped around his trigger finger.

Emil stood over him wishing he could take the bullet back. He kneeled down to say a prayer for him and lost all regard for his own life, utterly defenceless now, leaving his gun aside on the ground and praying for his enemy with a pool of blood edging like a slow, dark delta towards his knees. He closed the man's eyes and felt the stubble of his beard as his hand glanced across his chin. He could see the tan line around his neck. Then he cut the icon off with his bayonet. The icon would remain in Emil's possession as a kind of reminder of the man he had killed, a man he would spend the rest of his days trying to bring back to life. Gregor has the icon now in his apartment in Berlin. It's one of the only things which he has brought with him from his family. The white ribbon has gone beige and the brass is dulled with time. Occasionally, he stands it up on the hall table and opens out the doors on their plain hinges, a kind of duty that comes along with this precious possession, to think of the dead Russian soldier.

For Emil, the glorious moment of ecstasy came not long after that. He had been in a numb state for days, stepping over dead bodies from his own ranks and from enemy ranks, all lovers of their own nation now lying in the early agony of decay around the sandy roads and fields. Men lying in orchards, surrounded by apples and baskets. A cow grazing among the dead, as though they were farmers lying idle.

One morning, after another lull, they woke up with the enemy right in front of them, beyond a stand of trees. There was a mist across the fields and they could see nothing, only a family of deer leaping away through the dawn. Roosters crowing in the distance. Through the sleepy emptiness of the landscape came the sound of screaming. Phantom voices of women screaming from the trees with every variation of hurt and anger coming closer through the morning air. The moment had arrived at last. As the sun was beginning to break through, bringing a hint of colour back to the landscape, the screaming became even more shrill, more hostile, more terrifying, until they finally saw a battalion of women soldiers running straight at them out of the mist.

The men seemed unable to move. Men who were so eager to see women of any kind, had no idea what they should do. All that virile longing turned into a spurt of warm weakness. A hollow, immovable blue ache in the groin that made them unable to walk. Women of all shapes and sizes dressed in men's uniforms, some with their hair tied and some with their hair wild. Women with big breasts, women with boyish figures and fiery eyes, women with enormous open mouths gone hoarse with screaming. Mothers and daughters and wives and fiancées, charging fully armed, carrying their weapons like ladles, running with open arms, some gone crazy with the instinct of child protection and mother love and passion for motherland. Women running with their bayonets flashing like silver eels in the morning light.

By the time these female warriors came level with them, the men were all ready to submit. The officers ordered them to fire, which some of them began to do, but without any heart, because they were so confused. Unable to make out the difference between love and death, they waited for the warmth of these women to wash over them like a great big blanket of murderous affection. Some of the men dropped their weapons in shock and opened their arms in a great death wish as the women sliced through their straw stomachs. Women gone fierce with screaming, women with ancient kitchen skills wiping bayonets across men's necks, letting their lives flow out across the mattress of the September fields. Some of the men fought for their lives and were conscious enough of their own mortality to see these women as their enemies. But Emil never saw so many men accept death with such ease of mind. He felt like an infant boy waiting for his mother to wrap a towel around him after his bath, and before he knew it, he blanked out and fell down in the spot where he stood.

When he recovered consciousness in a field hospital, his body was deformed from the shock. His legs were twice their normal size, his face and neck like a bulging, sheepskin container of water. The first grotesque encounter with women was such a shock, he suffered acute kidney failure. A renal shutdown brought on by overwhelming fear, causing water retention and giving him that inflated appearance which he had for the rest of his life. He survived a battalion of women and eventually married the nurse who looked after him at the field hospital and vowed to calm his nightmares.

He should have been terrified of women, but then he made a remarkable recovery and turned it into his life ambition to be loved by as many women as possible. And that's what got him into trouble in the end, Gregor's mother said, as a warning.

'He was a great singer,' she said. 'He should have been on stage. He should have made records. Instead, he became a dealer on the black market.'

Gregor often asked her to tell the rest of the story about his grandfather, but she did not have the answers to that. He disappeared in the end, she told him. He never came back to the railway station to collect them.

Twelve

Daniel has arrived with his girlfriend, Juli. He is the image of his father, though Gregor cannot see the resemblance himself. He finds it hard to see his own reflection at this point. Daniel is tall, but he's got brown eyes, and he doesn't have the curly hair. Maybe it's the quiet, intense way they both talk, their smiles, their way of speaking with the head bowed a fraction to the side.

Daniel and Juli go around embracing everyone. They all stand back and admire this young couple, their perfection. Juli's father is a fruit importer from Istanbul and her mother is a true Berliner, born and brought up in the city, though Juli has become a rebel. She dresses in contradictions, wearing a white linen dress and dreadlocks in her hair that make her peer up at everyone through half-pulled curtains. In the sunlight, her white dress lights up like a paper lampshade and there is a stud in her lower lip which shines like a steel pearl. Daniel works as a chef, in a vegetarian restaurant. He is a little older than Juli, but she is the true environmental activist who has been involved in all kinds of protesting and has been arrested for obstructing the police.

They have taken a vow of frugality, refusing to get into private cars, using only public transport, eating only organic food. They intend to make their way to Africa by ship, first to Egypt, then on to the Sudan, so it seems like a long exile ahead of them. No quick flights home for Christmas or whenever the mood strikes them.

They are the new earth lovers for whom this fruit gathering is more like an elegy, more biblical than a simple day out in the country. They love the hand-to-mouth, subsistence notion of harvesting as much as the socialists of his parents' generation admired the company of the real working class, people with coal marks on their faces and dirt under their fingernails. They are the believers now. But where does all this purist logic square up with the self-destruction of alcohol and drugs and dancing all night in a techno fit around those clubs in Berlin? Gregor and Martin and Mara were those revolutionaries once, but maybe they all go soft in the end, because revolution is hard work. For the moment, Daniel's youth-bound principles have remained strong.

They live in this city full of contradictions. A place where nothing matches but where everything blends together in a strange conformity of clashing styles and biographies. The city is vivid with history. Layers of it in every suburb, coming up through the streets, in people's eyes. A chamber of horrors, but also a place of monuments and devotion to memory. A place that has no time for greatness any more and celebrates instead the ordinary genius of survival. A wounded place at the heart of Europe, eager to heal and laugh. A cut-price city full of mischief and functional chaos, full of thinkers and artists and extremists.

On the street where Daniel lives, there is an ecological slogan reminding them, every time they leave their apartment, to respect their environment. It's a city full of warnings from the past and warnings from the future. They live in an area of Berlin where the rents are down to nothing, where the punks and goths hang around outside the underground station with their bottles and their docile dogs, where everything is covered in graffiti like a film of thin paint along the walls and doorways. It's all very reassuring, like a running commentary of the city's life. When the Berlin Wall came down, the street art moved into these open spaces in a new search for belonging. Heroic, three-dimensional expressions, most of them making no sense at all. But here, across the street from Daniel's apartment, where the corresponding apartments have been missing since the war and have been replaced by a repair workshop, some artist has painted a striking image on a red-brick wall. A convex face of a dog with orange teeth and rectangular jaws. It's hard to say whether this enormous face is meant to be growling or smiling. Menacing or mocking? The dog is smoking a cigarette, a tiny stub balancing at an angle on the lower lip, with a thoughtful, almost human intelligence in his expression, speaking the jagged words of doom: 'Waiting for the flood.' A prophet with a sense of humour.

Gregor and Daniel are getting on better now than before, making up for lost time. They meet occasionally for a drink. But it's obvious at times that Martin has remained closer to Daniel, mainly because he became a surrogate father figure to him in Gregor's absence. They have an amiable duel going that seems lacking between father and son. Only Martin can get away with calling Daniel an ecological missionary.

Once every fortnight, during the summer, Daniel has brought Gregor a basket of fruit, sent to him by Mara with a note. It's her way of gently pushing them towards each other, getting Daniel to carry the fruit with him the three kilometres from the farm to the station because he won't accept a lift, delivering these certified, pesticide-free cherries along the least fuel-travelled route. Even if the cherries had little maggots doing back flips around the basket by the time it reached the city, Gregor must admire the effort his son has taken. It's a message of goodwill from Mara, passed on to him through their son Daniel.

Each time Gregor has invited Daniel inside, they've sat on the balcony, drinking coffee and eating fruit, listening to the mournful sound of the six o'clock bells tailing off in a sad, minor key.

'Are they still complaining about your students?' Daniel asked one evening.

'Not so much,' Gregor said. 'Maybe they're getting used to it.'

Gregor has a great reputation for private lessons, though he's got constant trouble with the people living below. It's a war of noise and counter-noise in the city. He makes every new student lie on the floor beneath the grand piano in order to listen to the full sound travelling downwards before he even begins to make them sit at the keys to discuss posture. His students love him and maybe parents have begun to trust the eccentric teacher more than the clean-cut, conventional type.

From the playground next door came the wild echoes of football players amplified around the empty court-yards at the back, preventing them from having much of a conversation. At times, the noise of screeching voices was like the seaside, with the ball banging against the fence being mistaken for the hollow thump of the surf folding on the shore. Cars passing by along the cobbles making up the raking swish of the retreating wave across a stony beach. And right underneath them, the people sitting outside the restaurant at the orange tables, chatting and laughing. When the winter comes, all of those sounds will disappear for another year as the acoustic landscape outside becomes every bit as muted as the visual one of bare trees and empty benches and abandoned playgrounds. Only the bells will remain with their holy, melancholy chords. In the summer, the noise of the city conspired to keep them silent.

Daniel has taken his shirt off in the heat, so he can start picking the apples in earnest. One of his shoulders is bigger, better built than the other, a strange physical anomaly that comes from Mara's side of the family and has been passed on at random. One of her uncles has the same feature and maybe they were all hammer throwers going back in time, or miners in the Ruhr valley with an overdeveloped right shoulder.

Quite suddenly, he is forced to drop his basket when a wasp hovers around him. Everyone else ignores the wasps, but Daniel feels exposed. He runs away. Fights off the unseen wasp in a silent tantrum among the trees, an irrational performance, lashing all around him, punching holes in the air in this peaceful place as though he's remembered some grotesque dream.

'Hit him with the rake,' Martin says. His big laugh fills the entire orchard.

'You must stay calm,' Thorsten advises. 'You mustn't make sudden movements. They won't harm you as long as you stay calm.'

'What are you going to be like in Africa?' Mara laughs.

'Look, Daniel,' Thorsten says. He digs his big hand right into the rotten apples on the wheelbarrow. Everyone turns to stare at his bare arm covered in wasps.

'They're drunk,' Mara says. 'Drunk on food. They are so heavy and full of fruit juice, most of them, that they can hardly even fly. They don't have the energy to get angry and sting anyone.'

'Look, they have droopy eyelids,' Martin adds.

Thorsten says that he's only been stung once, inside the house when he happened to put his arm right down on the table where a wasp must have been feeding on a spot of jam. Never while picking fruit. They often take up apples or pears off the ground with two or three wasps crawling out, embarrassed at being caught gorging themselves.

Martin turns it all into a larger joke, pretending that he has been attacked by the same wasp. He imitates Daniel's erratic motions of terror, chopping the air, kicking and running to pick up the rake to defend himself against an invisible monster.

'Down with this sort of thing,' he shouts, and it is Mara who laughs more than anyone else.

Thorsten mentions that they had bees for a while, in one of the barns. Nesting in the loam floor. A beekeeper came to transfer them to a proper hive out in the open, close to the orchard. For a few years, they thrived there until the colony died out. The hive was attacked by wasps and there was nothing left of them, only the dark honeycomb all empty and the shells of dead bees.

Gregor talks about a house he stayed in that was full of wasps, when he was travelling in the USA, out there in the mountains of Colorado, in one of those mining towns where the frontier men went to dig for lead and other metals.

'I swear, they were everywhere,' Gregor says. He speaks with a husk of protection around his words, without metaphor. It is not easy to extract any secondary meaning.

'It was a big old wooden house and they were crawling up and down the sash windows, trying to get out to the light. Desperate for water. I told the woman of the house about them, so she came and killed a whole load of them, then she tried to flush them down the toilet but they were still floating around when I came back that night after the concert. They were all over the bed, alive again, so I had to kill about a dozen of them myself. Next morning there were dozens more alive again at the window. Must have been nesting right in the walls.'

Daniel goes back to pick up the apples he dropped, still keeping his eye on every wasp in his vicinity.

'For an environmentalist,' Martin comments, 'you're very mistrustful of insects, Daniel.'

Daniel smiles. 'They have it in for me, those things.'

'He was stung by a hornet when he was a boy,' Mara explains.

Why does she mention the hornet? Why here? The mood has turned serious and Gregor finds Daniel staring at him now.

'They're protected,' Thorsten says, as a fact. 'It's illegal to kill a hornet.'

'How would you like to be stung by a hornet?' Juli says, turning on Gregor as though she felt the pain herself.

Her words reveal the hurt passed on. She must know that the hornet sting all those years ago is still associated with Gregor leaving. Daniel crying at night as a boy and the neighbours in the town where they were staying on holiday in the mountains coming over with aloe vera ointment. The pain is gone now, but the memory of it returns, prolonged by each year that Gregor spent away from his family. Daniel crying months later because his father was gone. Still asking for his father years later and pointing to the spot where the hornet sent the hot, poisoned sword into the back of his leg.

'You fucked off after that,' Daniel says. 'You left your family.'

The orchard is thrown into silence. The outburst seems at odds with the calmness and the intense hum draped over this gathering. The pain has come back and everyone looks at Gregor.

'Daniel, please,' Mara intervenes. 'You promised.'

Martin sucks the hostility out of the air by changing the subject. He smooths over the tension by ignoring Daniel's words, pretending there is some acoustic black hole in the orchard by which nobody heard anything. Instead, he mentions a Beach Boys' song he heard in the car on the way down. 'Good Vibrations'.

He begins to howl some of the words of the hit song. *'Good, good, good . . .'*

'That's your era, isn't it?' Daniel mocks.

'It's a classic that,' Martin says. 'I never knew that the wobbly instrument was invented by a Russian.'

'Theremin,' Gregor says. 'Leon Theremin. He tried to sell it in the USA, but then Stalin sent the KGB after him. Ended his days in the Gulag.'

'Then the Beach Boys got a hold of it.'

Once again Martin begins to imitate the sound of the theremin. Gregor joins in, adding the instrumentation and the harmonies. Martin picks up the rake and plays air guitar with it for a moment. When they calm down again, Martin leans the rake back up against the tree and quotes one of the lines from the hit song with a puzzled expression.

'I don't know where but she sends me there.'

He pauses for a moment and translates the words into German.

'Ich weiss nicht wohin aber sie treibt mich dahin.'

They laugh together for a while at that and then go back to concentrating on picking the apples.

Thirteen

He knows only that he was left alone a lot as a child. There are certain doorways, certain architectural features, entrance hallways and stairwells of a green or beige colour which will always remind him of the house where he stayed every day after school. Because his mother had to work in order to keep things going after the war, he was kept in a home until she came to collect him. For a while she worked at night, in a bakery, so then he had to stay overnight in the care centre. To this day, he still gets the chalky taste of pea soup at the back of his throat every time he's reminded of that place. He knows they were not very nice to him there. He knows that he was left for long periods in the cot. He knows that he was calling the nurse, but when she came it was already too late. She smiled as she slapped him in the face. She said it was the most disgusting painting she had ever seen in her whole life, a train at the end of the cot and tracks going all the way along the wall. He remembers them hosing him down with cold water in the bath. He must have been crying afterwards, because a woman came over to his cot. She was collecting her own son, but stopped to stroke Gregor's head and told him he would be collected very soon, too. He remembers the worried look on the other boy's face watching his mother sharing that precious affection around so indiscriminately.

His own mother didn't like him playing in the rubble with other children as he grew up. He had died in those ruins before. She preferred him to stay inside with her, making lists together. It was her way of dealing with life, holding everything in place, writing it all down methodically.

'Make a list,' she would say. And he would take out pencil and paper and put all the items down, ticking them off one by one. If something wasn't ticked off by the end of the day it would have to be placed at the top of a new list for the next day before they could sleep. Lists of things to do and lists of things they had done together. Even the simplest things that sometimes should be taken for granted were put down, maybe as a kind of reassurance that they were alive and that the world was still moving on. 'Will I put down brushing your teeth?' Gregor would ask. And 'Yes,' his mother would say, 'put down brushing your teeth,' because each one of those daily anchors drove away the fear that he could sometimes see in her eyes.

He was a nervous child, constantly peeing in his pants at school, always coming home wet and stinking. She traded with him, allowing him to sleep in her bed as long as he didn't pee. And that's how things stood for years, a close and sometimes suffocating relationship, until one day when he was suddenly banished from his mother's bed. A man from nowhere walked in the door and took his place. His father had arrived back from the war and took over the role that Gregor had enjoyed to himself till then.

The man bought him a scooter. And a mouth organ. He took him hunting and taught him all about nature. But maybe there was always something missing, some absence, some feeling that Gregor was never adequate. A failure in his father's eyes.

He retreated into his boyhood fantasies, mostly about trapeze artists. Circus women dressed in spangled tops and the string tights. It was not the animals or the clowns that attracted him as a boy, but the woman who could wrap her legs around the rope and flew through the air, smiling down at him from above. The circus came once a year in the spring and he could not tear himself away. He hung around all day and once saw the trapeze artist standing in the door of her caravan, smoking a cigarette and wearing a pink dressing gown. Another time, he saw her lying on the ground in a field nearby in the long grassy verge with one of the men from the circus, kissing and smiling at him as though she was still gliding through the air with her arms and legs and breasts just barely holding on to the rope.

Mara used to say that Gregor's childhood was like the dark side of the moon. There was little evidence of how he grew up. She did not have a single photograph of him when he was a small boy. No heroic images of him with sword or a bow and arrow. No shots of him and his dog. No first ride on his bike, no first day at school, no smiling pictures of him with missing teeth or with his arm around his mother.

He never talked about that very much. Only the mushroom picking and the endless hunting episodes. He said his mother could be a bit possessive. She could also be a saint sometimes, believing that the whole world was out to wear her down. Please, Gregor, I beg you, don't ask me any more questions, she would say. Please, Gregor, if you want a bicycle, draw it for yourself. Then she would do the singing yawn again, descending into a segregated mood in which she seemed beyond reach, inside her own world. She sometimes wished the worst on herself. He remembers how she broke her arm falling off a hunting tower in the forest.

He can still see the broken bone sticking out, bent like a stick underwater. But instead of calling for help, she became a stoic and proudly climbed back up the ladder with her lips tightened, biting back the pain in order to the show her husband what had happened. She was deeply Catholic. She was the kind of person who found some kind of elegiac, victim comfort in apocalyptic events. She had been forced to look at dead bodies, along with a hundred other women, paraded and photographed as they stood by decomposing corpses. It made her rejoice in calamity. A code of premonition in which she and her husband discussed world events with doomed enthusiasm.

There is a feeling of vertigo that comes along with memory. Or is it the apples falling? The sight of people high on ladders? The feeling of being upside down in this orchard after looking up into the branches for so long?

He has a fear of falling back into that emptiness. The strict ambitions of his father, the endless hunting days, the training for survival. When he was a teenager, he remembers coming back from a school trip in the Alps and finding his parents standing in the hallway. They looked him up and down in disbelief, speaking about him in the third person as though he had not quite physically returned yet. 'There is our son,' his mother kept saying, to make sure there could be no doubt about it. 'Make him sit down and tell us everything, slowly. On the balcony? No, make him sit at the table. Wait, don't begin yet.' They had to know everything, who he met, what mountains he climbed, what he ate, what mistakes he made, every detail of every day. He was their only child and they had always lived through him, just as he also had the feeling that his trip only became a reality through them, in the making of the story which he brought home with him. You must write all this down, his mother kept repeating. Make a list of everything, so you'll remember it all later.

He told them that he was nearly killed. It was a family test, the moment of separation when a boy tries to find out how much his parents would miss him if he was no longer alive. He had lost his footing and almost gone over a cliff. He was lucky, he told them, that they were climbing below the treeline because he was stopped by a single pine tree growing almost horizontally out of the side of the rock. He dangled there on this tree, the last coat hook on the mountain, looking down at cattle the size of grasshoppers in the fields below until his companions cautiously made their way down with ropes to rescue him.

He gave them the cartoon description, the light bravado with which the other boys put the shock behind them when they got back to the hostel that evening, knowing that he was safe. That fucking pine tree had your name written on it, they kept saying. They described it as though Gregor had suddenly decided to put on an acrobatic performance on the side of the mountain. They worked up the funny side and said he had an expression of surprise on his face as he leaped upwards, trying to do the cartwheel in the air. He looked so flexible, double-jointed almost, indifferent to gravity and immune to pain. Rubber man, or action man, with his head turned back one hundred and eighty degrees, his torso twisted to the opposite side, his legs and arms all belonging to different men who could not agree on which way they should be heading from now on. His right foot kicked upwards into the sky like an extremely clever soccer trick, a bicycle kick with which he was trying to score a last-minute goal before falling off the mountain. They described him waving his hand in a desperate farewell, before he began to slide towards the edge of the cliff. They embraced him and smiled at him, slapping him on the back like a hero for days.

'We thought you were gone, Gregor,' they said. 'You were a dead man there for a moment.'

His mother stood up and began to rifle through his rucksack. What was so urgent about the washing? Gregor remembers thinking. He thought his father would be proud, but instead he remained sitting at the table with fierce eyes while Gregor continued. He was expecting the sympathy of a family homecoming, the kind of back-from-the-dead welcome. Instead, he found their eyes bearing down on him as though he had been careless and damaged some precious belonging that he had been entrusted with. He felt like a family asset, such as the car of which they were so proud. Even the way they had explained the facts of life to him had a proprietorial basis. His mother was deeply Catholic and spoke about purity, while his father clung to a kind of fascist simplicity where sexual organs seemed more like state property, not to be abused or tampered with. A man was given one set of testicles and was under obligation to take care of them because they could not be replaced. They were like standard army equipment or like a passport which didn't actually belong to the person to whom it was issued, but to the larger family. You could not let anyone punch you there in that irreplaceable region because that would mean that you would never have children. With the result that Gregor sometimes felt his testicles were made of porcelain and should have been locked away safely in the glass cabinet with all those other figurines of miniature deer and miniature people in the costumes of another century.

Gregor told them his knees were shaking so much after the fall that he could barely stand up or even feel his own feet inside his boots. They had turned to liquid with terror. One of his friends stood him up and told him to get a grip of himself, to put the fear behind him or else he would live the rest of his life as a ghost. He said he could not even feel his bruises.

His father looked at him with great disappointment. And his mother kept pulling out the dirty laundry from his rucksack as the only true confirmation of life. Never before had Gregor been so disillusioned by his family. His father took the story as a personal offence while his mother stood clutching a pair of underpants as if that was the last thing left remaining of him.

'I've heard enough,' his father said. 'This is not my son.'

Did he always suspect something? Or was it just one of those phrases he had inherited from his own father, the kind of ventriloquism that goes down through generations with everyone repeating the same branded family admonishment in perpetuity. 'No son of mine would shake in his boots like that. And then be proud of it. Where's your courage, man?'

'Don't be hard on him,' his mother said. 'He's had a shock.'

'A shock,' his father bawled. 'He doesn't know what a shock is.'

His father expected a more heroic tale from the Alps and might have preferred his son to have been one of those rescuers. He wanted his son to talk tough, to tell it like a man with indestructible testicles.

'Be a man about it,' he kept repeating. 'When I think of what we went through in the war.'

Next thing his father would start going back over all the stories out there in the East with best friends dying in combat at the hands of a merciless enemy. Descriptions of survival against all odds in the bitter Russian winter, with scraps of newspaper inside the uniform to shield against the cold. Stories of sharing a last cigarette with fellow soldiers who never came back. The bottle of schnapps would come out and he would continue right into the night, clinging to the last few 'if onlies', hoping that things might have been a little different and the war would not have been so badly lost. Defeat supplanted in later years by hunting victories in which he would often photograph his son beside dead animals. Every deer, every set of antlers on the wall of the living room, every stuffed otter and every wild boar mounted on wood was a kind of consoling trophy which might settle the score of this vast failure in war. Followed by the whole slide of self-pity and blame, with his father still at war inside the family and finally pointing the finger at Gregor's grandfather Emil who had let the Germans down. And ultimately, the tears and the slamming doors and all that silence for days and weeks which made the home feel like the inside of an upholstered coffin.

'No son of mine.' The strange acoustic of those words echoed through his childhood, calling for him to be more like his father but actually pushing him away. All those fake memories collected over years into a phoney album. He no longer wanted to be the smiling boy in all the hunting photographs. The boy with a line of ten hares hanging behind him, or the boy with his hand shielding his eyes from the sun, holding on to the antlers of a recently killed stag. He began to reject all that bogus family folklore, all those duties of lineage and pride and expectation. He had tried to be an adequate son, tried to match up to the son that his father wanted to have, but he was always a disappointment.

Mara is looking over at Gregor now. She wants to tell him that all this has been sorted out now. There is nothing to fear from memory. No need to be on the run from your own life any more. She wants to send a message of calmness across the orchard, so she tells Johannes to go over to him.

'Go and ask Uncle Gregor if he wants to see the big anthill,' she says.

Gregor smiles back. He puts away the long pole and allows himself to be led away towards the gate. They pass by the compost heap and stop to look at the covering of rotten apples, layers and layers of miniature brown skulls strewn across the top. They leave the orchard and walk along the outside wall to a small stand of trees. Johannes tells him that you cannot go out into the field on your own, because that's how people get lost. When they come to the anthill, Johannes continues to hold hands because they must look at it together. It's heaving with movement. Gregor listens to Johannes explaining what ants do. He wants to show the boy something he discovered when he was small himself. He takes a stick and places it into the anthill, so they can watch the alarming reaction of ants gathering around it. He shakes the stick and the fury of the ants grows, spreading their toxic fumes to fight off the intrusion. The boy pulls his hand away and moves back. Gregor picks the stick out and plucks one of the ants off in his fingers. He tells Johannes that he is going to eat it. The boy smiles, but it's more a smile of mistrust.

'You can't eat ants,' he says. 'They will bite you. Inside in your tummy.'

But then Gregor calmly shows him that it can be done. He tells the boy that they taste a bit like marzipan with cinnamon. He shows him how to crush the ant a little and then places it into his mouth. He chews on it with his front teeth and nods to show that he likes the taste and that he has no fear of being bitten inside. 'Mmmmmm,' he says, but the boy finds it too absurd to try it by himself without the reassurance of his mother. He is being asked to believe something that is not safe. But it won't be long now, Gregor knows, when the boy will try it out for himself, even if his mother does not approve, exactly in the same way that he did when he was small.

'Uncle Gregor ate an ant,' he calls out to everyone in the orchard as he runs back in. He is horrified and boasting at the same time. 'Uncle Gregor eats ants.'

Daniel looks up with acknowledgement in his eyes. Because he also learned it from Gregor, the same way that Gregor learned it from his father.

Fourteen

Gregor's father would not tolerate the name of Stalin being mentioned in the house. Nor could he bear Gregor's grandfather being talked about very much. As far as he was concerned, Emil was a traitor. While he was out there defending his country on the Russian front, Emil was driving around aimlessly in his truck, wasting fuel. While his parents were killed as the Russian Army swept towards Berlin, Emil entertained all kinds of women up and down the country.

His mother and father didn't talk very much about these things around the dinner table. She spoke about Emil only when she was alone with Gregor.

Right at the end of the war, when it was only a matter of time before it was all over, she waited for her father at the train station. She had slept fitfully, with Gregor waking up frequently and people complaining about the noise. By morning his infection had spread into both ears and he could hardly hear anything. The waiting room was so crowded that many people had decided to sleep on the platform under the awning instead. They were not moving on any more because the news was going around that the American troops were very close and that the town would soon fall. There was no point in going anywhere, only waiting.

Emil had not returned yet. She was worried about him. But she was even more worried now that Gregor would go deaf with his ear infection. She had tried to swaddle him during the night so that he would sweat, but it didn't break the fever. He kept moving, trying to throw off his blanket, and when he began to scream again in the morning, she decided to go and look for some oil, hoping that somebody in the town could help. She stood Gregor up on his feet, tucked a spare vest in around his neck for a scarf and pulled his hat down. He was a good boy and didn't complain about the weather, just walked by her side holding her hand. She walked through the town, memorising her way so that she could make it back to the station again later on.

There was some reassurance in moving on. She found a school where charity workers were giving out food. It was even more crowded than the railway station, but she managed to get inside and find a nurse. Everyone else was concentrating on the food, so the nurse got Gregor to lean his head over and poured in some warm cooking oil. It made him whine at first, but the nurse had a quick way of calming him with a little rhyme that ended with a tickle. The nurse went away and came back with a new hat for him, more of a winter hat with a peak over the eyes and flaps that came down over the ears. She kept talking to him as she placed a piece of gauze over each of his ears and then tied the hat down under his chin.

It was noon by the time they went out into the street again, not knowing where they should be going now. There was an old woman sweeping the footpath, cleaning the stains of rain off the pavement, all the way to the edge of her property. With more clouds coming, the old woman looked up. There was a boom of heavy weapons in the distance, and maybe she had mistaken it for thunder.

Gregor's mother walked down the main street to the town, half hoping to see her father. And then she came across his truck, parked outside a public house.

She walked right up to the bar, holding Gregor with her hand. She looked in the window and saw nobody. When she knocked, a woman came to the door, shouting. Could she not see that they were closed? Did she have no idea what was going on in the town. There were soldiers running in the direction of the fighting, old men mostly, and young boys. The woman said there was nothing left to serve in her bar, no beer, no food, nothing. Everything had been bartered or taken from them. She was full of pessimism, almost envying those who had nothing at all, wishing that she could abandon everything and flee herself, then she would not have to worry about what would happen to her house and her business.

Gregor's mother said she didn't want anything, she was merely looking for the man who owned the truck outside. She was careful not to reveal too much about herself.

'My father,' she said. 'I'm looking for my father. A fat man, have you seen him?'

'Emil,' the woman said. 'If only he came back, then everything would improve. At least I'd have customers again.'

The woman became more friendly and invited them inside. The boy was drowsy and ready to faint again. She sat him down, explaining that he had a fever. His face was wet with sweating, but she tried to stop him taking his hat off.

They had not sat down for more than two minutes when three men from the Gestapo came in and told her to stand up.

'Papers,' the officer barked at her.

She produced her documents from her bag and held them out. The officer smiled and passed her papers over to the other men.

'Come with us,' he then said, and she had to get the boy up again. Carried him in her arms this time. One of the men held the door open and she was escorted across the street to the police barracks, though she hardly had time to work any of this out because she kept looking back into the street to see if there was any sign of her father.

At the police station she was taken into a room and questioned. Where had she come from? Where was she going to? It was clear that they knew everything about her father and his bogus mission. They slapped her and told her not to lie, because they already had the facts. Gregor huddled close to her, cowering.

The war was so near the end. In some parts of the country it was already over and soon these buildings would fall into the hands of the enemy, but still these Gestapo men had all the time in the world to interrogate her about her father. She had walked into a trap. At first they demanded to know where Emil was hiding. Then they turned it around and pretended that they had already captured her father, but that they were still looking for his companion, Max. And when she kept crying and repeating that she had no idea where her father was, they threatened to execute her and her boy for assisting deserters.

They told her with some pride that they had been after Emil for quite some time now. They even shared the information they had already uncovered about his 'pathetic' little scheme. They knew the location of various checkpoints through which he had passed over the last month.

'Your father thinks he can make a fool of us,' the officer in charge said with a triumphant smile.

She said nothing about waiting at the railway station and nothing about the fuel her father was seeking. But they continued bullying her with so many questions that she could not help herself admitting things they were putting to her. The officer in charge leaned in right close to her and she got the smell of wurst on his breath. Then he turned to question the boy. But Gregor was too young to know what was going on, only that something was wrong. His small body shook as the officer raised his voice.

'What's his name?'

'Gregor,' she answered. 'He's got an ear infection.'

The officer clapped his hand in a test and the boy flinched.

'He's almost deaf in both ears,' she pleaded. 'He can't hear a thing.'

She could not think of excuses. She was not clever with answers like her father. She knew from going to school that one excuse was always more believable than three excuses. The officer in charge continued to try and communicate with the boy, but he remained silent.

The officers looked at each other. They examined his clothes and took his hat off to look at him more carefully. The gauze was still stuck in his ears, but they fell out on the floor, thin pieces of linen with a golden nipple in each one where they had been fitted right into the eardrum with the oil. One of the men pointed at the boy's trousers and she understood this as a command. Unbuttoned his braces and pulled his pants down with the men looking on, examining him, then recoiling. He had soiled himself again. The room filled up with a sweet smell of excrement.

'Come on, let Mama take care of you.'

She took off his trousers completely, even though he was trying to pull against her. She could see that he was also totally wet, not only with urine but with sweat. He was coughing, a kind of hoarse cough that sounded like the bark of an old dog. Deep in his chest now, whistling every time he took in a breath. His groin was raw and there was a rash developing at the front of his legs.

'Come on, Gregor, my little sweetheart. It's not half as bad. Here, let me clean you up.'

She took his underpants off. She cleaned him off as best she could with the vest from around his neck and pulled his trousers up again. Then she hugged him again and rocked him back and forth for a moment, humming to him in a whisper, before she turned back to face her interrogators. They were standing in the corridor now, with the door open, smoking to clear the air and muttering among themselves.

She was worried that it would be her fault if they found her father. Worried about the look of disappointment on his face because she had not stayed at the railway station as he had asked her. And just as she rocked Gregor back and forth, waiting to see what the men would do next, she heard the main door opening and somebody shouting.

'We have him,' they repeated again and again. 'We have him.'

She turned round with an emptiness in her stomach. She felt herself going pale, ready to collapse. She kept her eyes on the door and on the corridor, waiting to see her father being brought in with his hands in manacles behind his back, a common criminal. She waited for that despairing glance that he would throw at her in the room, before he was pushed on past her door into some other cell. She was ready to run out into the corridor and beg for her father's life, but then she stood still.

Instead of Emil it was Max. She could not help feeling relief, but also a terror at the expression in his eyes. They pushed him along and he disappeared. She heard doors closing behind him at the back of the building.

Fifteen

Their hands are sticky. Their fingernails are dirty. They have flakes of bark in their hair and bits of stiff, dried-out leaves clinging to their clothes. There is a dryness in their throats and occasionally they can see by the light under the trees that the air in the country is not the pure void they believed it was but a dusty substance, thick with particles and hovering insects. They breathe in the scent of apples and deadwood and soil and rotting things all around them. The fruit flies are everywhere. Swarms of them in a veil around the wheelbarrow. Johannes is counting the sacks that have been collected so far, ranked along the side of the orchard. He keeps starting from the beginning, but there are too many for him, more than he has numbers for in his head.

He goes over to whisper in his mother's ear. Katia gets up slowly, taking her son by the hand. From his movements, it's clear that he needs to go for a pee. He's holding on to himself and dancing a little, pulling at her hand. She walks through the trees towards the edge of the orchard, carrying her belly the way she would carry a basket, heavy with apples. She finds a suitable place and helps him to pull his shorts down, but Johannes is afraid to pee because he's seen an ant.

'The ants are looking,' he says.

'The ants are not one little bit interested in your winkie,' Katia says to him.

But she has to move somewhere else. She carries him quickly with his trousers around his ankles, over to another spot at the rim of the orchard where the grass is longer, almost the height of the boy himself. And when everything is right, he finally sends a perfect, golden arc into a tall column of grass in the sunshine with his mother holding him.

'Is Uncle Gregor going to play the trumpet?' he asks her.

'You'll have to ask him,' Katia says.

Johannes runs off, straight over to Gregor.

'Are you going to play the trumpet, Uncle Gregor?'

'We'll see,' Gregor answers. It is the same answer that Gregor used with his son, Daniel, the same answer that he heard so often as a child himself from his own father, one that he hated hearing himself. But he can't help himself repeating the lines of his father. Once again that ventriloquism of generations, parents speaking through their children.

'We'll see. Later maybe.'

'Of course he'll play,' Martin says.

Gregor still allows people to speak for him, putting words in his mouth at times when he remains ambivalent. He doesn't want to promise too much, but then he smiles. How can he refuse? He has the trumpet in the boot of the car, everybody knows that.

'Yeah, maybe later.'

Johannes runs back to his mother, bringing the news over to her like a town crier, even though she's heard it already.

'Uncle Gregor is going to play the trumpet.'

It's how the news is received that gives it shape. Mara raises her arm, clenching her fist. The very same salute that she made when he put the trumpet to his mouth and blasted out his first chain of profane notes on his birthday one year. It was Mara who got it for him and secretly saved up for months without a word. Up to then he had always played on a trumpet he had borrowed from a friend.

The clenched fist is one of Mara's trademark gestures. A salute of determination and fun and mischief and support. Something left over from the revolutionary years which she does quite naturally, without any triumph or aggression. Not menacing so much as bolstering. She has always been a motivator and does it with a comic flair, with a hint of self-parody, to agree with something, to make her point in an argument, to show her emotions when she's listening to music or dancing with her head down and her hair in her eyes. She did it when she heard that Katia was expecting her second baby. She will do it again with tears in her eyes when Daniel and Juli go off to Africa.

Gregor recalls seeing her once, raising her clenched fist towards a bus driver on Wittenbergplatz. Daniel copied her, clenching his small fist at the bus driver, and maybe it was such a funny image of mother and son that instead of feeling offended, the bus driver was forced to smile. She was not merely raging at the bus driver, but at all those other things in the country that were wrong at that time and needed to be put right. At the government for the length of time it was taking to pay reparations to victims. At the way immigrant workers were treated. At the Berlin Wall. At the building of Stammheim maximum security prison. At the news that a young man was shot at a table in a restaurant while he was eating. At the news that the police raided the home of her favourite author. At the arms manufacturers in Germany sending weapons to Africa.

She has always troubled herself with these thoughts. Felt responsible for world events. Now she clenches her fist with more sanguine authority, but she does it in a gesture of fearless innocence that makes her look like she's just out of school.

It came as a surprise to Gregor every year in May, when Mara announced that it was his birthday. The date of his birth, the date on which he stepped into the place of another child. He remembers the conspiracy of kindness with which she saved up for that trumpet and kept it a secret, until Daniel blurted it out.

Daniel was almost four then, not much younger than Johannes is now. Mara placed a deposit on the instrument he once tested in the shop and which he said he would buy if only he had the money. She got a bit of help from her parents, but never admitted that to him in the end. A few days before his birthday, Gregor walked in the door and Daniel could not wait to tell him what was on his mind.

'Mama has got you a trumpet,' Daniel said right away, before Gregor had even taken his jacket off.

'Wait,' Gregor said. 'Was that meant to be a secret?'

'Yes,' Daniel answered with eyes wide open. 'It's your birthday present,' he said.

Gregor may have had a hint even before that, because he once mentioned the notion of buying the trumpet his friend had lent to him, but Mara discouraged that, saying they would start saving up for the best. Nonetheless, it was still a surprise when they celebrated with a cake and candles and tablecloth on the table and Mara dressed up. He unwrapped the gift pretending he knew nothing, carefully taking off the paper, embracing her with such life in his eyes. He could work out how long she had been saving up and how hard it was not to say a word.

How often has he played it all over the world, in so many bars and jazz clubs, never once forgetting that moment when she gave it to him, sometimes thinking about it all evening and then putting it out of his head so as not to allow the feeling to get the better of him. Countless bulging notes have been blown through that piece of brass. It has lost its gloss, but it still releases an exceptional musical scream in his hands. The horn has become dented by collisions along the way, but it has character like no other trumpet. A sweetness, a clarity, a pure, lived-in sound that only a well-played trumpet can have and that only fellow trumpet players can really appreciate. He's been offered money for that instrument. By well-known players. Enough to buy himself a whole suite of new instruments. In fact, he has bought other trumpets since then, for their own particular tone, but none of them play quite like this one. None of them have that much biography in them.

He has often spoken about the weight of it in his hands. The kiss of brass on his lips. He is known for swinging it over his shoulder like a shovel or a pitchfork in a momentary pause at concerts, a style that other musicians have since copied. He was born for that instrument, Mara always said whenever she heard him rip another deep, declamatory note into their small apartment, a note that probably shook the whole block into life, like the sound of a cow lowing in the courtyard. The neighbours must have said: 'Oh no. Somebody's bought a shagging trumpet.'

He still plays some of the clubs in Berlin when he's asked to join a reunion gig. He likes the relaxed companionship of musicians playing their stuff together and hardly speaking to each other. His big brass larynx. The unmistakable warm, half-drunk, country-wedding sound of the trumpet. A fat, laconic, outdoor echo. The whole inner road movie of feelings that comes out every time he lifts the instrument up to his lips. He jokes about making a big comeback, but he's really much happier doing his own thing now, playing for fun instead of for a living, listening to younger players, teaching and watching his own trademark licks passing on to another generation. He's had too many comebacks already. An entire lifetime of departures and comebacks.

Sixteen

It's lunchtime now. They have barely noticed the time going by in the open air, until Thorsten rings the bell from the house. They see the time only in the amount of apples that have been collected. They come down from the ladders and drop their equipment. They leave the orchard behind and glance back at the work they have done so far and feel that they have earned the break. Gregor is the last to leave, with Martin putting his arm around him.

'Mara looks great, doesn't she?'

'She does.'

Gregor is not really aware of these words or what they are asking him to think. There has never been any animosity between them over Mara. Too much has gone by to begin raking over the fact that Martin was her lover for a short while in the years when Gregor was absent. Friendship is too big a gift to throw away on pride. They have accepted each other's failures along the way and maybe these things have brought them closer in the end.

Gregor looks at Mara, walking ahead with a basket on her hip. She has remained devoted to those ideals of love and friendship and family, upbeat and optimistic to the extreme. She must have learned this from her parents in the Rhineland, from all the calamities in the past, the rush to put the war behind them, the memory of such loss, when friends were so easily taken away by the most whimsical fate of war logic.

Over lunch, Daniel has begun to needle Martin a little about his diet.

'You don't still eat all those meat products, do you?'

'As long as it's dead, I'll eat it,' Martin returns.

Mara gives them both a warning squint with her eyes.

'Look, you two,' she says, 'we're not going to have a discussion about GM products or about the agony of the poultry industry. And I don't want to hear about the ethics of long-distance food. We just want to eat and enjoy the food.'

They smile at her.

'What about the castration of pigs without anaesthetic?' Daniel asks.

'Absolutely not,' she says.

'I suppose that rules out force-fed geese too, does it?'

She smiles back at Daniel. Plates are offered around the table. Johannes is sitting on his father's knee. Katia finds it hard to eat and feeds her son instead of herself.

Martin eats heartily, with even greater defiance under the gaze of moral condescension from Juli. As he looks up, he spots Daniel sniffing some hummus and swallows what is in his mouth in order to go on the counter-attack.

'Hang on,' Martin exclaims. 'You can't sniff your food, Daniel.'

'Why not?'

'That's against the rules as well, Mara. Isn't it? Even for vegetarians. Sniffing your food at the table. Tell him that's not allowed.'

Martin slips easily into the role of surrogate father, a cool banter from which Gregor feels excluded at times. Mara has often said they don't talk enough, and maybe there are still one or two unfinished things between them that need to be sorted out before he can reclaim his place as a father. It was Martin who was always there to help when Daniel was growing up. Martin, not Gregor, who was there at Daniel's bedside in hospital when he had a seizure once after taking cocaine. Martin, not Gregor, who coaxed Daniel in from the balcony when he started holding his own mother to ransom.

For now, Gregor becomes a spectator in this game between Daniel and Martin. Perhaps there is a sign of regret in his eyes, that he forfeited this close relationship with his son over the years. There is a fine residue of anger in Daniel which comes out now and again in tiny serrated hints. He still blames Gregor, for abandoning him. For travelling off with his band and leaving them behind.

'Sniffing is an act of doubting,' Martin says. 'Isn't that so, Gregor?'

Gregor laughs and holds his hands up.

'I'm a chef,' Daniel replies. 'I sniff food all the time. It's part of the gastronomic talent, and the pleasure.'

'No, it's not. You make it look like the food's gone off.'

'You sniff your wine,' Daniel says after a pause. 'Don't you?'

'That's different,' Martin counters once more. 'That's a culture. There is no culture around sniffing food. And we don't sniff each other either, do we? When I introduce you to my wife, you're not going to start sniffing her, now are you?'

The laughter rushes in a Mexican wave around the table. Martin begins to sniff at Gregor like an animal, keeping the wave going. It's an aspiration of their time, to laugh, to enjoy the lightness. Perhaps even the peak of their culture, sitting alone watching somebody on YouTube eating marshmallows for seven minutes running.

Mara takes a detour in the conversation. She turns the discussion towards football and the recent World Cup.

'Amazing,' she says. 'Two months after the World Cup is over and the German flags are still up on the balconies everywhere.'

'You're right,' Gregor says. 'Never seen so many German flags in my life before.'

'All made in China,' Martin points out. 'I'm not joking. They couldn't keep up with the demand here and had to send for more from China. They have the production facilities over there to make flags quickly.'

'In the USA,' Gregor tells her, 'they think nothing of having flags on their lawns all year round.'

'To remind them of what country they live in,' Martin adds.

'Is that why you wear those sunglasses, Martin? They're like big American cop sunglasses,' Daniel says.

Martin gives Daniel a menacing glare over the top of his sunglasses.

Juli puts her arm around Daniel with exaggerated protection.

'We had forgotten what country we were living in,' Mara thinks, 'until the World Cup came to Germany.'

'Dreamers,' Daniel cuts in. 'Pack of dreamers. With a team like that.'

'Ah now, Daniel,' Gregor argues. 'We didn't do that badly.'

'Ploddy,' Daniel reinforces, with the assurance of a football commentator. 'Methodical and lame. No imagination. We didn't even deserve to get to the semi-final.'

'We were always dreamers,' Martin agrees. 'You're absolutely right there Daniel.'

He takes his sunglasses off completely at this point, then pauses.

'The Germans have always been the world champions at dreaming. For years, we were forbidden from having our own dreams. Only American dreams. Capitalist dreams, Communist dreams. Rock and roll dreams. Greek island dreams. Biggest dreamers on the planet, the Germans. You should be glad, Daniel, that at least now we're dreaming about football again.'

They pause and think about this for a while.

'Still a crap team.'

Mara looks away into the sky.

'Such a fantastic day,' she says, this time with a tiny, free note of joy releasing itself from her voice. 'Thorsten, can we not take a break for a while and come back to the apples later when it's cooled down a bit?'

It's not really all that hot, just the idea of exhaustion descending over them. Looking up at the sky over the roofs of the farm buildings, there is only one feathery cloud to be seen, a vague white streak, like the wipe of a cloth left on glass. Even though it rained a few nights ago, it's only a small relief and the landscape is burned out, hoarse and silent, waiting for water.

In the orchard, everything is quiet, a long sustained note stretching into the afternoon. The air is humming in there now. The fruit gatherers have fled and left everything behind them. The ladders. The long poles. The rake leaning against the tree. The wheelbarrows and the boxes and the lines of sacks, full and bulging with red apples. The birds and the insects and the beetles on the ground sneaking back to have a look at what is left, once more reclaiming the place for themselves.

Seventeen

Looking back now, Gregor feels more like an invented character, swept along a predestined narrative. He wishes he could go over his own life with an omnipotent hand, to intervene at vital moments.

It was the year of the hornet sting. Late November, when Daniel was still only five, Gregor received a letter from home. The sender's name on the back of the envelope was Maria Liedmann, with an address in Nuremberg.

Gregor was out recording in a studio that morning, so the letter lay on the table unopened, with Mara staring at the female handwriting, wondering what was going on. At first she felt the excitement of discovering that Gregor might have an aunt or a cousin still alive. But then it also revealed that Gregor was hiding something.

She stared at the letter, took Daniel to school, went to work and remained inside her own world, unable to get it out of her head. When she got home it was gone.

'The letter,' she asked quite innocently. 'Who is it from?'

'It's nothing,' he answered.

How could he have thought he might get away with this? She pursued it, naturally, but Gregor went mute as a stone. For a man who could make up good stories for children, he seemed more and more incapable of speaking to adults. She could ask as many questions as she liked, but he sat in front of her, strumming chords on his guitar in answer. Rather than explain things, he sat with Mara in a kind of meaningless twilight, plucking the strangest of notes while she continued to place words in his mouth, as if he came from a different country where it was only possible to communicate through music.

'Are you hiding something from me, Gregor?' she asked.

'Speak to me, Gregor, please,' she begged him, before breaking down at last in tears. 'It's very lonely for me sometimes, when you don't speak. I never know what you're thinking, Gregor, unless you say something.'

'I can't talk about it,' he replied. 'Trust me, Mara. It's nothing. It's from the past and I don't want to go back there.'

She sat wiping the tears with the sleeve of her woollen cardigan over her hand.

'What am I to think, Gregor? If you say nothing, then you give other people the right to speak for you. If you don't explain things, then I will start imagining things that might be untrue. Please, Gregor, tell me what it is.'

'It's a letter from the past, Mara,' he repeated. 'That's all I can tell you. It's a long way back in the past, before we met.'

He refused to say any more. Got up and went over to kiss her. She didn't resist his embrace, but she gave only a half-smile and her eyes were full of questions.

The following evening, she searched for the letter, turning the whole apartment upside down. Finally found it in the bin outside in the courtyard. Smiled at neighbours and explained that she had accidentally thrown a pay cheque out with the rubbish. Found the tiny torn-up pieces of truth at last and salvaged them with great care, bringing them up the stairs to reconstruct as a real-life jigsaw. Later, while Gregor was playing in a bar, Mara put the letter back together, patiently gluing each portion down on a clean sheet of paper, matching the words up with the eagerness of an archaeologist.

It had come from Gregor's mother. Maria Liedmann.

'*Your father is dying,*' the letter said. '*This will be his last Christmas.*'

She felt the shock of the words in her stomach. It was bigger than any revelation about a secret lover. He had not broken the silent pact in the railway station after all. She was thrilled to find out that Gregor's adoptive mother was still alive, but the reasons why he had concealed this from her scared her. Afraid that she no longer understood the man she was living with.

What great emptiness did he construct behind himself? It was easier to deal with no knowledge whatsoever than it was to know that there was something which he was suppressing.

'Why is he denying everything like this?' she asked Martin on the phone. 'Why doesn't he want to talk about his mother, the woman who rescued him and brought him up? How can he turn his back on her?'

There was something fascinating about deceit. This was an infidelity. Though it had nothing to do with sexual deception, it contained all the subterfuge and secrecy that goes along with being unfaithful. No giveaway signs in the bedroom. This was more about family detective work, about the longing for knowledge, the wish to know everything about him.

For the moment, she kept it to herself.

'Do you still love me?' she asked him.

'Of course,' he said with some humour. 'Goes without saying, Mara.'

But since the letter had arrived in their midst, there was some stronger affirmation required.

Was he incapable of integrating in a family? The trapdoor opening up again and taking the ground from under his feet? The disability of an orphan, unable to trust the human trade of giving and accepting love?

Did he find it hard to return that invisible substance that passes between people and which is impossible to measure? Are there people who have no talent for love, just as there are those who cannot sing, or dance, or balance a plate on a stick? Some devastation in their history. Some coldness in the heart. People who have had that precious substance withdrawn from them at one point or another. Those who have found no way of expressing it or receiving it. Was love nothing more than a sign of insecurity? Some form of self-preservation or human investment, dressed up as virtue in movies and books. She had been told by poets and revolutionaries at the university that unconditional love was a myth. Like the lost half of a tea set, like sabre-toothed tigers, like Major Tom drifting away into space. But wasn't it impossible to live without love, like living without breathing, without water, like trying to survive on a loveless planet without trees?

Mara decided to go to Nuremberg herself. There had to be some reason why Gregor was denying his own mother. She wanted to see where he had grown up. This was her chance to imagine his childhood at last, the house, the surrounding streets and shops, the school and the traffic lights where he must have crossed over on his way home every day. She wanted to see the stairs he walked up, the hall door, the surname on the bell. Stalking a living ghost made her feel light-headed with excitement, something she had not felt in years.

She told Gregor that she would be away for two days, visiting her sister who was ill in Köln. She left Daniel with

Martin and his wife, Gisela, and drove to Nuremberg with the address she had taken from the letter. A neighbour informed her that Frau Liedmann had gone to visit her husband in hospital. It was too late to come back and call again, so she had to leave it to the following day, and even then she was afraid to ring the bell this time. Afraid of this tidal wave of information which would emerge from the meeting.

She waited until Gregor's mother came out. Followed her to a nearby café. It was December by then, just before Christmas. The Christmas markets were open and one of the streets was blocked off from traffic. There was snow falling and Gregor's mother wore a grey woollen coat with imitation fur around the collar. She had on a pair of short brown boots with rings of beige fur around the top. She slapped some of the melting snow from her coat with her gloves and put them away in her handbag, which was kept inside a reusable shopping bag. She opened the buttons of her coat and left her hat on, a purple cashmere hat in the shape of a sugar-coated jelly sweet. With the straw grey hair under the hat, it was possible to imagine her as a small girl, with red cheeks. She seemed nervous and ate her piece of cake, a cream-filled tart with strawberry mousse, in a slightly furtive way, glancing around her first to make sure she was not being watched. Other women greeted her curtly, hardly even looking at her, as though 'good morning' meant 'stay where you are'. Frau Liedmann remained very much on her own, and maybe there was a hint here of Gregor's solipsism. She consumed the cake in a mechanical way, looking away into the street where the cars were hissing through a lacklustre shower of white, frozen rain.

Mara waited until Frau Liedmann was finished with the cake, then worked up the courage to make a discreet approach. After all, it was Gregor's mother who had made the first move, sending the letter.

'Frau Liedmann,' she said in a quiet voice, smiling. 'We got the letter. I am Gregor's wife, Mara.'

There was a shocked exchange of looks between them. It had the effect on Frau Liedmann of being caught by the police, something she had been expecting all along and almost wished for so that it could be over at last.

'There is nothing wrong, Frau Liedmann,' Mara reassured her. 'I don't want to alarm you. It's the letter. We got your letter.'

'Gregor,' was all that Frau Liedmann could utter.

'He doesn't know that I've come here,' Mara said, and maybe that was an important initial connection, a conspiratorial friendship between these two women, two mothers. 'He cannot find out about this. Gregor is like that, you know, very fixed in his mind about things.'

'Can we go somewhere more quiet, maybe?' Frau Liedmann said politely, again searching around, glancing at other people for permission almost.

They walked a hundred metres through the snow to another café where they sat down in a corner. It seemed important to her not to be overheard. Did Frau Liedmann feel that her background did not match up to those of other people around her? Some inadequacy in the black market of confession and gossip and home truth?

The waitress brought better coffee this time and they sat looking at each other with Mara doing all the talking, filling in the absent details. They had a five-year-old boy, named Daniel. Gregor worked as a musician, as well as teaching music part-time. She didn't tell Frau Liedmann that Gregor had told everyone that his adoptive parents were dead, only that he had started a new life.

'You have a son,' Frau Liedmann said. 'That makes me very happy.'

There was emotion in her voice. Mara searched in her handbag for a photograph, a picture of the three of them together on holiday in Spain that year. Frau Liedmann looked at it for a long time, while Mara told her that it was just after Daniel had been stung by a hornet, which explained why he looked a bit sulky. Frau Liedmann swallowed the image, unable to connect to it across the time gone by.

'I've never seen him with a beard before,' she said.

She took off her coat at last, and her hat, adjusted her hair and examined the photograph once more in greater detail.

'You're welcome to keep it,' Mara said, but Frau Liedmann placed it on the table in front of her, propped against a small can of milk, perhaps not fully sure if it could really belong to her.

Eighteen

They fell into conversation and agreed to address each other informally as Mara and Maria. That alone made Mara feel like a lost daughter returning home. She was brought back to the house where Gregor's mother prepared something to eat. Surrounded by antlers, they sat looking through the photographs and Mara rested for a long time on one particular image of Gregor as a boy, trying to teach the dog to jump through a hoop. His curly hair rising up in a wave on top of his head. His eyes looking at the camera. It was almost too much to absorb in the space of one afternoon. And yet she wanted to see more, everything. Another picture of him with his own head concealed under his jumper and the dog's head under his arm as a joke. A further picture of Gregor and his mother standing on the steps of the house beside Uncle Max.

Why had all this been so hidden? Why had Gregor erased this part of his life with such brutal determination? Was there nothing from these tranquil family moments worth keeping?

'He told me about that dog,' Mara said. 'Fritz was his name, am I right?'

'That's true,' Gregor's mother said.

'Didn't he have a big war going with the postman?'

'That dog was a terrible nuisance. My husband hated him because he used to bark in the forest and chase all the wild deer away. The postman was terrified. Very nervous man, after the war. I don't know how many official letters of complaint we received over that dog, and the postman had to deliver them himself.'

'He was run over in the end, wasn't he?'

'The truck driver gave Gregor some money to get a new dog. But he never did.'

'Why not?'

'The postman still believed he was alive. Gregor had this funny idea of telling him that the dog was locked up in the back.'

'So he lived on in the postman's imagination.'

'Until I blurted it out one day. The postman asked me where the dog was and I told him he was long dead. Almost a year later. Imagine. And Gregor blamed me. Said I killed the dog by telling the postman.'

The two women scraped over the details like two historians, sharing knowledge, exchanging facts and eccentricities, a well-informed jury examining things from opposite viewpoints. At times it seemed like they were not even talking about the same person. Again and again, there were trademark features which they both recognised and made it feel like an odd reunion of complete strangers. And maybe there was not too much harm done by the fact that Gregor had denied his adoptive mother, as long as Mara could engineer the reconciliation.

'Gregor hates shopping,' she said. 'I buy all his clothes for him because he can't bear being inside a shop.'

'He picked that up from his father,' Gregor's mother replied.

'Funny,' Mara said. 'Gregor thinks shop assistants are like hyenas, stalking customers, preying on the partner.

He physically pulls me out of the shop and I feel like a shoplifter being arrested.'

But there was something more serious to be discussed.

'His father was very good to him,' Gregor's mother said. 'He would like to see him again before he dies. He's forgiven him.'

'For what?' Mara asked.

'He threatened us with a hunting rifle. Just before he ran away. My husband doesn't hold that against him any longer. If only he would come to see us.'

These new facts began to overturn everything. Gregor's mother spoke about the bond between father and son. How her husband had helped Gregor to bring home an injured hawk and encouraged him to nurse it until it could fly again. How he explained to him that hunting was not always about killing but also about conservation. There was a tone of regret in her voice as she explained why she had to leave Gregor in care so often, before her husband came back from captivity. She even had a second job cleaning offices at night to keep things going.

'What else could you do?'

When Gregor's father returned from the war, he was depressed. Found it difficult to discuss things. He had terrible headaches, so the house often had to be silent. Gregor grew up as a quiet boy, making lists all the time, separate from other children.

'They used to fight with him because he was so tall,' she said. 'But he was always a big softie. He could never stand up for himself.'

As a child he liked looking at gardens. When they went for a walk together through the suburbs of Nuremberg, he would lead her on a trail mapped out in his head in order to pass by the best gardens. He liked growing things. He became a reclusive teenager, interested mostly in his music.

Her husband was an accountant, a good man, with strong principles. Perhaps it was hard for people who came through war to adjust to life in peacetime. They overcompensated. They loved their son with too much force. Gregor's father was a survival artist and she laughed at the way he sometimes made his family go through fire drills at the weekend. Maybe life was more about enduring than about living. She said her husband could not bear to see food going to waste and sometimes forced Gregor to eat up, telling him what it was like to starve and to live on ants. Gregor had to be spoon-fed until he was ten. She spent her life running after him with food, with his school lunch box, his jacket, his homework. She described how he often left his scarf behind or lost his coat on the bus, and each time, her husband bought him a new one, an even better one, with better lining and a detachable hood and more inside pockets.

'He loves his son,' she said. 'He's the only friend he's ever had.'

'I'll speak to him,' Mara said. 'I'm sure he'll come round. It's just that he's had so much trouble coming to terms with the fact that he's an orphan.'

'I beg your pardon?'

'He's adopted, isn't that so?'

Gregor's mother looked straight into Mara's eyes, blinking, unable to grasp what she had just heard. She paused for a moment, sighed, shook her head.

'That's totally untrue.'

They looked at each other in disbelief. Now they really were talking about two different people. Gregor's mother stared across the photographs and family artefacts spread out on the dining-room table. A lifetime turned into fake.

'It's a complete lie, Mara. I should know, I'm his mother.'

'You're saying Gregor made this up?'

'His uncle Max made it up. He put all that stuff into Gregor's head.'

A mother's word against that of her son. Mara put forward Gregor's argument in his absence, describing in detail the story that she had got from him. The journey south on the truck with Emil, the long wait in the train station, the interrogation by the Gestapo. It all seemed to match in every aspect except for one essential detail. The child lost in the bombing. The replacement.

'But he's Jewish,' Mara said. 'He was rescued by your father. You adopted him in order to replace your lost son. Isn't that why there was so much trouble with the Gestapo?'

Gregor's mother stared back, unable to reclaim possession of her own life. The rejection was too much to bear and there was hostility entering into her voice.

'He's no more Jewish than me, or his father,' she said. 'He's German. He's the image of his grandfather Emil. For God's sake, look at the photographs. He's a musician and a singer, just like Emil, isn't that so?'

'He told me that he came from the East, with the refugees.'

'He can make up whatever story he likes. I can't force him to go and visit his own father on his deathbed.'

The truth left nothing to be imagined. The facts were incontrovertible, changing everything, dislodging the entire basis of Mara's marriage. Maybe his story was more elastic, more redemptive. How often had she passed by the building in Berlin where Gregor died in the bombing. How often had they looked up at the windows where his mother lived during the war and lost her only child while her husband was away at the front. Gregor's birthplace. His place of death. His moment of immortality.

'But he was circumcised,' Mara said. 'As a baby.'

'What are you talking about?' There was a cynicism in her voice. 'I would have noticed, don't you think?'

'At birth,' Mara said. 'I thought he was circumcised at birth.'

'Nonsense. That's all part of the fabrication. He must have got that done to himself after he ran away. I thought he would have grown out of that fantasy by now.'

'I don't understand anything any more.'

Mara cried openly, holding nothing back. She had spent all this time living with a ghost.

Nineteen

Driving back along the autobahn from Nuremberg, Mara became involved in a strange, disembodied argument with another driver. She had not been concentrating and must have done something stupid. The roads were wet, coming up to Christmas, dark early. She drove in a bruised and remote way. In silence, without the radio on so as to avoid the sentiment of music. Staring past the windscreen wipers sweeping off flakes of snow. Seeing nothing but the watery tail lights of trucks ahead and the crop of water rising up from their wheels. Aware only of how much her world had changed in the last forty-eight hours.

Perhaps she had overtaken without indicating or maybe slipped in ahead without giving enough room. The offence was hardly worth mentioning, but the reaction was instant. Horn screaming, lights flashing right behind her. She slowed down and allowed plenty of room to pass. After you! she muttered to herself. Go ahead, pal, kill yourself. She remembered the funny phrases of her own father, telling her to be careful because there were always 'other idiots' on the road. What should she have said? Excuse me, I've just found out that my husband is a liar. He's not an orphan after all. The driver came right alongside, just to hammer home the road courtesy lesson, long enough for her to see his face. A young autobahn idealist with

144

furious eyes. Get off the road, you fucking asshole, he was shouting, or miming, with his mouth clearly pushed into the shape of a curse and his middle finger raised in supreme insult.

There was a rage in the country. It was there on the autobahn, in the people's hearts, in the newspapers and in the music. It was a time of self-loathing and self-accusation, a time when everything was being exposed and examined. The science of failure. The lonely momentum of truth. The guilt spreading horizontally, reaching into every heart and every home. Their shame was their identity. Their misery had become their poetry.

At home, she felt exhausted, unable to conceal the distance in her eyes.

'What's wrong?' Gregor asked.

She didn't know how to start. Or end. Waited until Daniel was asleep before she could work herself up to the right words. Looked at Gregor as though he had just walked in off the street and she had to ask him what he wanted in her home.

'You can't lie to me, Gregor,' she said. 'I can't live with lies.'

'What are you saying?'

'I've met your mother. She's told me everything.'

Gregor reeled backwards, as though a door had slammed in his face. It took a moment before he could find the words to reply.

'What? I don't believe what you've just said. You went behind my back and spoke to her. That's unforgivable, Mara.'

'It's all untrue, isn't it? You're not Jewish. You're not an orphan. You made the whole thing up for some scabby reason I don't understand. Just to make yourself look good or feel good, is that it? You lied to me, Gregor. And now I don't know who you are any more.'

Gregor did not reach for his guitar this time. He remained silent for a moment, clearing the situation in his own head before responding.

'This is very unfair, Mara.'

'I believed everything,' she said, looking at the floor.

'You went to see her. That's such a betrayal.'

'You can't even speak about betrayal,' she replied. 'How can I ever trust you? How can I believe anything you say, ever again?'

'You have decided not to believe me,' he said. 'You've decided to believe her. What did she tell you? All lies, I bet.'

There was a long pause. Mara went around the kitchen, clearing things away, stacking plates, doing things that had no urgency. Gregor sat at the table with the newspaper opened out in front of him, staring down, but not allowing any of it to enter. His credibility in shreds. His identity gone. The trapdoor underneath him had opened up and swallowed him.

'She's your real mother,' Mara said. 'Why would she lie to me?'

He waited for a while in silence, only slowly realising how serious this was. She talked about a fraud. She accused him of destroying the family.

'What am I supposed to tell Daniel when he grows up? That I married a con man who said he was a Jewish orphan? What will I tell everybody, all our friends? That you live in a fantasy?'

'Tell them what you like, Mara.'

'For whatever reason, you made up a story about being Jewish, because you couldn't face up to the truth. You preferred to be the victim, is that it? You fabricated this story about being replaced as a child, so you could escape from our history, isn't that so?'

'Stop it,' Gregor said. 'If you continue like this, I'm leaving. I'm not going to listen to you accusing me like this.'

'Answer the question then,' she said. 'Are you an orphan or not?'

'She's lying, Mara. Don't you see it? I found out, believe me. She's making this whole thing up. She never told him, her own husband. Now she can't get out of it.'

'It's hard to believe that a mother would lie about her own child.'

'There you go,' Gregor said. 'You want to believe her instead.'

'Can I call her?' Mara said. 'Can you discuss this on the phone with her at least?'

'No. I will not speak to her.'

'You told me they were dead. You told me you had no relatives. You told me you were circumcised at birth. All lies, Gregor. You're no more Jewish than I am.'

'Is that all you married me for?' he then said. 'Because I'm Jewish?'

They were throwing everything at each other now and it was difficult to see how they could find a way back from this confrontation. Soon they would fall over the cliff and bring the marriage to an end. Or maybe it was already over and they were merely justifying themselves to some invisible family tribunal.

'You have to get your story right,' she said.

She was crying. A helpless burst of tears, full of fatigue. She sat down at the table opposite him, looking up every now and again to see him through a watery prism. He stood up and came round to her side, placed his hand on her shoulder. Tried to embrace her, but she didn't want to be touched.

'You see, there's no proof, Mara,' he admitted finally.

She listened without looking up.

'That's the problem,' he said. 'I told you that. There's no proof, only what Uncle Max told me. It's her word against mine.'

He went over his story again. His entire existence was in Mara's hands, in her imagination, in what she agreed to believe and what she would dismiss. She held him like a porcelain figure, at her mercy, waiting to be dropped to the floor in tiny pieces. He placed the facts in front of her, holding on, desperately trying to save himself.

'Let me ask you this,' she said finally. 'If what you say is true. If you were adopted and your mother saved you, then how can you treat them like that? How can you turn your back on them?'

'Because they lied to me, Mara. Don't you see it?'

'Your father is on his deathbed and you can't get yourself to forgive him. That's not something you are entitled to do if you're an orphan. You can't be that cold-hearted, Gregor.'

She could not understand the ruthlessness with which he had cut them out of his life. Was that part of the self-loathing? He had walked away and now she was afraid that he would also walk away from her and Daniel.

'It's over, isn't it?' she said. 'It's over between us.'

She uttered those terrifying words in the hope that they were not true. She desperately wanted him to contradict her, to give some explanation which would allow her to believe him again. He tried to disarm those terrible words by saying that they would soon get this behind them. He swore that nothing had changed between them and that he felt every bit the same about her as he always did. All that mattered was that they stayed together.

'I'll find you the proof,' he said. 'Give me time, Mara. I'll get the proof, you'll see.'

He stood behind her and kissed the top of her head. He placed his hands under her arms and lifted her up from the kitchen chair. Her elbows were planted on the table and her fists glued to her cheeks, and they remained like that for a moment until he released the tension which had locked them in that position. Her face was indented with knuckle marks. Blotches around her eyes. She could hardly stand with the weakness in her legs, as if the truth was the only thing that kept people alive.

He virtually carried her into bed. Left the light on in the hall. Took her shoes off and helped her with her jeans. And in that drowsy swirl of thoughts before she fell asleep, she turned to put her arm around him.

'You looked so sweet, Gregor,' she said, half dreaming, half crying. 'You must have been such a sweet little boy.'

And maybe it was too soon to spring to conclusions. What did it matter now? she thought to herself in a blur of emotions. Everybody needs an identity, a disguise, a story in which they can feel at home. He had managed to knock a good enough life out of that survivor body of his, whoever it belonged to. Was he not making good use of the name he was given by his mother, regardless of his true origins? Whether he was inhabiting the soul of a dead boy or a living boy, he had made it his own now. And maybe he was not unlike all other people in that respect, part human, part fabrication. Part ghost, part living being. Part real, part invented. Existing mostly in the minds of those around him, his family and friends, his fellow inhabitants in the city where he lived. He claimed a place in their imagination. A semi-successful, semi-failed individual with a complex narrative which was perhaps a little in the vein of fiction itself, something you want to believe rather than something you have been told to believe.

Twenty

She was sitting on the black-and-white chair in the bedroom when he announced that he was leaving. He had found and bought that chair for her in a basement junk shop. It had come from a notorious Berlin café which existed in the late 1890s and which was considered respectable only before noon. The chair was painted black, with striped upholstering and a grip for waiters built into the frame. The name Café Bauer was written underneath the seat and it was mentioned in the famous novel called *Effi Briest*. They had seen the film. It ran for years in the city. Its portent of family betrayal had not entered their minds then. But they could remember the remoteness with which the characters spoke to each other, and the heartbreaking voice of Effi, after she was banished by her husband, saying: 'I hate your virtue.'

Dressed in a towel after a shower, she sat sideways with her arm over the back of the chair. In the weeks since the revelation about Gregor's identity, the innocence had been taken out of their eyes. The lightness had gone out of their language and when they reached each other with words, they were tinged with sharpness, accusation, doubt. Everything seemed to have been said before. They felt the weight of history dumped on them, subverting everything she believed, his lifeline, his survival, his entire credibility as a person. Each time they spoke to each other, the emptiness seemed to enlarge. Christmas was an impostor, a pageant re-enacted to postpone the inevitable.

'You want me to leave, don't you?' he said.

'Now you're trying to blame me,' she said. She was speaking in that laconic, disconnected tone, as though she was the only person left in the world. After all the arguments, she spoke with exhaustion in her voice, not even looking in his direction but at the foot of the bed.

'You want to be able to say that you were driven out.'

'I can't stay,' he said.

'The only way you'll sort this out is by finding out the truth, by going to speak to your mother.'

Mara had some problems with her health at the time, an ache in her joints, possibly from being bitten by a tick in the mountains that summer. She was on medication for it and sometimes had to stay in bed.

'I've got this invitation to play in Toronto,' Gregor said. 'I think it would be good for us both if I went away for a while. I want to sort this out. I'm going to get the proof.'

In the meantime, he had teamed up with a new band. He had met an Irish musician by the name of John Joe McDonagh, and there was some chemistry between them, going back to the basics with blues, jazz, folk. After a lacklustre response to Gregor's compositions, he needed to engage in something more real. John Joe had come to Berlin in a cheap car bought in Holland, parked it outside a bar in Kreuzberg where it remained as a billboard where people left messages under the windscreen wipers until it was towed away.

Why was he so impressed by John Joe? Was it the ability to celebrate? The instant friendship? The way John Joe placed his arm around Gregor's shoulder when he asked him if he had ever heard of a song called 'The Lover's Ghost'. John Joe knew the song well, 'but don't ask me to sing it.' Gregor felt welcome. He found a wildness inside himself, a longing to start all over again without looking back. That spontaneous energy around John Joe gave momentum to his life. 'For a laugh', on a late-night tour through city bars, John Joe dragged him and some other Irish musicians into a sex club. And once inside, they had nothing on their minds but more beer. John Joe even bought drinks for the three women who sat on bar stools in the reddish gloom. Then he got out his harmonica to play a tune. Over the sound of breathing and groaning on-screen in the background, he started huffing and bending the notes of a familiar train song, with a cigarette between his fingers. The rest of the musicians joined in like a strange band of missionaries, getting out their instruments and ripping into a frantic reel which was in complete contrast to the tired sexual signals all around them. The bar stools were pushed back. The women came to life. This small, moribund bar, where the decor had lost its decadence, was transformed into a country dance hall, heaving with perfume and perspiration and smoke. One of the women said afterwards that it was a long time since she had been swung around so mercilessly and now her yellow blouse was sticking to her back. John Joe yelped and they moved on again to the next bar.

It was so easy for Mara to descend into bitterness. She discovered a cynicism creeping into her words. 'Next thing you'll be telling me that you're Irish,' she said. But that was not her style and she punished herself for saying it. Hard as it was, she would have to become more encouraging and stop Daniel from being infected by the negative atmosphere. She was determined not to let anyone see her sadness. Already, their friends were discussing the news, talking about the doubt over Gregor's origins. Martin spoke to him about it and said he didn't want to come between him and Mara, but he felt it was his duty as a friend to warn him.

'You would tell me if I was being an asshole, Gregor, wouldn't you?' he said.

'What do you mean?'

'Look,' Martin said, 'I want to tell you something. I have always had a suspicion that my mother was raped by my father. He was in the Russian Army and I have a feeling that at least it was not entirely voluntary on her part, that she went along with him because there was no alternative at the end of the war. I can remember him bringing us to Berlin once when I was small and she didn't want to go. He insisted and when we came to the city to go shopping, she was crying all the time. Didn't even want to get off the train, I remember. She's never been back to Berlin since, even though we lived only an hour and a half away on the train. I asked her about all that much later, but she would never tell me anything. Maybe she knew it would turn me against my father.'

'What are you telling me this for?'

'I still have that suspicion,' Martin said.

'And so?'

'Suspicion is all I have,' Martin said. 'What can I do about it? I can prove nothing. So I just have to live with it.'

Gregor waited for him to make his point, the advice of a best friend.

'You can't live your life on the basis of some hunch,' Martin said, 'that's all I'm saying.'

But none of this had any impact on Gregor, other than to send him deeper into himself, making him even more of an outsider even within his own circle. Mara decided instead to try and pull him back. Rather than holding on like one of those Velcro women that musicians spoke about, she laid on the support. She went to see his new band playing, waited for him afterwards, in an empty hall, with the crew carrying the equipment out and a door banging in the background. With the roadies moving in and out behind them, she put her arms around him and told him that she loved him.

'And there's nothing I can do about that,' she said.

At moments when they were discussing things at home, Daniel often stood in the doorway in his pyjamas, saying he could not sleep, so they had to snap out of their crisis and behave as though nothing was happening. She would turn to the boy with excessive kindness. He would tell a bedtime story with such enthusiasm that even a fairy tale sounded contrived.

And while Gregor put Daniel to sleep on that night, she sprang out of that dreamy, devolved mood which had slipped like a virus into her blood and stood up from the black-and-white bedroom chair. She got dressed and went into the kitchen to prepare the dinner. A discipline returned to her eyes. He had made the right decision. She was afraid of being alone, but she knew that with Gregor in the apartment, she was already alone.

'You're absolutely right, Gregor,' she said when he came into the kitchen some time after. 'It's good for you to go to Toronto.'

Gregor was surprised by her sudden conversion, and waited for the twist. He expected her to reveal some new plan or admission that she had always wanted him to go away. She blessed his decision with a clenched fist.

She had prepared a beautiful meal. The table had already been laid with great style, because she didn't want the parting to be like an escape or a banishment. But just as she was about to serve, placing small sprigs of parsley on the fish and readjusting the slice of lemon, the whole thing turned into a disaster. Reaching out to hand him two water glasses from the cupboard, one of them fell, shattering into a thousand beads all over the counter.

'Jesus, I'm so sorry,' she said, holding her hands over her mouth. 'Oh God. How stupid of me.'

She tried to remove the glass from the plates, but there were too many tiny splinters unseen to the eye, hidden in the beautiful black-bean sauce she had made to go with the fish. Glittering diamonds mixed in with the rice.

'It's all right,' he said. 'Don't worry about it, Mara.'

'I'm so fucking stupid,' she kept saying. 'God.'

'No. Look,' he said, 'we can go out instead.'

'I've ruined everything now.'

He cleared the plates away, dumping the lethal food into the bin, hoovering across the counter, while she got the woman next door to look after Daniel for the evening. The normal arrangement was that if they arrived home before twelve, they would drop in and pick him up. Gregor was such an expert at lifting the boy out of the bed with the blanket still around him. He was able to carry him out onto the landing and in through the hallway of their own apartment, then lay him down in his own bed without ever waking him up. He would slip his hand under Daniel's neck, holding up his head, not allowing his arms to fall down. While Mara rushed ahead opening doors, he held his head to ensure that it was not exposed to the draught, sheltering his eyes from the light.

They chose a restaurant in another part of the city, a place where they had never been before. The disaster of the splintering glass changed to an accidental celebration.

Mara spoke with renewed enthusiasm. And this time, her anger was beginning to turn into something else, into a kind of desperate loyalty to the story she once believed. If she could no longer hold on to the person she had loved, then she could at least carry on believing his story, as though the biography had always amounted to more than the person to whom it belonged.

'I want to believe that you're Jewish,' she said. 'While you're away in Toronto, I'm going to go and meet your mother again. I'm going to go through the whole thing with her and get to the truth. If she's hiding something, then I'll find out.'

And with this declaration began an obsession. She seemed to have entered into a private crusade, conscripting herself into a lifelong duty to establish the true facts so that she could rescue him from oblivion. It was like some oath of allegiance to the family, to the truth, to the past, and she sounded more excited again, full of energy, as though she couldn't wait to begin her quest. Already she was dreaming of digging up some vital piece of evidence to prove his true identity which might allow him to return to her. With his imminent disappearance, she seemed to cling to this crazy undertaking, to bring him back to the real world, to establish his story at least, if not his physical presence.

'Mara,' he said, 'leave it.'

'No, I'm serious, Gregor,' she said. 'You've got to let me do this. If you're Jewish and she's denying it, then that's something that needs to be cleared up.'

The other guests in the restaurant looked up. The word 'Jewish' echoed across the tables around the restaurant like some illicit term. There was nothing Gregor could do to stop her resolve to pursue her investigations in Nuremberg.

Besides, it was only right for Daniel to get to know the people Gregor had grown up with. It was impossible to get Gregor to go and see his father, so she and Daniel would have to do all that on his behalf.

In the car outside, just before she started the engine, she could not help herself asking one final question that was close to her heart but which had not been formulated before. She waited as though she could not drive until she got the answer.

'There's one thing I need to ask you,' she said, looking him in the eyes. 'Don't take this the wrong way, Gregor. I just need to know for myself. Is this about dealing with the past? Some kind of atonement?'

Was this something she admired or was it an accusation? He didn't answer. An entire history had been placed into his mouth. Everything that had gone on in their country, everything that was being spoken about in the media was hanging in the silence between them. She had dared to suggest that by declaring himself to be Jewish, he was turning himself into some kind of human monument to make up for the past. Perhaps she intended it to sound more supportive, but he was trapped by the taunt inside the words.

She switched on the engine, but he told her to stop.

'I want to walk,' he said.

'I'm sorry, Gregor,' she said. 'I didn't mean it like that.'

He got out and walked away. She watched him turn the corner and drove after him for a while, like a police tail. But he marched on and she then decided to drive home.

He drifted through the city for hours, in a wide arc. But he was merely stalling the moment of return when he would have to answer her question. The walking brought exhaustion in his mind and, with it, a clarity, a submission.

He only allowed the streets to lead him home again when he was sure that Mara was already asleep. She would have gone in to the woman next door and brought Daniel back. She would have woken the boy up and put on his slippers and made him walk on his sleepy legs, shuffling through the corridor. She probably made him go to the toilet while he yawned and rubbed his eyes and shivered with the warmth of his pee escaping from him. She would have put him into the cold bed and tucked him in with a kiss on the forehead. She might have made herself some camomile tea with honey and waited up for him a while, but then gone to sleep in the end.

When Gregor finally turned the corner onto the street where they lived, he glanced up at the windows. There were no lights on. He had the keys in his hand, ready to steal in like an intruder. But then, at the last minute, before stepping up to the main door with silver graffiti over the carved oak features, he turned to the parked beige Renault and found her sitting inside.

She had been waiting for him all this time, frozen, staring ahead with that ghostly sadness, beyond crying. There was no escape from those eyes. The questions in them. He walked up to the car and opened the door.

'Mara, what are you doing here, sitting alone?'

He brought her inside and linked arms with her on the stairs going up. They went straight into the bedroom. She dropped her clothes on the black-and-white chair as usual and got into bed, exhausted, without words. They made love. A farewell love. On the eve of departure. With fatigue in their limbs and with hot tears rolling across his chest. The genius of it. Staying in the car all night and waiting for him to come back. Sitting there with the keys in her hand, staring ahead, knowing that some time, sooner or later, even if the dawn was coming and the noise of refuse trucks was advancing through the streets, he would eventually have to walk past and find her there. The courage it took her to see it through, to be noticed by neighbours coming out to walk their dogs. Waiting only for his tall, familiar shape to appear, with his ghostly face coming up under the street light to ask her, 'Why don't you come inside?' Keeping herself awake inside the cramped car, hoping that he would not go in without seeing her, as if it didn't matter.

Twenty-one

The good apples have already been stored away. Thorsten has stacked them up on a wooden trolley and taken them over to one of the barns. He has opened the big sliding doors and wheeled the trolley in, carrying the sacks into the basement with Johannes following him all the way, watching everything.

The others are wandering around the farm in the early afternoon. Katia has disappeared for a rest, while Mara has taken Gregor and Martin by the arm, one on either side, on a guided tour. In the yard, Juli is trying to get the pump going. It squeaks like an old donkey and she keeps laughing with the effort, pumping the big lever up and down but not drawing any water. Daniel watches her with a condescending smile, enjoying the way she struggles with such a redundant piece of cast-iron equipment. 'Does this not work any more?' she asks, smiling, with the stud under her bottom lip reflecting the sun. Daniel nods, but refuses to show her because he likes to watch the furious determination on her face. The laughter has taken the power out of her arms and her lips are pursed in mock distress, but she tries once more, throwing back her hair to put in one more genuine effort and prove that she can figure this out by herself.

'You must put the water in first,' Thorsten calls out from the door of the barn. Juli is not really all that pushed about getting water and he fails to notice that there is a game going on here between them.

Thorsten connects the yellow hose to the tap and explains to her that the tubular upright sink has to be filled with water first, otherwise the lever will only pull up air. When that's been done, he asks her to start pumping again and the cool underground water comes gushing jubilantly across the stones. She takes a drink from her cupped hand. Then she fills an enamel basin with water to throw over Daniel. And even though he wouldn't mind cooling down, he flees like a chicken across the farmyard, still laughing. Most of the water from the basin spills on Juli herself and on her white dress, so that her thighs now look as though they are wrapped in cling film. But she has also managed to hit Daniel with some drops of water across his bare shoulders. She heaves the basin back down and walks away in triumph, bowing to an invisible audience with her hands silently clapping above her head.

Is this a high point? An afternoon in the sunshine with Daniel and Juli laughing helplessly and the clang of the empty enamel basin echoing around the farmyard? Are the contortions of history not mere pilgrim stations on the way to this peak of freedom?

They are taking it easy now. Juli and Daniel leave the pump behind to go down to the lake with Johannes. In winter, they threw a rock out onto the lake and it remained suspended on top of the frozen water for weeks before it sank. Now, Daniel says he's going to dive down to see if he can bring it up again.

The others intend to follow later. In the meantime, Mara is pointing out some of the war damage on the farm buildings. Facing east, on the outer wall of the barns, they can see the holes in the bricks. The bullets have taken chunks away, leaving shards and dust in a red line on the ground along the wall. Nobody has ever swept it away. At the corner where the artillery fire blew large gaps into the side of the barn, it has been repaired with yellow brick replacing the original red ones. The farmhouse itself got the worst of it, almost completely destroyed because the red roof offered such a perfect target. And the barn where the horses were burned alive is still standing as a ruin with no roof.

Martin is smoking a cigarette. So calm is the afternoon that the smoke rises straight and he even manages to blow an effortless smoke ring, making the air seem interior. His sunglasses make him look like a dragonfly stopping to reflect, staring into the distance at the forest on the far side of the field.

'That's where the Russians were,' Mara explains, 'in those trees.'

'Us Russians over there,' Martin says. 'And us Germans over here.'

'It took them eight days, apparently, to take over this farm.'

Mara says there were seven German soldiers holding out here, to the last man. The fire came from the trees, day and night, with intervals in between, waiting for the artillery. One night, the Russians sent a young man over to steal his way into the farm, but he was caught by the Germans and when they searched his rucksack they found nothing but a book by Pushkin. He was held hostage, but the Russians eventually swept over all these farms with the sheer force of numbers, even though they suffered great casualties. A minimum of sixty Russian soldiers were said to have fallen in the fight over this farm alone. By that time the house was in ruins and there was nothing much left to defend, but the Germans still refused to surrender. The farm was conquered eventually. The Russian intellectual was found dead and the two remaining German soldiers were taken into captivity before the army moved on in the race to Berlin.

Thorsten's aunt had fled as the battle over the farm began. Every edible animal had already been slaughtered to provide food for the front, some of the horses turned into sausage. She wasn't even allowed to take one of her own horses and had to join the thousands who were fleeing to the west on foot. And then she soon found herself overtaken by the advancing army. The war was effectively over and she decided go back to try and hold on to the farm which had been in her family for hundreds of years. But that was her mistake, because she was then at the mercy of a new war of looting and rape. In her twenties at the time, only recently married, alone facing a wave of revenge.

'It must have been horrible,' Mara says. 'They tied her by the neck to the pump.'

And when all that was over, she was forced to defend the farm once again during the GDR times, because it was sequestered by the socialist state. After she and her husband had managed to rebuild most of the buildings, the state took possession and ran the farm while they fought to be allowed to live there. They were offered work at a printing firm in Leipzig, but refused to leave, saying they would kill themselves. Eventually they were kept on as labourers on their own farm. And each day, she must have walked past that pump, trying to forget the memory of those dark moments. It was only after the fall of the Berlin Wall that she finally managed to claim back the farm and then handed it on to Thorsten.

The farm is a bit of a mess now. Maybe it was always like that, even when it was in full swing with cattle moving in and out and the grain being stored in the lofts and the sweet smell of manure all around. It's a place where nothing was ever finished. Some of the old farm machinery is still lying around, idle and rusted now, like the horse-drawn soil leveller with its thick, heavy wooden wheels and a seat for two people to sit on while driving. Everywhere, items waiting to be taken away or put somewhere else. A car wheel leaning against the wall of the house. A pile of yellow bricks left by the side of the grain store, and further away, a stack of grey slates intended to fix the roof damaged by a storm when the chestnut tree lost one of its branches. Closer to the house, there is a stack of logs and an axe leaning against the wall. Somebody must have decided it was time to have a go at getting the wood ready for the fire but then got distracted and considered something else to be more urgent.

The yard is enclosed in a rectangular shape by buildings on all sides, leaving access to the fields at each corner. Everything seems to have moved on and left this farm behind now. A barn owl comes in the late afternoons from time to time to sit on the roof or in the plum tree at the centre of the yard. The weeds are growing everywhere and maybe nature may yet manage to have the last word.

Could the old fairy tales be coming back? Or did they ever disappear? Once a year in a nearby village, the women wear their traditional dresses, claiming that the legend of Red Riding Hood sprang up here centuries ago. They have marked a place in the forest where they believe a small girl in her red cape was abducted on her way to see her grandmother. Was there something darker about the original story that made it too difficult to tell in any other form but in a fairy tale? Is it possible that the tale of Red Riding Hood was invented in answer to sexual predators of the time, and that the wolf became loaded with all the unspeakable crimes of society? Just as some people now believe the story of the seven dwarfs was based on child labourers working in the mines. Mara has seen the women in the village, around fifty Red Riding Hoods of all ages gathering together. They march into the local bar and order schnapps. Old and young women in red hoods, celebrating the day when the predator was defeated and ended up in the well with a meal of rocks in his stomach.

'Thorsten was brought up in Berlin,' Mara says. 'Katia told me that when his mother was taking him to school on the S-Bahn, they used to pass by the Berlin Wall and see the soldiers and the dogs below them. He would ask her questions and his mother would answer them quite honestly.'

She reconstructs the surreal conversation which Thorsten and his mother had going to school, with everyone on the train listening to the banal, but absolutely correct answers.

'Mama, why are the dogs there?' Thorsten asked.

'To stop people going over the Wall,' she answered.

'What is the Wall there for?'

'To protect us from the capitalists, son.'

'Who are the capitalists?'

'People who love money.'

'Do we not like money?'

'No,' his mother answered. 'We hate money. It makes you sick. It makes you want to buy nice things.'

Mara says there was nothing that anyone listening in on the train could argue with. But the innocence of the questions and the answers must have sounded absurd, mocking the entire socialist system even if what she was saying was absolutely bang in line with Communist dogma. The clarity of the child's questions and the simplicity of the mother's answers always revealed the lies inside the system.

'Are they all sick over there?' Thorsten asked, pointing across the Berlin Wall to the other side.

'Yes,' his mother would answer. 'They're all sick over there because they want to do nothing else but shop.'

It went on for weeks like that, his mother answering every question correctly and innocently, everything going along with a socialist view of the world, but all the passengers listening in knowing that the answers sounded completely daft.

'What did the other passengers say?' Martin asks.

'They kept their mouths shut, mostly,' Mara says. 'They stared ahead and ignored it. Except for one man, who once said her attitude was disgraceful and that she should stay quiet. So she barked back at him and asked him what he would answer to all those questions. "You answer them," she said. After they got off, another woman quietly came up to her and, without saying anything, shook her hand. Thorsten kept asking the same questions every day going to school, because he was fascinated by the sight of the soldiers and the dogs and the barbed wire and the lookout towers. But even more than that, he was obsessed with the strange answers that his mother gave. Eventually, an official came to the house one day and told her she was no longer permitted to travel on the S-Bahn. And it was not long after that that only special people could travel that close to the Wall.'

With the large doors open on both sides of the building, the farm almost looks operational again, as though the cattle are merely out in the fields and will soon be returning for the night. The sunlight slopes into these dusty, forsaken halls now, along the loam floor and through the empty pens, casting shadows. The air is full of sound memories, hooves, chains, clanging buckets, the lowing of cows and the whistling farmhands. The reimagined smells of dung and straw. Old leather straps and blinkers and cobwebbed harnesses still hang on the walls. At the centre of the doorway onto the fields, a swing has been erected on long ropes.

'How do you think Daniel will manage in Africa?' Gregor wonders.

'He'll be fine,' Mara says. 'Don't worry.'

'As long as they get all their shots.'

'He's got Juli with him,' Mara says. 'And she's a tough one.'

'Like a bodyguard,' Martin says. 'I don't think Putin has a better security team around himself than that.'

Mara steps towards the swing and sits in the wooden seat. Martin stands behind her, ready to push. They fall into the roles of children without giving it a thought.

'Remember that rash he got once,' Martin says.

'What rash?' Gregor asks.

'He got this terrible rash behind the knees,' Mara explains. 'Lasted for about a year. We took him to all kinds of specialists.'

'Leprosy,' Martin says.

'I actually thought it had something to do with the hornet sting,' Mara says. 'Had to get him a dozen different ointments. We even tried acupuncture. In the end it just disappeared again. Complete mystery.'

Gregor becomes aware of how much has been lost by his former absence. He would like to claim back some of those details, but they don't belong to him. She has used the word 'we' to incorporate Martin into those intimate family episodes, because he was there to help at the time when Gregor was abroad. Looking out into the fields at the stubble and the blonde rectangles of straw still waiting to be picked up and brought in for storage, he feels what is missing.

'His outburst this morning,' Gregor says. 'There's something he wants to get off his chest.'

'He hasn't mentioned anything to me,' Mara says.

'He's never really forgiven me,' Gregor says.

'Why do you say that?'

'I feel it. There's something on his mind,' Gregor says.

'You haven't really talked much recently, have you?'

'I thought we'd sorted everything out,' Gregor says. 'But there's something wrong. I know he still blames me. I can feel it coming. From her, from Juli as much as from Daniel.'

'He needs to go away and clear his head,' Martin says.

'Maybe Africa will change him.'

'He's just like you,' Martin says. 'He has to travel and discover himself. You'll see. He'll come back in a year's time and the two of you will have so much to talk about.'

'Maybe it's better if he gets it off his chest before he leaves,' Mara says.

She settles into the seat and begins to swing in and out. With the help of Martin, she sails into the open air. Her dress rises up in the breeze and she appears to go right out into the landscape with her bare legs pointing towards the lake. The ropes are very long, four metres at least up to the frame of the doorway, and she swings like a young girl defying all instincts for safety, feeling the narcotic, funfair rush inside her stomach. Out into the blinding sunlight and right back into the shade of the farm building, speeding back and forth through the entrance full of hovering dust and flies. Higher and higher with her eyes closed, as though she wants to continue going all the way up to the sun. Leaning back with the ropes in her hands and her feet stretched out in order to gain the maximum height. Returning with her hair going forward and knees folded so as to keep going, almost up as far as the heavy wooden beams crossing under the roof.

Twenty-two

There was a frightening moment soon after Gregor left. Coming back from shopping one day, Mara parked across the street from the apartment. She let Daniel out and went around for the groceries, handed him one of the bags and before she had time to remind him not to cross, he disappeared. She heard the screaming tyres. Saw the car skidding. Daniel shivering and clutching the bag with both hands up to his chin, still waiting for the impact, almost smiling with fear for a split second. She smelled the burning rubber and ran out to grab him in a panic, even though she had all the time in the world now. The car had come to a stop at a slight angle. The driver sat with his hands on the steering wheel, unable to move, unable to speak.

She's gone over these details a thousand times, trying to put them behind her. The dry mouth, speechless aftershock. Measuring and remeasuring the short distance between luck and disaster. The compound range of confusing emotions springing up between rage and passivity. The urge to kill the driver. Followed by an equal wave of guilt and compassion as he stepped out of the car and leaned over to be sick. The spectators raising their heads over the parked cars in judgement, converting the scene into a parable for their own children. And the sudden awareness of her own vulnerability. That cold feeling around the shoulders. She had dropped the keys out of her hand. Some of the groceries rolled under the car. Afterwards she discovered that somebody had made off with her purse, while she stood in the middle of the street lifting Daniel up in her arms and turned, out of sheer habit, to say something to Gregor, even though he was no longer there.

'I thought you were watching him,' she wanted to say, though she cannot remember if this was actually said out loud or only inside her own head.

Back in the safety of the apartment, she kneeled down and shook Daniel by the shoulders. Clenched her fist, telling him never to do this to her again. Then she cried and hugged him, saying: 'I'm sorry, Mama didn't mean to be cross with you.'

She wrote to Gregor and told him about that incident. They were in contact all the time, by letters and by occasional phone calls from Toronto. She would pass the phone to Daniel and allow him to speak to his father for a few precious moments, but there was nothing much to say at that remove. Gregor remarked on how tall the buildings were. How cold it was in the winter. But it was making no sense to Daniel that his father was away and not coming back soon. Gregor sent gifts for them on their birthdays. Mara assured him that Daniel was very happy and well taken care of. He spent time with her sisters, and Martin was also being very good to him, often inviting him to stay overnight with his family.

Daniel sometimes woke up at night, dreaming of hornets. She had to take him into her bed to calm him down, tell him the windows were all shut and there was no possible way that a hornet could enter the house. He heard buzzing. He imagined them hiding behind wardrobes and nesting in the curtains. Brightly coloured creatures with sickle blades ready to attack as soon as he went to sleep.

They avoided the obvious questions of fidelity. Of course, Gregor would meet other women. The music business was full of drifters and casual adoration and promises of uncomplicated love. It was hard to discuss it on the phone and too blunt to put into letters. The conversations were tough and tearful enough as they were. So they maintained that proxy, long-distance marriage which so many immigrants and seasonal workers all over the world live with all the time.

The only way of getting closer to Gregor now was to go back to Nuremberg. She took Daniel with her on these visits and rebuilt a family relationship from the evidence of ruins. It was soon clear that Daniel meant the world to his grandmother.

'Look,' she said, smiling at the boy. 'He's the image of his great-grandfather, Emil.'

Mara looked sceptical.

'Before he got fat, that is.'

They placed the photographs alongside Daniel's face. A strange family science, comparing eyes and cheekbones and mouths, wishing the resemblances to life.

With all this added attention, Daniel became fond of his grandmother. They formed an immediate friendship, perhaps actively encouraged by Mara so that she could spend more time investigating. A family spy, hoping to uncover some vital piece of information. She took Daniel to the funeral of Gregor's father when he died. And in the following summer, while Gregor's mother was grieving, they often stayed over the entire weekend, even going up to the mountain lodge where Gregor and his father used to spend so much time when he was growing up.

Mara had taken Daniel to see Gregor's father in hospital before he died. And maybe the time had come for an open discussion. Perhaps Gregor's mother had only been obedient to some post-war pact with her husband and would now be in a position to reveal the real story. As they became more familiar, Mara brought up the subject of Gregor's origins more directly.

'Why would he have made up a story like this?'

'I can't answer that,' Gregor's mother said. 'Only Gregor can tell you that.'

She ran into a dead end each time. It was depressing to find nothing at all. They went over the war years and Mara noted every detail in her head, often writing things down afterwards in a notebook. Then she would send letters off to Canada again, though Gregor refused to get into the circle at all and said he was not joining a history club. What amazed Mara during these long discussions in Nuremberg was how close the story of Gregor's mother tallied with that of Gregor, apart from the one essential fact. He was not an orphan. His identity was clearly that of a German boy, an only son, who had grown up in Nuremberg and began to fantasise about having a different life.

'Strange,' Mara would say. 'Very strange, don't you think, that he would have made up such an elaborate story?'

'I blame Uncle Max,' Gregor's mother said. 'I'll never forgive him.'

'For what?'

'For putting all that stuff into Gregor's head.'

'And why would he do that?'

'Because he was going mad. Because he was guilty. Don't ask me. All I know is that Gregor started becoming obsessed with himself, looking in the mirror, asking endless questions and imagining things that were completely outlandish.'

Mara was conscripted by this family duty, not so much for Gregor's but for Daniel's sake, bringing a lost family back together. She was charged with the task of establishing Daniel's true identity, even if Gregor's was beyond reach already.

Sometimes she felt the futility of all this. Was your identity not something you chose, as much as something you rejected? Characterised by those elements you admire as well as those you deny. Daniel's identity was not so much inherited any more. It had little to do with religion, with history or with geography, even less with his place of birth or his ancestors. His identity was something in the making. Already, Martin was taking Daniel to football matches, buying him a blue-and-white scarf, giving him a feeling of belonging in the city, a family of inhabitants, a spooling of emotions into one large unlikely commune.

She found herself walking around the house in Nuremberg, imagining Gregor when he was Daniel's age. She observed the reactions of her own son to the antlers on the walls, the guns lined up in a rack behind glass, the hunting prints depicting dogs and men jumping out of bushes to pounce on a wild boar with gleaming tusks. The unimaginable height to which a heavy wild boar could jump to get away from his pursuers. She noticed that, just like his father, Daniel was afraid of the stuffed badger on the landing, until Gregor's mother finally agreed that the claws looked a bit threatening and placed it somewhere else.

Everywhere the household items that would have been so familiar to Gregor. Were they not part of his identity as well, the fridge, the TV set, the shape and position of the radiators? The visual content of his memory, the logo of family possessions and home smells and peculiarities. The radio in the kitchen on top of the fridge. The carved wooden pastry print with the faces of Max and Moritz on the wall. The piano in the living room with the pictures of Emil above. The ring of glass trinkets and vases and ornaments on the sideboard every time somebody walked by. Even the handprints and finger marks around the light switches.

She wondered what it was like to have no identity, the loneliness of belonging to a people who had no disguise.

In the hallway, there was a full-length mirror which Gregor had told her about, how he stood there and imagined where he came from in the East. His mother confirmed that he had always been an insomniac. It may have had to do with the antlers. Or maybe it was the clock chiming every half an hour in the living room.

Gregor used to get up and wander around the house at night, creeping down the stairs so as not to wake his parents. He knew every creak in the floorboards. He had to reimagine all the furniture in the dark so that he would not crash into the coffee table or the sideboard. He took fright at the shape of animals on the wall as if they were not quite dead yet. A speck of light coming to life in the eyes of a dead deer. The grimace of a mountain goat. The antique hunting rifles hanging over every doorway. The coat rack in the hallway like another set of antlers with coats hanging down like dripping skins. And the shoes and boots left just inside the door which always made it look as though his parents had evaporated.

'He used to stand in front of that mirror at night,' Mara said.

'I know that.'

'He told me that he would see no reflection in the dark.'

'Naturally.'

'He stood there wondering if he existed at all.'

And when the dawn came up, Gregor would see himself coming back to life again slowly, along with all the other dead things around him in the house. Gradually the image in the mirror would gather light and he had the feeling that he came from nothing.

Twenty-three

There was something unwelcome about Uncle Max. Gregor remembers his mother being quite nervous whenever he came to the house and his father remained aloof, even hostile. His presence created an uncomfortable tension and everyone was relieved afterwards when he was gone. A quiet, introverted old man who was not actually related, only called Uncle because he was a family friend. Perhaps it was his physical appearance that made him seem so grotesque. Uncle Max was missing one eye and his false teeth didn't fit very well, so he smiled awkwardly and lisped and spat across the table whenever he spoke. Bits of food occasionally landed on the tablecloth at dinner and Gregor remembers the fascination and revulsion of watching his mother discreetly sweep away some offending morsel or hiding a stain with the jug. On top of that, his missing eye wept frequently so that he had to wipe away the discharge with his handkerchief, and perhaps it was that sad appearance that made everyone feel afraid of him.

Uncle Max brought a big silence with him. There was something even more absurd about his chronic inability to speak freely about ordinary things. He asked questions, how Gregor was doing at school, how his music lessons were going. The visit often revolved entirely around that staccato question-and-answer session. 'Tell Uncle Max about your new piano lessons,' his mother would say to fill in the space, and Gregor would be left searching for something to report. It seemed like an extraction each time. Gregor couldn't imagine how it would interest Uncle Max to know the name of his music teacher. His parents were not very skilled at keeping a conversation going either, so the evening with Uncle Max staggered through a series of agonising silences in which everyone glanced furtively around the table avoiding each other's eyes. His father sometimes let go in a tirade on some current political issue, but Uncle Max never joined in the debate. His mother didn't allow herself to have political opinions either and when she asked Uncle Max what he thought, he usually gave a neutral answer like: 'That may be right.' Sometimes they all got going together on some major road-building project nearby, but the discussion always ran aground. Sooner or later, they would end up looking at Gregor again for relief. Then his mother would ask Gregor to perform something. 'Play something for Uncle Max,' she would say and, for a while at least, the room had a communal focus, followed by an applause that made Gregor feel even more self-conscious and eager to get back to his own room. Uncle Max clapped longest and then brought his handkerchief up to his eye again.

Finally, his father would seize the opportunity to end the evening by offering Uncle Max a lift in the car, and then the house could breathe again.

Afterwards, Gregor would ask questions. 'What happened to Uncle Max? How did he lose his eye?' But his mother normally answered with one polite sentence.

'He was treated very badly during the war,' she told him. Once, she even used the word 'torture' but then regretted having said it. She told him that Max had no friends and that's why she called him Uncle, so he wouldn't feel left out.

'You're not to ask him anything,' she would say. 'Do you hear me now? You don't ask questions like that.'

Gregor's father could not bear this kind of talk. As far as he was concerned, Uncle Max was another deserter who betrayed his country. And maybe there was some deeper disgrace in his deformities that could never be discussed around the table. Gregor knew that the piano was a gift from Uncle Max, though his father didn't want to accept it because the family might be beholden to him. And perhaps they were. His mother spoke with regret, as though there was something shameful which brought up an unimaginable pain of her own.

When he was a teenager, she told him about the bombing of Berlin, the flight from the city when Gregor was three years old. How his grandfather Emil came to collect them in his truck, and how she was questioned by the Gestapo in a small village, right at the end of the war.

'Your grandfather was not a bad man,' she said. 'Only dealing in things on the black market, Gregor, do you understand me?'

She didn't take any pride in the fact that her father had tricked the Nazis. She didn't describe it as an act of heroism, only bad luck.

'Uncle Max was Grandfather Emil's best friend from school,' she explained. 'They had all kinds of cracked ideas for getting into business together. They got a delivery business going and during the war they invented a scheme to avoid being sent to the front. It was awful at the front.'

'Was he a deserter?' Gregor asked.

'Yes,' she said. 'He broke the law and they slapped me and asked me where he was hiding. I was afraid. I'm not very clever. I didn't have any intelligent answers to give them.'

'Did he escape?'

'I didn't know where Grandfather Emil was hiding,' she said. 'Only Max knew that.'

'Did they take his eye out?' Gregor asked.

'You were only a baby,' she said. 'You didn't hear anything. You had a terrible ear infection.'

She stared Gregor in the eyes.

'What could I do? I was afraid they would take you away from me. I was no good at keeping things quiet. I had to tell them about Uncle Max, but they knew that already.'

After saying it she would suddenly change her mood. She grew angry, regretting her confession. Afraid of the power which this information gave Gregor over her, the ability to hold her to ransom with her own biography. She withdrew into her martyred frame of mind, begging him to stop 'tormenting' her with stupid questions for which she had no answers.

'Did Uncle Max tell them where Grandfather Emil was hiding?' Gregor asked.

'I don't know,' she said in desperation. 'Gregor, you're asking me things I don't know.'

In the absence of hard facts, Gregor began to imagine things for himself. At the next visit, he stared at Uncle Max with open curiosity. The table was set with the usual care. The same ritual silences. The same questions from Uncle Max and the same minimal answers from Gregor. When the conversation came to a standstill, his father took over and spoke at length about hunting events, giving Gregor a chance to examine Uncle Max's thin features on the opposite side of the table. His hands and his fingernails, the socket of his missing eye. But the greatest sign of torture was not physical at all but his silence.

Uncle Max would be asked a courteous question about his health. He said he was working part-time in a bookshop, but that he might have to give it up. Health was not a subject that interested Gregor, but he was aware enough to imagine that the torture Uncle Max had endured might be impacting on him much later. All through dinner he imagined him calling out for mercy. The only clue to his suffering was in his good eye. A sensitive thermometer of human feelings. It expressed latent fear, or maybe great strength, he could not tell which.

Gregor understood endurance in the face of extreme physical tasks, from cycling and climbing mountains. Games involving survival instincts and inner strength. In the battle with the environment, mental courage was the ultimate challenge, more than the mountain itself. But torture was inflicted with great imagination, precisely in order to edge past that threshold of endurance. The victim was driven to the edge of reason and kept there. A mountain could kill you, Gregor recalls thinking, but a torturer was an expert at keeping you alive.

Gregor was only three years of age when all this happened, but he was present nonetheless at this man's worst moments. He was a witness and that produced its own pain. The bystander pain. Uncle Max could, if he was strong enough, put the suffering behind him, but Gregor could not. He stared across the table and felt the obligation to reimagine that moment of torture with obscene clarity. He knew it was impossible to measure suffering. But the pain of the witness went on without stopping, because he had no entitlement to put it behind him.

He remembers trying to make Uncle Max feel happy. He told him with great enthusiasm about the new guitar he had bought with his own money. He ran up to his room and brought it down, along with a folder of lyrics which he had collected from the American Army radio station. All carefully maintained with photographs of rock stars pasted in.

After dinner, Gregor performed something on the guitar first, then on the piano. While they sat around the living room sipping coffee, his father smoked a cigar that sent bonfire clouds through the forest of antlers and skulls and grimacing faces. He played Bach. A gust of chords and interwoven notes. When the piece came to an end, he watched Uncle Max take his handkerchief out again.

'He certainly brought the music with him,' Uncle Max said. 'Aren't you lucky you have found such a talented boy.'

The room went silent. Shocked glances flashing between their eyes, searching the linguistic tilt in the words. An atonal melody left hanging in the room, refusing to fade out.

'He got it from his grandfather,' his mother responded. She was indignant. She had a worried expression on her face.

'I'm sorry,' Uncle Max said. 'I thought he knew.'

'Knew what?' Gregor blurted.

Gregor's mother burst into tears and left the room. His father became angry, standing up and moving towards the door.

'What the hell are you saying? Why do you come here to upset her like this?'

The evening came to an abrupt end. An atmosphere of crisis all around the house that night. Gregor remembers hearing his parents talking in raised voices in bed. He remembers not being able to sleep and going downstairs while they were still discussing things, wandering around the house in the dark and coming across the mirror in the hallway, looking at himself and not finding his own reflection, wondering if there was another version of himself that was being kept from him.

His mother explained the following day that Uncle Max was not right in his mind. She placed her arm around him and said Uncle Max was starting to imagine things. She blamed the ill treatment and said he had begun to ramble and say things that didn't make sense.

Instead, she told him a little more about his grandfather Emil.

'He could remember the words of every song,' she said. 'Even English and Italian songs. You're very like him, learning songs on your guitar. He was known in every bar and could drink for free anywhere he went. That was his problem, Gregor. That's why he was separated from my mother. All the women loved him. When he sang, they sighed and had tears in their eyes.'

Gregor was distracted from his enquiries.

'Everybody wanted him for their birthday parties,' she said. 'He even got invited by the military to sing at a party for Hitler's birthday. And maybe that's why they were so enraged when they discovered he was tricking them all the time.'

There was nothing more said about Uncle Max. A forgetful old man. But not so forgetful, it seems, because he sent Gregor a package on his birthday almost six months later. His birthday falls on the second of June, the date on his passport, on all his documents. On his seventeenth birthday, Uncle Max sent him a recording of Jewish music. Gregor was more interested in pop music, but he listened to the raw energy of the record, trying to extract some meaning from this gift. It contained a coded message, a virus that became slowly more active with each playing.

On the cover, there was a picture of men in suits, standing under a tree in summer, holding their instruments and smiling at a dog lying down asleep nearby in the shade. There was a card alongside bearing the words, '*Good luck with your music, Uncle Max.*' The affidavit of a delusional man who never came back to the house again.

Twenty-four

They walk slowly along the edge of the field towards the lake. They leave barn doors wide open and the swing still going to and fro a little in ever reducing motion. The afternoon is moving on at the same pace, never coming to a complete standstill even after it appears to have come to rest. They have reached a wall of poplar trees with their tambourine leaves, jangling high on the breeze. They have stalled to look at the sunken roof of a wooden hut which has begun to fade back into the landscape. They look back in a sweep of one hundred and eighty degrees to the orchard and the farm buildings and the forest beyond. They can already hear voices from the lake, and the splashing. They talk and laugh and remember and move on. What else can they do now but talk and remember and swing back and forth, suspended along the axis of their own lives?

Mara wears her sun hat and carries a basket containing cake and coffee, everything including silver forks and a tea towel to spread out on the ground. As they move on, Gregor picks up a long blade of grass and turns it into a green reed between his thumbs. He brings it up to his lips and produces a familiar, boyhood country call.

'Do you remember how Daniel was afraid of that sound?' Mara says to him.

Memory is like stored energy which has not been spent yet. It comes to life in family folklore. It produces a special kind of identity, like all things collected among people to mark the time they spent together and the times they have been apart. The photographs, the treasured objects, the family medical records, the entire composite of shared experience. They recall the time when they were camping in the mountains and Daniel had no idea where that sound was coming from. He imagined a monster, a prehistoric bird, with a great serrated beak and scaly talons. Ran straight back into the arms of his mother and she laughed, telling him it was only his own father making silly noises with grass.

A shrill echo comes back from the lake. Daniel has taken up the signal and decided to answer with his own croaky screech. A long extinct crane with luminous eyes. As they move closer to the lake, the grass cries converge. Father and son once again making their signature calls to each other across an imaginary distance.

When they come in sight of the lake, Daniel is hanging from one of the trees above the water. His naked body ready to drop, screeching like a boy with legs kicking out in mid-air, penis and testicles dangling free like exotic fruit set in black fur, holding on to the branch until his hands can no longer take the strain and he lets himself descend into the clear water below with an exaggerated splash. Juli comes out of the lake and stands with her body gleaming. Her breasts shimmering and her pubic hair shaped like a black steel arrowhead, pointing down. She picks up a mobile phone from the bank, throws back her head to get the shower curtain of hair out of her face. A mist of tiny droplets fills the sunlit air around her. She turns round towards the lake to say hello, then listens, looks at the caller number before throwing it back onto the grass again. On her lower back there is a piece of body graffiti, also pointing downwards. She dives into the lake again and disappears.

Thorsten is standing some distance away under a tree with Johannes. They have made a boat out of twigs, father and son both crouching in the same posture, same physique, same square buttocks, same belly and bony chest, only thirty-odd years is the difference. They squat down to launch the ship on its maiden voyage. Johannes calls out to his mother in the middle of the lake, lying on her back with her round balloon belly floating on top of the water. A lost beach ball, inflated at the naval, drifting away so that somebody will have to swim out later and steer it back to shore again.

Daniel's head comes up with the bark of a seal, shouting, overqualifying the beauty of the water, telling those who have come late to get in as quickly as possible.

'You don't know what you're missing,' he says, his green legs dancing a warped foxtrot under the surface.

Mara shouts back, removing her clothes as though she will never need them again after this. She takes a giant evolutionary step backwards, becoming fish. She is naked all at once. Just one brief moment of involuntary sexual lingering as she steps out of her underwear. Her body is strong, healthy, and as she walks into the water, no signs of age can be noticed. Only two small incisions in her right breast for biopsies. An ash-grey bruise on her thigh. She sinks into the lake and floats out with hardly a ripple.

Martin cannot wait to fling himself into the lake after her. He jokes about how much water will be displaced by his body. He hops around, darkened by foreign holidays, trying to get his foot out of his trousers, dragging a bear trap behind him before he finally frees himself. He throws himself into the lake with a splash that sends waves across the surface, reaching a new high watermark along the dusty trunks of the willow trees at the edge.

Thorsten tells them that the lake contains a rare species of crayfish which goes to prove how pure it is. Swimming in mineral water, Martin responds, before he spins away in a fierce, one-man race to the far side.

And Gregor with his long indoor limbs, disrobing himself of all that time spent in half-lit, smoky jazz clubs, all the anonymity of public spaces and air-conditioned interiors. He removes his clothes as well as all that long accumulation of solitude. He immerses himself into this quiet baptism of belonging, with his goat-like genitals dangling low between his thin legs, visible from behind as much as from the front as he sinks down into this sacred, unspoiled font. A scraggy, elongated, soft leather sack which has carried his testicles around the world and a circumcised penis, dipping cautiously into the lake. The water like a cool hand fondling before he turns and throws himself on his back.

They have rediscovered the lightness of their true nature, this half-human species of people-fish. They have returned to water as though to a primal memory, to the outer limits of their freedom. They swim and float and remember and move on, with the clear water washing away all catastrophes gone by and yet to come.

When they have finished swimming, Mara spreads the tea towel on the ground and shares out slices of cake. The smell of coffee rises up to overpower the scent of the lake and the earth around them. They eat the tart, with a fault line of marzipan in the middle and wild berries on top. They sit gazing across the lake, at the insects buzzing.

The wasps are back as well, alerted by the smell of cake. Martin lights a cigarette to fight them off and Johannes watches the smoke rising and dipping as it veers across the water.

They have come to a standstill. There is an afternoon courtesy in the silence, to all things growing and resting around them.

Thorsten talks about how he and Katia went up to the Baltic coast for a few days. He speaks with great enthusiasm about their trip, with Johannes listening, remembering everything for himself. He says they went to Rostock and then took an old steam train across to Heiligendamm. It was wonderful to look out at the sea and there were some great fish restaurants where they ate in the evening.

'Very windy up there on the coast,' he says.

After a pause, Daniel talks about how he and Juli went to visit friends in Jena recently. He says they woke up in the morning and stepped out onto the balcony and found dozens of police trucks lining the street, with hundreds of policemen in riot gear below their window.

'Sounds familiar,' Mara says.

'They were like gladiators,' Daniel says.

'I hope you never get into combat with them,' Gregor says. 'Your head is no match for those truncheons, take it from me.'

'Didn't do us that much harm,' Martin laughs.

Mara pours the remains of the coffee.

'Police everywhere,' Daniel continues. 'On the main square we saw a big crowd of anti-fascist protesters.'

'Counter-protesters,' Juli says. 'They were demonstrating against a crowd of neo-Nazis.'

'This part of the country needs time to adjust,' Thorsten puts in.

'They're everywhere,' Katia says. 'Believe me. It's nothing but thug pride.'

'Funny,' Daniel says. 'Less than a hundred neo-Nazis, four times that many anti-fascists, and about five times that many policemen in riot gear.'

'They're like an endangered species,' Martin says.

'That's what you think,' Juli says. 'I find it very scary.'

'I got a photograph of one of them,' Daniel adds, 'giving us the finger.'

'That's scary all right,' Martin remarks.

'Don't be an asshole,' Juli snaps.

'He's only joking,' Mara says.

'It's not the Third Reich coming back, Daniel,' Martin says. 'The past is not fixed. It keeps changing. Look at how everything has changed since the Wall came down. And 9/11. Nothing is the same since 9/11, since America lost its two front teeth.'

'That's the problem with you people,' Daniel says, getting up. 'You're more afraid of the past than you are of the future.'

'We have to protect the past,' Martin says.

'I'll tell you what's scary,' Juli says, joining Daniel and turning round to face Martin once more. 'On the train going back, two of them got on and started yelling abuse at our Sudanese friend. We were very lucky the police got on and threw them off.'

Daniel and Juli begin to walk away.

'I'll give you a hand in the kitchen,' Martin calls after them.

Daniel has agreed to take on the cooking for the evening. The rest pick themselves up and pack everything together, then drift back slowly in small groups. Johannes carrying the basket and Gregor carrying the towels, talking to each other about dinosaurs. Mara walking barefoot at first, then stopping to put on her shoes while Martin whips the air with a stick, leaving Thorsten and Katia lying alone on their blanket for a while longer in the evening sun, both facing towards the lake, their bodies hooked into each other and his arm across her belly.

Twenty-five

By the time Gregor was seventeen years of age, he was convinced that there was no resemblance between himself and his parents. He had examined all the family photographs and studied himself in the mirror many times. He had brown eyes. He was tall. He had become a giant, a monster belonging to a different species. What began as a normal suspicion in the minds of many children at a certain age, had become a raging obsession.

He started rooting through his mother's possessions looking for more evidence. All the contents of her life stashed away in her dressing table. Broken watches, old reading glasses, garter clips, concert tickets, odd jewellery, single earrings kept in the hope that the match would turn up. Outdated medication. Discoloured packets of sleeping tablets. A strange instrument with which he once saw his mother sanding off dead skin from her foot. He discovered things without knowing much about their provenance, items with no story attached. He didn't know what he was looking for and even when he found something worthwhile, he didn't understand the significance.

Until he came across the letters from Uncle Max.

The letters were polite and restrained. Even in writing, this old man was full of silence. The early letters expressed a wish to come and visit, asking about Gregor and how he was doing. In one of the letters, Uncle Max said he was too ill to work in the foundry any more and had taken up a part-time job in a bookshop. A more recent letter said he had given up the job in the bookshop as well.

Gregor was convinced these banal words contained some hidden message, as long as he read carefully. But it was only the last letter that revealed anything, an apology. Uncle Max said it had not been his intention to hurt anyone. It was a letter of farewell, acknowledging his mistake. He wished them well and said he would not intrude on their lovely family again. And finally, something that made Gregor even more curious.

'Maria, please believe me. I did not tell them anything.'

He read these words over and over again. What did Uncle Max want her to believe? And what did he not tell? The words had a begging tone, desperate for an answer.

'Please, let me hear from you, Maria. I can't sleep until you tell me that you believe me.'

It took Gregor some time to work up the courage to pursue this. But instead of asking his mother, he decided to visit Uncle Max. He had always been afraid of him and unable to interpret those silences from the past. Afraid to ask him questions. Convinced there was some information being held back from him, but still unable to ask the right questions. He needed to speak to Uncle Max alone, without the presence of his mother in the background. He copied the sender address on the back of the last envelope, took his bicycle from the shed very early one morning after his school holidays arrived and rode away from the house without looking back.

He brought a map with him, and some money, but he forgot to bring any food, only water. Full of great enthusiasm he sped through villages, memorising the chain of names behind him. Cloud shadows raced alongside him on the road. He freewheeled into warm valleys filled with sunshine. Breezes pushed him up the hills and in his mind he invented bicycle sails, spinnakers that could send him speeding as fast as any of the cars that passed him along the way. Rain stopped him once or twice, soaking and stiffening his knees. But nothing could keep him from pressing forward on this mission. Up to a radius of around fifty kilometres he had cycled many times before, both on his own and with the cycling group. But this journey went far beyond that, leaving behind everything that was familiar to him, pushing on and on, repeating the words 'find out' in a flat musical cadence inside his head. The more he began to tire the more persistent the melody echoed.

'*Find out, find out, find out, find out.*'

He found himself going in the wrong direction for a while and wasted an hour coming back to the road again. He blamed himself for not looking at the map more carefully. He had never learned to celebrate his own mistakes, only to be hard on himself, to regard everything with merciless self-scrutiny. His parents, his schooling, the history of his country had elevated fear of failure to extremes. He was taught to minimise exposure to error. Everything had to be mapped out. Consequences examined. For once he wanted to do something utterly reckless, to claim the right to make his own mistake, the freedom to be wrong.

Instead, he was worried about his own future, his ability to know what was right and wrong. He recalled some of the taunts of his father, phrases such as 'waste of intelligence' and 'he'll come to nothing'. Perhaps it was nothing more than physical hunger manifesting itself, lack of food translated into self-doubt.

He told himself that he would become a musician. It was the beginning of a journey of artistic endurance. He intended to be like his grandfather Emil, who was looked on as a waster in the family. He would claim the right to create something utterly useless. In fact, he would write that up on the wall of his bedroom as soon as he got home again. '*Do something useless today.*' Because music was failure turned into virtue. He would become a musician and travel around the world, free to play without regret.

It was evening by the time he reached the town were Uncle Max lived. He underestimated the journey, over a hundred kilometres. He was lost and confused by the rain. A car leaped out from the side of his watery vision and sent him skidding across the cobbles of a square. Losing balance, he hit the ground and saw the bike rushing away from him, with a terrible noise that caused more pain than his own injuries. The blood on his elbow meant nothing to him, only the sight of the bike lying on its side with the front wheel spinning.

A female motorist stepped out appealing her innocence, an instant outdoor courtroom in which he felt guilty, with nothing to say.

Gregor picked himself up, straightened up the bike, hastily checking that it still functioned. He was afraid the police would come and they would contact his parents, send him home again to face the ultimate failure, so he fled from the scene, limping, running, then jumping on his bike the best he could with the woman driver shouting behind him to come back.

He stopped by the wall of a graveyard to examine the bike more carefully. The journey was a disaster. This was the shape of his life from here on, running away and crashing. Until the woman in the car stopped again right beside him and got out, full of concern. He was afraid of sympathy. Afraid to give in to self-pity. But she asked to see the cut on his elbow.

'Where are you from?' she wanted to know. She wore a shiny black raincoat with a yellow collar and looked him straight in the eyes, understanding him in leaps, saying: 'You've run away from home, haven't you?' She explained that she had a brother who ran away and never came back. Even changed his name.

She took him the rest of the way to where Uncle Max lived, with his bike in the boot of the car, stopping to get him some cake, which he ate silently in the passenger seat, staring ahead. He held the address, copied out neatly on a piece of blue paper. A shabby apartment block on the edge of the town, beside a foundry. The orange glow of the fires could be seen through the gate.

There was no answer from Uncle Max, but then one of the neighbours came out to bang on his door. His hearing wasn't very good and he didn't respond to the bell any more. When Uncle Max opened the door he looked tired, even shocked at this late visit. The neighbour told him not to play his TV so loud.

Gregor had always seen Uncle Max in a suit before. Now he was unshaven, wearing slippers. The apartment was a mess, with a window looking out over the yard of the foundry, where men worked with their shirts off in the heat, shouting to each other over the noise. Living alone in one room, with a sofa against one wall and a bed against another and a small TV on a table. Uncle Max turned the sound down and the football players continued to glide around the green pitch in silence. Shaking, turning away, looking at his watch, he hardly knew what to do with this visitor. He took out his handkerchief constantly to wipe his eye, stared out through the window at the glow from the foundry and then turned round like a condemned man.

'I didn't betray him,' he said. Sitting down at the table, he placed his hands together in prayer almost. 'I didn't tell them anything. You must believe me, Gregor.'

The outburst was frightening. Gregor could not think of what to say in reply. He apologised for coming so late.

'Thank you, for sending the record.'

Uncle Max could not recall any record.

'The record with the music from Warsaw.'

Uncle Max turned away, examining his memory, his good eye rolling around, searching.

'Would you like a drink?' he finally asked.

He began fussing around, getting out a bottle of apple juice and pouring two glasses, then forgetting to hand out the drink.

'Are you hungry?' he asked.

'No thank you. I've eaten,' Gregor said.

Uncle Max wanted to know how long the journey had taken and where he was going to stay the night. War language. Questions from a time of great distress and upheaval. Fear and pain which had slipped into his body, like a tropical disease entering through the soles of the feet.

It had been a mistake to disturb him. How could he ask any questions? He got up to leave again and said it was time he was heading back home.

But then Uncle Max became more rational. He looked at his watch and said Gregor could get a train, there was still time.

'It's been so long,' Uncle Max said. 'How is your mother?'

'She's fine,' Gregor said.

'I know why you've come,' he said. He began to speak about Emil. He was rambling, saying things that Gregor already knew. Emil should have been an actor. 'He would have made a great film star. He could make people think day was night.'

And then Uncle Max left one of his great silences.

'Emil always went too far,' he said. 'With the women, with the Nazis. He wanted to see just how far his luck could hold out.'

Gregor had not asked a single question. He listened to Uncle Max weaving through his memory, spitting as he talked, then wiping his eye, then going in circles and starting from the beginning again.

'We just wanted to survive, do you understand me? And have a good time. That's what everybody wants, isn't it? The place was full of women without men. They all wanted to hear Emil singing. They threw themselves at him. Emil brought gifts with him, meat and cognac. He was great on the black market. Nowadays, he would have become a successful industrialist or a property developer or maybe even an impresario, running a theatre company or a film company. Your grandfather would have been a millionaire if he had survived the war.'

Uncle Max drew into himself.

'Then he started helping people. And that was dangerous. Emil wouldn't listen to me. When all those refugees started coming from the East, he started doing things for non-profit, do you follow me?'

The clues began to fall into place.

'Your grandfather – if I can call him that – he went to get your mother and bring her to safety in the south. She had lost all that she had in the bombing.'

'Am I an orphan?' Gregor asked.

'Emil didn't tell me everything,' Uncle Max said. 'The Gestapo were on to him. It must have been one of the husbands who came back from the front who pointed the finger at him.'

He explained how he had managed to get some more fuel and how they were ready to move on. They had arranged to meet, but then Uncle Max was arrested by the Gestapo.

'They questioned me for a long time. They wanted to know where you had come from. They kept asking me if you were Jewish.'

'If I'm Jewish?'

'Yes,' Uncle Max said. 'They suspected you were Jewish.'

Gregor felt like a fraud, an impostor dwelling in the human frame of another person. He didn't know how to react, with fear or with rage. How could he ever return home again? How could he ever take part in the fake family that had been created for him? How could he live in this country any longer, in this language which had been imposed on him? He didn't belong here. He had no contract with this country.

'I told them I didn't know anything, but they started beating me.'

Uncle Max began to descend into his own fear once more.

'You must believe me,' he said. 'I didn't tell them where Emil was hiding.'

They were in such a hurry, right at the end of the war, Uncle Max explained. They had to use torture to try and get the information they wanted. He didn't describe the details, but the proof was there in his missing eye.

'I swear to you, Gregor, I didn't tell them.'

'I know,' Gregor said, trying to reassure him.

This was everything that Uncle Max needed to hear. Somebody had come at last to take his suffering away. Gregor had become the bystander, taking all the information home with him. Already he was maximising each tiny detail inside his head.

It was late at night when Uncle Max took him to the train station. He bought the ticket and got him a pretzel for the way home as well. He told him to take his best wishes to his mother. He asked Gregor what he was going to do when he grew up and Gregor told him that he had made up his mind to become a musician. Uncle Max clapped his hands together and said that made him so happy to hear that.

'You'll be like your grandfather, Emil,' he said. 'One of these days I'll see your photograph in the paper.'

On the platform, Uncle Max smiled and waved. As the train pulled out, he took his handkerchief from his pocket and held it up to his good eye.

Twenty-six

Even on the train coming back from Uncle Max, with his bike strapped to a hook, he knew that he was leaving. With the night landscape of early-summer fields rotating by his window, he thought of the big atlas on the wall of his classroom moving in the breeze. He thought of schoolboy theories of people moving forward on trains, travelling faster than the speed of the train itself. Of being able to see into the future as the train curved round a bend. Of theoretically being able to wave out the window to himself if he ran fast enough from the front of the train to the back. Of the discovery that there was only one thing faster than the speed of light, and that was the speed of thought. He was going back to put his parents on trial. He would expose this fabrication of home with which he had lived for so long and define his real origins at last. He would become a separate being, an individual, with an identity of his own.

As he got off the train and made his way through the familiar suburbs in which he had grown up, there was a triumph in his walk. Limping with his broken bike, he had outgrown this place.

His mother stood in the kitchen showing her anger.

'Where were you?' she demanded.

'I went to see Uncle Max,' he said, and he could not help an involuntary grin erupting on his face.

'You what?' she returned with a sigh. 'Now why did you do that? He's suffered enough, that poor man, without you tormenting him.'

'He told me everything,' Gregor continued. 'I'm not your son.'

She looked him in the eyes, then turned away. He watched her ironing a shirt, trying to give it a factory neatness. He accused her of not paying attention, until she said: 'I'm listening all right, go on,' urging him to get it all off his chest. He made his speech, going through the scant facts, adding all that he had surmised on the train. He didn't speak very well because he was nervous. Concentrating hard, jumbling his words like an inarticulate child. He reached blank areas in his knowledge and began repeating himself. Ran aground with lack of evidence and blindly accused her of deceit.

'Why didn't you tell me?' he said with tears rising.

'What?' she asked.

'That I'm adopted,' he said in despair. 'You're not my real mother, are you?'

She sat down with her apron covering her face, hands trembling, suppressing an agonising cry that seemed to come from somewhere else in the room, a distant wail, far away in a different street. Her weeping was an admission.

When she finally dropped the apron from her eyes, they were red. She coughed to clear her throat, turning round to Gregor, unable to find the starting point to explain her life.

'I'm so sad now,' she said. 'I don't know what to say.'

Gregor didn't know what he wanted any more, further information or just comfort, reassurance, love.

'Poor Max,' she said. Then she stalled again, shaking her head, reliving the events as though they had never gone away. 'You had no right to visit him and put him through all that again. He's never got over it. Still living with all those ghosts, still suffering from what they did to him back then.'

Gregor waited.

'I never blamed him,' she said. 'I never accused him. He just kept trying to convince me that he never said a word.'

'But he didn't. He said he never told them anything.'

'It destroyed him,' she said coldly. 'Losing his best friend like that, having to tell where he was hidden. He denies it, but why did your grandfather Emil not survive the war? How did he disappear? That's what he cannot answer.'

She came over to embrace Gregor, but he moved away. Called him 'darling' and 'sweetheart' and 'dear Gregor', as though she was writing him a letter instead of speaking to his face.

'Uncle Max has lost his mind now,' she said. 'He's going insane with it. I tried to help him after the war. We gave him the old apartment here in Nuremberg, but he became impossible.'

She seemed calm now. Either she was telling the truth or else she was a brilliant actress. Had she inherited the gift of cunning from her father? Had she rehearsed this answer for years or just spun it out honestly?

'My darling, Gregor,' she said. 'You can't believe a word of what Uncle Max tells you.'

Her endearments were condescending. Her denial brought out a helpless rage in him, thrashing out accusations. She told him to calm down and said he shouldn't say hurtful things.

'Please stop,' she said. 'Right now. Don't let this fantasy get any louder in your head, not one more minute.'

And when he continued, clutching at suspicions, she merely spoke over him, turning him into a child.

'You have no idea what things were like in those times,' she said, with a finality that excluded him from voicing any further opinion. He had no answer to that. He came from a generation with no experience of war, only questions and attitude and conscience.

When his father came bursting in from his study, they spoke about Gregor as though he was not even in the room, ganging up as they always did, loyal to their own generation, defending themselves against attack from the outsider which he had become.

'He's been with Max,' she said. 'He's got it into his head now that we're not his real parents.'

His father flew into a rage.

'How dare he?' he said. 'I've a good mind to go straight over to Max. With my gun. Silence him for good.'

He marched in a state of war around the living room underneath all the dead animals, making a speech with a tremor in his voice.

'Are you accusing your own mother of being a liar?'

He listed off the great hardships of their lives, the balance sheet of survival, how they saved and worked their backs off so that he could enter a life of choice and luxury. His mother had done everything after the war, when Gregor's teeth were grey from malnourishment, keeping everything going until he returned from the Russian camps. She hardly had anything to eat herself.

'Skinny as a knitting needle, she was. I want to show you something,' he said, taking Gregor's hand and forcing him to feel his mother's knees. 'She spent half a lifetime on her knees for the Americans, just to keep you fed.'

Gregor had been shamed. A coward defaming his own family.

'Just think of what you're doing,' his mother begged.

Gregor was torn between pity and anger, between forgiveness and rejection.

'I'm Jewish, isn't that right?'

'What?'

It was the final test.

'This is outrageous,' Gregor's father said.

Gregor had never heard his parents say a bad word about Jewish people. Professionally, at least, his father had nothing but respect for them. He had started his apprenticeship in accountancy with a Jewish firm in Berlin until the Nazis came to power. He always said he had learned everything he knew from Jewish people.

'I'm Jewish,' Gregor said once more. 'I know it.'

'Gregor,' his mother said, going across the room to win him over with an embrace. 'This is insane. I love you more than anything in this world.'

Her love was frightening. He was afraid he would suffocate in it. A possessive, claustrophobic, killer love, strangling him slowly until he could not breathe any more.

Gregor ran to his room. While they went into the kitchen and continued talking, he collected a few things together in his rucksack, took his bank book with all the savings, his passport, some of his books, his guitar, a number of cards he had written out with the most memorable lines of songs.

He chose not to leave them a note. That could all be done later. Instead, he stood in the hallway with the bag on his back and decided on one last heroic act. He found himself striding into his father's study and taking out one of the hunting rifles from the glass case, the one with which he was meant to shoot his first deer.

Gregor had begun firing practice at the age of thirteen, an essential skill, according to his father, like learning to drive. In a factory warehouse belonging to a friend, they set up a firing range and held competitions which Gregor soon won. His father said he was a born marksman. But target practice was nothing like shooting the real thing. Nothing like those hunting prints all over the house. Nothing like the sound of a gun discharging right beside him and the echo wrapping itself around the trees and the sight of a life-less animal on the ground with its eyes still open. Gregor had seen the blood around the fresh bullet hole. He had heard his father talking about this sacramental moment, the great ecological balance of nature.

Gregor had carried that same gun through the forest, pointed downwards, with the knowledge of the wild in his bones, listening to every shift in the undergrowth. Every footfall. Distinguishing ground noise from aerial noise. This is where the faculties of hearing and vision evolved many millions of years ago, when vibrations turned into sound, shadows into sight. It was here that Gregor's musical ear received its most intense training, in this minimalist auditorium of creaking trunks and sibilating leaves. But with the afternoon lantern light coming through the trees, he allowed the deer to escape. He aimed the gun, shot in the air and watched the animal leaping away.

His father said he could not believe he had missed it. His migraine returned with great ferocity. Blinding zigzag patterns. Kaleidoscope eyes. Along the way back, there was no friendly hand on the shoulder. It was the end of all that companionship in the forest.

Now Gregor stood in the door of the kitchen holding that rifle in his hands once again, pointing at hip height. It was no way to hold the gun. His mother looked up in shock. She was ready to become a martyr at last.

'I want you to tell me the truth,' Gregor shouted.

His eyes were fixed. The rifle gripped much too firmly in his hands, knowing how worthless the truth was when it came by force.

His father must have believed it was impossible for him to die. After all his miraculous escapes in the war, he rushed forward with great anger, ready to take the rifle away from his son.

'You fool,' he said. 'You have no idea how to use that.'

Gregor was determined to prove him wrong. He turned the rifle at the door of the kitchen. Pulled the trigger and shot at head height through the wood. The room jumped. The crockery sang. The cutlery droned inside the drawers. Great vacuous blasts of aggression came back from the walls, slapping their faces, shouting at them to wake up. The sound filled the entire house like a deafening curse, so foul and so saturated with bitterness that it left a hole in the wood and lumps of plaster all over the kitchen counter. The top half of the door was scorched and the spice of the explosion spread like the pungent mixture of mustard and mint and cigars and used matches. They swallowed. His mother whispered the words, 'For God's sake.' Their mouths were dry, incapable of language. The gap in the door became the only organ of communication between them. A screaming mouth. It must have crossed their minds to say it was a miracle that nobody got killed, but such was the irony of the thought that nobody uttered it. They stood there, with the lingering gunshot hum still fading away, absorbed in their clothes and their hair and their skin. Gregor disappeared almost without anyone noticing. He took on the shape of a ghost. With his mother and father left behind in the kitchen, erased himself out of memory and out of existence.

Years later, Mara discovered that spot where the bullet had lodged in the wall of the kitchen. It had been plastered over and repainted, hardly noticeable. And the hole in the door where the bullet had passed through had been replaced by a diamond-shaped piece of stained glass. A practical, aesthetic solution to take the place of the mute family mouth blown into it by the gun.

Twenty-seven

In his absence, Mara continued to keep in touch with Gregor's mother. Each time she and Daniel went to Nuremberg, they came back with a new piece of information, a memory of Gregor's childhood, a photograph of him in the lunar canyons of post-war ruins. Family details such as Gregor's attempt to grow an apricot tree from the kernel in his room under lights. How Gregor had once organised a home-made raffle in the neighbourhood and ended up giving the prize, a climbing rose, to his own mother. A moment when his father was fixing the car, leaning down over the engine under the bonnet, when Gregor got into the driving seat and blasted the horn, frightening the life out of his father and bringing the bonnet down on top of his head.

Daniel developed a great fondness for his grandmother. They played cards, late in the evening. An uncomplicated relationship in which a grandparent can play the role of temporary guardian without choreography, without wondering how Daniel might be affected by her influence. The result was a wise, funny, companionship between them which had none of the normal family obligations attached.

Daniel noticed her habits and began to mock his own grandmother in ways that Gregor would never have been allowed. He imitated her accent. He copied the trademark, sing-song yawn that she made from time to time and got her to laugh at herself. He even played tricks on her and put a stuffed otter into her bed one night before she went to sleep, with a hat and glasses on his head. Daniel was good at drawing and passed the time by sketching. He concentrated on gory scenes and his favourite images involved cartoon depictions of chainsaws cutting off legs and blood dripping down the page. People being decapitated. Insides spilling out. Limbs flying through the air after an explosion. A wolf chewing on a human leg. A crocodile with its jaws around a girl's head. All the stuff that obsessed a young boy. And when his grandmother saw these pictures, she was horrified that Daniel could be entertaining himself with the kind of thing that she had actually witnessed in reality during the war. She was afraid he would grow up and become a killer.

'It's very disturbing, I think,' Gregor's mother said to Mara. 'How can he sleep with so much violence in his head?'

'He's only exercising his fantasies,' Mara replied.

'You don't know where this is going to lead to,' his grandmother said. 'You should stop this before it goes too far.'

'Better that he draws the stuff than carries it out in real life, don't you think?' Mara said.

But Daniel's grandmother didn't see the difference between fantasy and reality. She began to hide some of the worst pictures, saying they were disrespectful. And when she saw a drawing of a man with his eyes gouged out, she'd had enough.

'I don't want pictures like that in the house,' she said.

'But look at all the antlers and stuffed animals,' Daniel replied.

'That's different.'

Mara was eager not to interfere and alienate her. And maybe Daniel found his own way of disarming his grand-mother who had already come up with her own solution in the meantime, asking him to stop drawing and rather make a few lists of his favourite things. So Daniel drew up lists of nonsensical things, often with sharp instruments and body parts included, groups of ghoulish items which were more acceptable than the sight of blood and often made his grandmother laugh instead.

Mara was given the cap that Gregor wore for years when he went hunting with his father. Daniel was given a little hunting knife, with a deer's hoof as a handle. Another time, Mara returned with the letter Gregor had sent from London, saying that he was never coming back. The tone in that letter shocked her and made her feel it was directed at her too. But the collection of family artefacts seemed to bring him closer. She had become a curator. Gregor's childhood became an archaeology of shards and hints of evidence, guessing, deducing, still hoping to find out the absolute truth.

She once managed to invite Gregor's mother up to Berlin for a visit. She was getting older by then and Daniel was already a teenager, a tall young man, like his father. It was a shock to her to be back in this city for the first time since the war, but she took a great interest in everything she saw, knowing she could have remained part of it herself if only history had turned on a different plate. The city had changed so much. Trees everywhere, she commented, more than before.

They stood on a wooden parapet to look across the Berlin Wall to the other side. They went to see the house where she had lived during the war before it was bombed. They stood in front of the peeling façade and she remembered fleeing from the city. When one of the occupants came out, Mara rushed forward to keep the door open.

'Come on,' she said, encouraging her to go into the courtyard.

Gregor's mother was reluctant, but Mara took her by the arm and took her right inside. They looked up at the windows of the second-floor apartment where the bomb destroyed the entire back of the building. The trees at the centre of the courtyard had been replaced since then by a young walnut and a cedar which had almost grown to maturity. Mara waited for her to say something, but she remained silent, swallowing her feelings. Mara suggested going up the stairs, maybe to knock on the door to see if the occupants might let her have a look around, but that was going too far.

'That's enough for me,' she said.

On the underground going back that evening, Gregor's mother examined the passengers. Two girls sharing a plate of pommes frites and ketchup, stabbing them with tiny coloured forks, like a game. A homeless man dragging himself onto the carriage, speaking gently to his dog, politely addressing the carriage to sell his magazine. She gave him money. In the next carriage, there was a man silently playing the saxophone as though he was very thirsty, drinking back an enormous gulp from a long, S-shaped brass bottle.

She was beginning to think of her own death. That evening she told Mara that she had made her will and said she was passing everything over to Daniel, the house, the cottage in the forest, everything, including the savings that her husband had built up. She spoke with some bitterness. She was at the mercy of those she had cared for, the vicarious accumulation of people she had kept in her thoughts throughout her life.

'He never went to his father's funeral, so he needn't bother coming to mine.'

She chose Mara as executor. She left it to her to decide what she wanted to do with the contents of the house when the time came. She wrote down the name of a lawyer friend who would come and take the hunting gear, since Daniel expressed no interest in them.

Gregor came back to Berlin once, but he never went to see his mother in Nuremberg. He only returned to see Mara and Daniel, but even that became like a strange seance in which they stared at each other like strangers across a room. It soon became clear that he hated being back in the city, that it made him feel uneasy, like a ghost or his former self. And she could make no real investment in these rare visits because she knew he would disappear again. It would cause too many tears.

Though it was hard to admit, she realised that some of her happiest moments were spent with Daniel, just the two of them together, joking and talking. When Daniel came into her room on a Saturday morning and woke her up, putting headphones on her ears in order to play his favourite track, she seemed to need nothing else.

She was no fool for Gregor, it has to be said. She decided to get on with her own life and had a number of partners over the years. The companionship with Martin asserted itself when he became a surrogate father to Daniel. Even though he was married with children of his own, she began to depend on him and they became lovers on and off over the years, or was it deep friendship with physical love included, less like betrayal, more like an act of loyalty which spilled over into great sexual need? She wanted the fun of life to confirm that she was living in the real world, not only the imaginary. That human certainty, the affirmation of touch. She wanted to laugh and dance and be watched, to feel the music in her arms and legs, somebody to provide the guarantees of toll-free sex.

At first it was all done in great secrecy. They didn't want Daniel to be burdened by betrayal, of friendship as much as marriage. But then these things had a way of coming out into the open, and even though Daniel never said much, only to ask one day if she was screwing Martin, he internalised it along with everything else.

Martin's marriage broke up, though it was heading that way all along and Mara was not the only one to blame. What troubled Martin was that she could never make the emotional transfer needed for them to become real partners. He was careful not to say too much against his friend, but he became impatient with her at times.

'How long are you going to hold out for Gregor?'

'You're right,' Mara would say. 'I just want Daniel to have a feeling of knowing his real father, which Gregor never had.'

She was lying to herself. She was lying to everyone around her, including Daniel. She had become obsessed, like an addict, unable to give up the search for something which would always remain nothing more than imagined. Even if she had got used to Gregor's absence, she could not do without the great adventure of solving the mystery of his origins.

'You've got to be realistic about this,' Martin said to her at one point. 'You've given yourself a crazy mission. You've got to let it go, Mara.'

'I want to find out the truth, that's all,' she said.

'What truth?'

'The truth about his real identity.'

'You mean, him being a Jewish survivor?'

'Yes.'

'That's become irrelevant at this stage.'

'How can you say it's irrelevant? He could have died in the camps.'

'Mara, look. His identity is not what he was or what the Nazis thought he was. His identity is the people he's been living with, but he's denied them each time. He always ran away from anyone who gave him any sense of identity.'

The relationship never went any further than this argument. Martin felt she was wasting his time, abusing his loyalty. Accused her of merely playing the role of somebody who was following her own free will, re-enacting the ecstasy of sex rather than living it.

'You've become obsessed with this thing,' he told her. 'You're infected by this sickness. You refuse to live your own life, basically, because you want to prove some spectacular hunch that he's a Jewish survivor.'

'But what if it's true, Martin? What if he really is a Jewish survivor? Then I would never forgive myself for turning my back on him.'

'You're crazy,' Martin said. 'This is like some terminal illness. It's going to destroy you.'

She was unable to live for herself, which was not unlike most other people, except that her quest had gone beyond life, into an obligation to resurrect the dead. She had become a fake, a hologram, a reflection of history, still hoping that some sliver of proof would bring him back to life.

'You're trying to catch moonlight,' Martin said to her. 'Look at the story he's told us. The Nazis had a hunch that Emil was up to something. They started torturing Max and asking him where the boy came from. Maybe there was something about his clothes or his appearance. They suspected this was a Jewish child being smuggled back with the refugees. That's how Max got it into his head and passed it on to Gregor. That's how delicate the trail of evidence is, Mara.'

'They must have known something,' Mara said.

'This is it, exactly, Mara. I believed it myself. In the end you are trying to substantiate a suspicion in the minds of these Gestapo thugs. They had this notion that Gregor was Jewish and that notion has led all the way to you. You are trying to prove them right. It's nothing more than a Nazi fabrication.'

He had gone too far. Gregor, the product of Nazi imagination. The idea was much too hurtful and obscene for her to accept, so they separated after that, vowing never to speak to one another again. It had become a contest, her devotion to herself against the loyalty to the past, her oath to happiness against this oath to identity in which she had become a powerless conscript. Martin apologised to her. Begged her to forget what he had said and allow them to remain friends. Said he could not understand what had come over him and promised never to speak like that again about his friend.

'Mara, please accept my forgiveness,' he said.

'What?'

She laughed out loud. Could not stop herself. She was back to herself again, shaking her fist at him and laughing helplessly.

'I accept your forgiveness,' she repeated.

She needed him to make her laugh. But the doubt which he had planted in her mind had the opposite effect in the end, driving her even further into this mission to establish the truth.

Twenty-eight

There are people who live their entire lives in exile. People who are never at home. Gregor had turned his life into a search for belonging, though it always remained a distant thing, a vague, utopian memory. Maybe luck and artistic timing were against him. When the band in Toronto split up and his friend John Joe went back to Ireland, Gregor drifted once more from one city to another. He made another attempt to go back to Berlin, but it was hard to find the song-line home. He was at odds with his family and hardly recognised his own son. Daniel remained aloof, cool, never showing any emotion or excitement in his reaction to Gregor's gifts. Merely thanked his increasingly absent father dutifully and got on with his life. The longer Gregor stayed away, the more the distance grew between truth and memory. There was a threshold of estrangement beyond which it became increasingly difficult to go back. And in the end, he always found himself escaping again, this time going over to Ireland, following his friend John Joe to Dublin in order to see if he could start a life there.

What would it take to turn a lifetime of running away into one great returning?

Gregor arrived in Dublin with a mouth organ belonging to John Joe, an excuse for reunion. He wanted to give it back because he knew it was a very special instrument which had witnessed many of their craziest moments together and which had emotional value in their touring history. John Joe had lost dozens of harmonicas, many of them mislaid on his travels, but Gregor knew this was quite unique, with a sweet, gravelly sound, best for bending notes. The worn black plate had the words 'Cross Harp' written on it, and the brass vents through which John Joe had drawn and pushed his breath had darkened with time. Carrying this small instrument in his pocket, Gregor was hoping to relive some of the times they spent together. They would remember John Joe bartering with a fast-food vendor on the streets of Toronto once, offering a song in exchange for a hamburger.

But the reunion in Dublin was a disaster. What had been billed in his mind as such a high point, became a colourless event. John Joe had given up the music. He had put all that behind him and become a computer technician. Lived in a suburban housing development on the edge of the city. The houses all had the same neo-Celtic stained-glass panels in the front door. The ceilings were low. There was a deep-fry smell settling in the hallway and the radio in the kitchen competing with the TV in the living room. The glass back door was covered in paw marks where a dog made a recurring appearance in the small yard.

It was John Joe's wife who answered the door and brought Gregor into the living room stepping past a baby's buggy in the hallway. John Joe was sitting on the sofa, watching the news. He didn't get up. Asked his wife to get Gregor a beer. Remained in a position of languid mistrust, as though he suspected that Gregor had come to take him away from his family again. With his legs thrown across the armrest and his neck cushioned by the back of the sofa, he appeared as though he was lying in a hammock. His hand brought the nozzle of a beer bottle up to his mouth, tilting it with his fingers to take a drink.

'I couldn't do it any more,' John Joe said, meaning the music, the late nights, the foreign cities.

He didn't encourage Gregor to stay. Hardly moved more than once on the patterned sofa and kept his eye on the news as though it was more important than anything else in the world. A remarkable height of friendship had sunk to a remarkable low.

Gregor finished his beer. He held the mouth organ inside his pocket, warmed by his hand, but something stopped him from giving it back. It had become a companion to him, much the same as his grandfather's brass icon, taken from a dead soldier. He decided to keep it. He left again and walked away with the instrument in his firm grip, knowing that it was more alive, more real, closer to him than the man who once played it could ever be.

In a Dublin bar that evening, he understood for the first time in his life what it meant to be homesick. He drank his beer, aware of his own presence in time and space. He had no story to live inside, no place in the imaginary world. He craved that belonging, something beyond the limitations of his own physical state.

'You're not from around here,' somebody said, and then he was drawn into conversation with a group of office workers.

They asked him questions. It seemed absurd to them that somebody was sitting alone without talking. They had a peculiar gift for creating an ersatz feeling of home.

He decided to stay in Ireland. Rented a cottage from an old woman some distance outside the city. It had a great rose garden which had become neglected but which he cultivated and brought back to life for the time that he lived there. He found a job working part-time in a recording studio in the city, creating tunes for radio adverts, mortgage companies, insurance brokers. Happy tunes to which people drove to work every morning, jingles that entered into their subconscious traffic-logged stares and adhered like sticky tape to their minds. He made them up and forgot them right away, hardly even remembered composing them when he heard them on the radio himself.

He found a few clubs where they played jazz and managed to get some stand-in gigs. Ultimately, he found a regular spot, too, but there was no money in it and maybe the will to make it was gone. He was only doing it for his own pleasure now, and that lifted a great weight of expectation off his shoulders, allowing him to play more freely.

He was away for the most important years when Daniel was growing up. He had missed key events in his development, only hearing about them in letters from Mara. He was absent when Daniel had his teenage crisis with drugs and only heard about it weeks later when it was all over.

One day, Mara received a phone call at work to say that Daniel had been rushed to hospital after suffering a seizure. Martin was in the emergency ward with him.

'He's all right,' Martin assured her. 'The doctors are examining him right now, doing all the tests. He just keeled over in geography class. His classmates said he was shaking and his eyes were rolling around.'

'My God,' Mara said. 'What are they saying?'

'They suspect it's epilepsy,' Martin said. 'But let's wait and see.'

She was forced to drop one of her own patients in mid-treatment. Raced over to the hospital and found

Daniel sitting up in bed with Martin beside him, already joking about things. He was out of danger, but had to remain under observation until they had done a CAT scan and various other tests.

When Mara finally got to speak to the registrar herself, she asked lots of anxious questions. She was told that Daniel was a suspected epileptic, and if this proved to be the case, he would probably have to go on lifelong medication to prevent further attacks. They had ruled out blood pressure issues. She was told that seizures like this could mean only one of two things, epilepsy or drugs. People sometimes got seizures from taking cocaine, but they had already ruled that out because Daniel denied taking anything.

She had recently found hash in his bedroom and had told him to be careful.

'You're only fifteen,' she said to him.

She explained that she and Gregor had done all of those things as well, but that you could not allow it to take a hold of your life. She spoke wisely, like a recovered addict, knowing all the trapdoors of addiction, but still unable to get away from her own obsessions which had also made her very detached from reality, still trying to substantiate the life story of a man who had disappeared out of her life.

Around the hospital bed she eventually got Daniel to admit that he had taken cocaine along with a substantial quantity of alcohol.

'You're lucky to be alive,' she said after speaking to the doctors once more.

Was this a cry for help too? While Martin and Mara brought chocolates and childish gifts, delivering all his needs, his music, his books, his games, trying desperately to turn him back into a child, what became clear to them all was that Gregor was absent from this crisis in his life. It was Martin who was present for that remarkable incident and Martin who collected Daniel from the hospital and brought him home. Gregor only heard about all this much later in a letter, as though it was some passing event in life which had already been sorted out by the time the news came.

Twenty-nine

The people in the town must have wondered why it was all taking so long. It was only a matter of hours before the town fell into the hands of the Americans. They were already on the far side of the lake, probably only waiting for the dawn to come. Already there had been quite a number of air attacks. Bombers on their return from city infernos had casually dropped an excess load on the post office one morning. The bakery had also been hit and fifteen people killed while they queued up for bread. All week the sound of heavy weaponry could be heard in the distance, echoing across the lake, absorbed by the forests. Now and again, the urgency of battle came closer with the abrupt presence of fighter planes overhead and the immediate response of anti-aircraft guns. Trucks racing by. Soldiers running. Orders bawled out in the streets. A tired assortment of old men and boys dragging themselves towards the enemy lines while others watched them carefully for signs of weakness and surrender. It made little sense defending this cluster of streets with nothing more than a church and a graveyard and a public house. A few villas by the lake and a railway station full of refugees. And still the business of holding the lines dragged on endlessly, hour by hour, through the night.

At the same time, they must have been wondering how all this could be over so soon. It was only a few years ago that all the dreamy optimism swept through the streets like an immortal carnival and everyone hung out their swastikas. Some of the children who were just starting in kindergarten at that time were not even out of school yet. The boys who were in school then hardly had enough time to grow a stubble on their chins before being sent to the front line. It was coming to an end before it even began, and still there was unfinished business in the town. In that last moment before peacetime and justice, they held on to the logic of invincibility with even greater tenacity, defending their own transgressions with suicidal obsession.

In the police station, Gregor's mother had been allowed to go to the toilet. The corridor was heavy with smoke and kept dark. Only the rectangular outline of light around the door at the back where they were holding Max. An officer directed her with a torch and she was able to clean the boy up in the dark and wash out the soiled cloth. She heard the interrogation, men speaking with great patience one minute, then raising their voices suddenly to a frightening bark that made her jump. They laughed as though they were at a party.

'Don't worry,' she heard one of them bawl. 'We'll have him before the night is out.'

As she came back through the corridor again she heard the voice of Max, pleading with them.

'I don't know,' he begged.

'Who gave you the fuel?'

There was no answer to that, only the sound of a fist, hard and soft, no more than a light click coming from a sports field or a playground, but with incredible violence concealed inside. How breakable the world was. How unfair the game rules. How much the force of the blow was felt by herself, imagined beyond all proportion in the dark.

'Muncher,' they shouted. 'Useless muncher.'

Their failure to find answers was being converted into rage. And their rage needed more justification, more abuse, more derision. They railed in grand terms against all schemers and deserters, defrauders of the Reich in its greatest hour of need. They knew what Emil had been up to all along, singing the right songs on Hitler's birthday like a great patriot. They vowed to comb every street until they found out where he was hiding. They knew about his trail of lovers. Some of them had already confessed their pathetic treason of bedroom acts.

'Why don't you tell us where he is?' she heard them say.

She tried to obscure the voices by speaking, calming herself as well as the fear she saw reflected in the boy, rocking him back and forth. And when she began to hear the voice of Max, turned into the helpless cries of a child, she began to sing softly. Even if the boy could not hear a thing, she hummed in his ear. He was fidgety and would not settle down. She tried cradling his head in her lap, but he kept getting up and pushing her away and then moving close again. Whimpering for a while and stopping and then remembering to cry again, louder than before.

She found some bread and tried to feed him, but he shook his head. She hummed more forcefully in order to obscure the terror of intimate screams coming down the corridor, stripped of all dignity. Cries beyond endurance, beyond submission, on the extremity of reason, close to death and sometimes almost beyond death itself, but all the more desperate to hold on. Inflicted by men whose confirmation of life came from the debasement of life. Whose self-esteem came at the expense of dehumanising others. Whose merciless skill in keeping people on the edge of life had become their only validity to power.

She could hear nothing any more. She remembered something and began to search in the boy's pockets until she found the sweet, the green sweet he had been given by Emil and told to keep for later. She took it out and placed it in the boy's mouth. It calmed him down right away and she rocked him while he sucked on it and stared with his eyes open into the dark.

And then it came to an end. Quite suddenly, she heard them running through the corridor. For a moment she thought they were coming back for her. But they ran past, out into the street. They left behind a crushed silence that went on for hours. She thought it was a trap and could not gather the strength even to call out his name, to say: 'Max, are you all right?' She feared the ugliness of human suffering. She feared his silence. Heard nothing until some time near dawn when American soldiers burst in, pointing rifles, finding her sitting on the floor in the corner of the room with a boy fast asleep in her arms.

She was standing in the street when they brought Uncle Max out on a stretcher. The medics must have given him something to stop the pain, but his face terrified her and she didn't want the boy to see any of this. She turned his face in towards her with both hands, almost suffocating him in her coat. Max held a stained cloth up to his eye, and then leaned up on his free arm to speak to her. A cloudy cough, full of gurgling, broken words, spilling blood and saliva down his chin.

'Emil,' he said. 'He's with Gertrude. Down at the lake.'

It was only years later that she could talk about this to Mara. Details that emerged bit by bit, as though they were in danger of bringing back all the pain once more. The American soldiers questioned her briefly with a translator interpreting her words. They escorted her to a villa close to the lake where Getrude lived, but it was too late and the unfolding events could not be recalled.

The Gestapo officers had gone to the villa in the early hours. They had found nobody there, only the signs of recent occupants, the smell of a cigar, an empty bottle of wine and two glasses. An unmade bed. An old woman, Gertrude's infirm mother asleep in another bedroom. Max and Emil's plan had been uncovered earlier that night. The canister of fuel was of no more use to them, so Emil made an alternative plan. Over the last farewell toast with Gertrude, he knew it was time to escape, this time by boat. He would not leave his friend behind, but Gertrude implored him to go before it was too late.

She made up a white flag for him. She went down to the wooden fishing pier with him, to where a small canoe was tied up waiting. They embraced and looked across the lake to where the Americans were, confident that Emil's white flag would be clearly visible but also afraid they might not take any notice. He was in German uniform after all as he pushed the small boat out from the pier, wobbling a good deal from side to side before he sat down and began to row silently away into the darkness across the calm black water. She stood there until he disappeared out of sight.

Mara has been to visit the town and the villa. There are very few people from that time still alive now. She went to the railway station and stood in the waiting room. She saw the public house on the main street, but the owners had changed hands right after the war, serving schnitzel and hamburgers, converting to a disco bar late in the evening. What used to be the police station had been turned into a fitness centre with kick-boxing classes, extended for weightlifting at the back.

Down by the lake, the town had spread out along the shore with cafés, restaurants, jewellers and designer stores.

A pizza restaurant with the smell of charcoal coming from the oven. The lake had become the high end of the town and some Americans still lived around there, even though the US troops had pulled out of the area. As she walked out along the lake, Mara heard children speaking English with an American accent. They were bouncing on a trampoline and there was a small dog underneath barking. She watched as the children lifted the dog up onto the trampoline, but the dog jumped off again because he preferred to bark and jump on solid ground.

The lake was not round but more kidney-shaped, with parts of it wrapped around the forest, disappearing from view. It was hard to get to the water in many places because the land was owned right down to the shore, but she found a place in the forest where she could stand and look back at the town from the other side. There were quite a few sailing boats out, even though there was little wind. They were almost stationary, with their sails flapping. Back in the town, she could see a sailing club with long windows onto the water, reflecting the sun and throwing the light into her eyes.

Standing on the shore, she worked out that he must have rowed straight towards that point where she stood. She wonders what happened. Did he lose the white flag? Did the moon come out suddenly from behind the clouds to expose him?

He must have seen the orange glow of cigarettes in the trees behind him on the far shore, but how could he be sure they belonged to the Americans and not to the Germans. Was he not rowing to his own death all the time? Ever since he woke up in the field hospital after the nightmare of screaming women in the First World War, he had lived in the minds of women, in the optimism of his songs.

It was a fatal decision. With all eyes and all military binoculars scanning every inch of water, it was a bad choice, but fully in character with Emil's life, to risk everything on that final gamble. At some point, a shot must have rung out across the lake, though it could hardly have been distinguishable from the gunfire reaching right into the town and through the streets until it was all over at last.

His body was never found. He must have slumped over in the boat. The oars must have slipped out of his hands and drifted on the water to go their own way, turning up in different parts of the lake, on a reef or a sandy ledge, depending on the currents and the direction of the breeze. Who knows where his little white tea towel went to? His weight must have taken him over the side of the boat, like somebody asleep in a chair. He must have gone silently into the black water and left the boat rocking for a while, leaving it to drift around for days, possibly even arriving right back where he had started from.

Later, Mara searched through some of the books written about that time. One published in Great Britain covering the very end of the war and the immediate aftermath. While glancing through illustrations and maps, she came across some photographs. One plate held her attention, a black-and-white shot of the body of a large man lying face down in the water. His head was not visible, submerged in the silted water. His trousers had come off and his grey buttocks could be seen, above the surface. The caption underneath read: *The corpse of a German soldier.*

Thirty

They have all returned to the house now, and in the kitchen, Martin and Daniel are preparing the evening meal. They talk among themselves, sharing hints, remembering to cut the fresh herbs but not to crush them. With the stickiness of garlic on their fingers they plan out the sequencing. Mushrooms picked over. Green beans lying on the counter, washed. Rice soaking. Fruit waiting to be cut up into a fruit salad in a blue porcelain bowl.

The meal will be constructed like a stage play, in acts, with intervals and plot. A performance of dialogue and laughter linking everything together. The big kitchen table has already been laid, with candles and a large jug of water with a mint sprig floating on the top. The windows are left open so the wasps that have come in during the afternoon will now make their way out again towards the light. Thorsten tells everyone once more to check for ticks, especially those who have been lying on the ground or walking through long grass. There is a polite queue for the shower. The house has begun to fill up with the smell of cooking from one end and the smell of soap and deodorant and skin creams at the other. Some have taken the time to have a quick sleep. Some have been making phone calls, or sending text messages to a remote world beyond this farm. Thorsten takes a quick look at the news on TV, but the events seem unreal, as fictional as the pale blue light from the screen spreading around the room. Johannes plays a computer game and the blip and drip sounds float through the corridor.

There is a reluctance to turn on the lights. They want to hold on to the available light left in the rooms. They put on fresh clothes. Their bodies have changed indoors, more self-conscious, more exposed, more in need of privacy and personal space.

They look in the mirror for reassurance. They construct their physical appearance in the way that they also compose the way they want to be remembered. A face is not so much a physical thing but a story which unfolds in the company of others, a book of interactions, full of smiles and frowns. They should rehearse a range of emotions in the mirror to get any idea of what they look like in company. They should laugh out loud, grimace, cry, give suspicious glances, dagger looks, send hidden messages. The full catalogue of human expressions.

A clang of serving spoons signals that it is time for dinner and they all emerge. All these faces come together around the table. Martin is wearing a bright blue shirt. Mara has put on a necklace with what looks like a hanging plum. Gregor is now wearing a brown linen shirt and Thorsten has draped a white kitchen towel over his arm to show that he is the waiter.

They sit around the long table in the kitchen and talk about Africa.

'Have you had your shots already?' Gregor asks.

Martin talks about a time when he visited Dar es Salaam. At the train station, a taxi driver put his suitcase in the boot of the car and sat in the driving seat while eight men came to push the car three hundred yards to the hotel.

He talks about immigrants who have come from Senegal and Guinea, all the way around the coast to the Canaries and on to Germany. In his law practice, he represents an asylum seeker who clung for days onto the rim of a tuna net before he was rescued.

The sun has gone down now, but there is light left in the sky. In the orchard, the ladders are propped up in position, waiting for the big crowd next day. New bottles of wine are being opened. Martin sniffs the wine. Then he sniffs Daniel to bring back the recurring joke. They move in a circle of jokes and facts and anecdotes, a dinner table, web page of consumer advice and gossip. They talk about the closure of the inner-city airport and what an opportunity it would be to create a parkland, an urban green lung, part of the Amazon rainforest reclaimed at the heart of Berlin. They talk about holidays and sport and cooking. They praise the meal. The mushrooms are wonderful. They listen to Gregor talking about how he collected them, how he learned to identify them.

'I found a bomb crater,' he says. 'In the forest.'

'I'd love to see it,' Mara says. 'Is it far from here?'

'It may not be a crater after all,' he informs her right away, almost retracting the image again. 'You know, it may be just one of those dumping pits. Though this one was empty. Right in the middle of the forest, far from any farmhouses.'

'We could go there early in the morning,' Mara says. 'Before they all arrive. Do you think you can find it again?'

'I think so,' Gregor says.

And then the argument finally breaks out around the table. It has been brewing all day, all their lives.

'I can't believe it,' Daniel says, confronting his father at last. 'You're still leading her up the garden path with this bombing story.'

233

'Daniel, please,' Mara attempts, but she is unable to hold back the debate any longer.

'You made all that up,' Daniel says. 'Why don't you admit it? The whole thing about being a Jewish orphan. It's all a fabrication, isn't that so?'

'What makes you so sure?' Gregor asks.

'Because there is no proof, is there? There never was any proof.'

'Daniel, it's important where you come from,' Mara says.

'Give me a break,' Juli snaps.

'If it's so important,' Daniel continues, 'then why don't we do a DNA test? Get it over with. That will solve the mystery once and for all.'

'What,' Martin bursts in, 'you want to exhume your grandmother?'

'If that's what it takes. I've got the money for it and all.'

'Jesus,' Martin says, 'she doesn't deserve that.'

'At least it would clear up this uncertainty,' Daniel says. 'Look, I don't give a shit where I come from. All I know is that my father wasn't around when I was growing up.'

He turns to Gregor, once more, pointing his finger this time.

'Why don't you do the decent thing and finally tell us that it was all made up?'

There is silence at the table. Mara gets up. She goes around to take Daniel by the arm. Then she goes around to Gregor and takes his arm also.

'Come on,' she says. 'I want to show you both something.'

While the others remain seated, she escorts them down the corridor to a room at the end. The house was built to accommodate a family of twelve, maybe even more, two sets of grandparents and perhaps a number of other relatives who came to work on the harvest each year. The last room

234

has been used by Mara to store all the furniture that came from Gregor's home.

Gregor enters like a child. In one corner by the window stands the round dining-room table and chairs which stood for years in his home in the suburbs of Nuremberg. On the walls, the same photographs of his ancestors which stared down on him as a child. It was impossible to escape their gaze.

'I took photographs,' Mara says.

'This is insane,' Daniel says. 'Do you not see what you've done to her?'

'Daniel,' Mara says. 'Wait. Be patient for a moment. I want you to see this thing I've found. Don't say anything more until we go through this.'

In front of them is the home that Gregor disowned. The curtains, the rug at the centre of the room, the entire nausea of home come to life. The fatigue in the furniture, the boredom trapped in the embroidered tablecloth, the raised voices, the long sigh of Gregor's teenage years, the martyred silences, all the false hopes and frail family achievements clinging like a musty scent. Plates and knives and napkin rings. Even some of the antlers. All the worthless objects of a lifetime elevated into a family documentary, containing human breath.

'I tried to keep as much as I could,' she says. 'I've gone through all the letters.'

Against the wall stands the sideboard, with neat stacks of letters on top. Each pile bound together with a ribbon and marked with a small card. Letters from Uncle Max. Letters from Gregor. Letters from people on the far side of the Berlin Wall. Magazines from the sixties. Gregor's school reports. A box full of rubbers and pens and nibs and jars of ink that have gone dry by now. A sharpener and a glass jar full of colouring pencils.

'Look, your records,' Mara points out. His first collection of albums. There were posters on the walls. Bedroom graffiti. Music scores. Notes taken down from books at a time when there were so few words in his life he could trust.

There, too, the photograph of his grandfather Emil, laughing. A tall, handsome man, thin as a pin, standing in his uniform before he went off to the First World War. Alongside it, the other photograph of the same man in later years, almost unrecognisable, after he had put on so much weight. The fat man who lifted him up on the truck and gave him the red sweet to eat right away and the other green one to keep for later. All the recurring dreams of searching for that second sweet and never finding it. All the unanswered questions. All the gaps filled by his own imagination, guessing what was out of reach.

Thirty-one

After Gregor went back to live in Germany, they found the door of his cottage in Ireland wide open. A young boy wandering around the fields by the shore on the east coast discovered that it had been abandoned and reported to his parents that the German was gone. The boy had heard him playing the trumpet a number of times in the distance and spoken to him on occasion on his way home from school. He had asked him questions and Gregor had told him that he was from Berlin. The boy was impressed by the fact that he had played in bands and said he would love to go and hear him play, but he seemed too young to be allowed into bars at night. Instead, he managed to get Gregor to play the trumpet for him one afternoon outside the cottage. But when he went back again on another occasion, he found the door open and nobody inside. Cats had got in and already sniffed over everything to see if there was anything left to eat. The place was unoccupied, only a few books left behind, and some newspapers, nothing of any value, just enough to indicate that the place had been inhabited up to a particular date and then suddenly abandoned.

Did this Irish boy remind Gregor too much of his own son? Did he perceive in these random meetings, all that time and all the conversations which had been lost with

Daniel? The innocence. The admiration. That loose way of talking without obligation.

The local people wondered what brought him to this remote place by the sea. They said he kept to himself pretty much. They often saw him cycling to the train station and they heard him playing the trumpet and some of them said it was like a miracle growth promoter, because it was great for the roses. What was he hiding from? they asked themselves. And what made him disappear so suddenly, dropping everything and leaving without a trace? Some of them got it into their heads that he might have been a war criminal. They must have uncovered his hideout and he was forced to find himself a new sanctuary, possibly in South America. Older people, better at guessing his age, knew that he would have been too young to have taken any part in the Second World War. So maybe he was more a spy, from the East German state.

His colleagues at the basement recording studio in the city shortened his name to Greg. They don't remember him being all that reclusive. He had a quiet sense of humour and could make people laugh without changing his expression. He made a name for himself writing clever jingles for radio ads. He had a lot of trouble with his teeth and used to swallow painkillers with his coffee. In the pale basement where no daylight ever penetrated, where the air was full of smoke and static, people lived on biscuits and takeaway food. Noxious curries that were left lying around on the floor by the mixing desk to be found by the late-night cleaners.

One of his molars had been giving him trouble for years on the road. He said he could well understand why cowboys in the American West used to have all their teeth removed before they went out to work on the ranches.

And possibly why they sang sad songs to the longhorn cattle all night to stop them from stampeding. A rotten tooth was like the enemy within.

He sat in agony one day, holding his jaw, and finally decided to go to a dentist. One of his colleagues recommended an old dentist in the suburb by the name of Eckstein. He had regular appointments from there on, stopping off on his way home. The dentist took on a reconstruction job, sorting him out after years of neglect. His gums were in a terrible state, red and inflamed with periodontal disease.

'Your two front teeth are already as long as your legs,' Eckstein said.

The dental practice was on the main shopping street, above a TV and hi-fi shop. The door was green. An old, dusty green that people no longer use, except on garden sheds. The buzzer automatically let Gregor in each time and he walked up the stairs with the green carpet and the scent of disinfectant in his nostrils. Every time he arrived up the stairs, Eckstein would come out and usher him into the waiting room, saying his assistant was off ill. He would sit down on the leather sofa and stare around the green walls, listening to the sound of the water drill working in the room next door. On the walls, a number of strange art objects, giant shells and molluscs made of wool and wax and other substances that turned out to have been produced by the dentist's daughter.

After a number of visits, Gregor began to suspect that the dentist had no other patients. The waiting room was always empty. He never heard any other voices. He had the feeling that Eckstein was only pretending to run a busy practice, keeping him waiting, making all the usual drilling sounds, telling some phantom patient to chew on the other side for a day before finally coming to show Gregor into the surgery.

Eckstein did all the talking, while Gregor stared out through the blinds at the upper windows of the house across the street which had no glass in them and where the pigeons were flying in and out, nesting in the upper rooms. Gregor's mouth wide open, forced to be silent, while the dentist told him how he came to Ireland from Poland before the Nazis came to power in Germany. Some of his family had made it to America but his grandparents and most of his cousins were killed in the camps. When he was finished, Eckstein spent a lot of time clearing up his equipment, still talking, saying he would love to go to America to visit all his Jewish relatives, but he could never take the time off. Eventually he would say: 'That's it for today,' but they would keep on talking for a while longer, because there was no other patient waiting. With a swollen cheek, drooling from the corner of his mouth, Gregor told his own story.

Gregor asked what the treatment would cost, roughly, so he could prepare himself.

'Don't worry,' Eckstein said. 'The bill is never as bad as the toothache.'

Eckstein fitted a crown and when the treatment came to an end, Gregor felt like the last man ever to sit in that chair.

Some weeks later, the trouble started again with the ache coming back in the same tooth. Every time he got out of bed and stood on his feet. A constant throbbing as he walked along the pavements. Vibrating like a tuning fork every time he played the trumpet. Gregor felt he had gone to an incompetent dentist who had done a bad job. He had paid and would have to go back to get it put right.

'You cannot have pain there,' Eckstein said. 'There is no nerve left in that tooth, Gregor. You cannot be experiencing pain in a tooth that is dead.'

He tapped at the crown, dabbed it with a swab of ether, compared it to other healthy teeth which instantly sent an icy chill shooting into the roof of his mouth.

'It's only a stump,' he kept saying.

'I'm not making this up,' Gregor said. 'It's killing me.'

'Tell me exactly where the pain is,' Eckstein asked.

Gregor pointed at the crown.

'This is impossible,' Eckstein repeated. 'It is physically impossible for you to have pain there. Unless it's a phantom pain, like an amputated leg.'

There was nothing Eckstein could do. Gregor left again, but the pain returned. He was back to swallowing painkillers. He went back, telling the dentist that the pain had shot up into his eye. Eckstein carried out more investigations, even going so far as to remove the crown and replacing it.

'I can take it out if you like,' Eckstein said finally. 'If it's giving you that much trouble. Maybe I can put in a bridge instead.'

Gregor began to suspect that Eckstein had done all this deliberately in order to keep his practice going. He couldn't bear to have any more work done. He decided to try and live with it. Pinched his cheek sometimes to distract from the pain. And finally, when it got so bad that he could no longer endure it, he went back one more time to get it extracted for good.

Around the same time, the news was out that the Berlin Wall had come down. In the TV shop downstairs from the dentist, Gregor saw the pictures of people standing on top of the Wall duplicated twenty times across the various screens. Again and again the same images of people driving through the barriers, embracing, drinking champagne, while bewildered border guards stood by. The first section of the colourful Wall being removed by crane, reminding him of his own imminent extraction. He put his finger on the buzzer and walked up the stairs along the green carpet. This time he was not asked to go into the waiting room and the door of the surgery had been left open. Eckstein was sitting in his own dentist's chair, reading the newspaper.

'Have you seen this?' Eckstein said.

'You mean the Wall?'

'Yes,' Eckstein said, slapping the paper. 'You must go. You should be there, right now.'

'It's hard to believe all right,' Gregor said.

'If I were you, I'd be over there like a light. I'd go myself but for the practice here. Can't let my patients down.'

He pointed at the pictures. He didn't get up and Gregor never sat down in the chair again. They never talked about the tooth and it was never extracted.

'You have to go home,' Eckstein said. 'You've got to be there to see this thing happening.'

The first Mara heard of Gregor's return was a call from the nursing home in Nuremberg. Mara phoned to see how Gregor's mother was getting on and was told by the nurse that Gregor was there with her.

At that point, she could no longer tell the difference between him and Daniel. She was very frail and her mind was going. She didn't speak any more, only looked up to see who was in the room. They were all present when she died. Gregor, Mara and Daniel. A rainy night in autumn. Rain that stopped and left the chestnut trees outside the hospital stained in streaks of liquorice black. A strange reunion, sitting around the bed, watching her last moments, holding hands, all four of them in a circle, free-falling like parachutists and finally letting her go. They stayed on after she was gone, sitting without a word while Mara cried. They embraced each other in that great emptiness with the long, final breath still lingering like an inaudible whisper in the room.

Thirty-two

Coming back is the hardest thing. After such a long time away, the moment of return seems awkward, mistimed, only half fulfilled. It's not easy to step back into the physical world, to feel the substance of life rather than the dream of life, to match up the touch world with the inner world. The returning partner has become a ghost, a shape in the imagination, a desire, a longing waiting to be converted into reality.

When Gregor's father returned from Russian captivity after the war, he was unable to feel anything. He had learned to suppress his dreams in order to survive the extreme hardship of the prison camp. He had watched other men succumb to the heights of longing and turned himself into an expert at wanting less, a denier of desire, a brilliant underestimater, sustained only by what mattered most, the thought of his wife and son waiting for him.

After his release, when he found his wife in Nuremberg and finally walked in the door, it felt like a fake. The embrace seemed unreal. It was too much to believe and he was unable to enter into his own luck, could not understand how he was still alive while millions of others had died. He hardly noticed his surroundings: the table, the two chairs, the stove and the bed at the opposite end of the single-room apartment. There was no sink and the water

244

had to be carried from the bathroom on the landing. And although these alone were luxuries beyond his imagination, he could only see what had been lost and what needed to be improved. She seemed in shock as much as she was in happiness, cried repeatedly and tried to smile, thanked God for bringing him back and said he looked very gaunt. He remained in a kind of waiting room, like a deep-sea diver spending mandatory time below the surface to decompress before being permitted to rise up.

Gregor stared at him constantly. He knew how lucky he was to have a father, to be crushed in his arms with misjudged force. He was excited to see this man shaving and sitting down at the table, eating bread slowly, chewing with a blank expression. He listened to him coughing, watched him lighting up a cigarette, examined hands, ears, nostrils, taking everything into his belonging with such eagerness that his mother had to tell him to stop, to give his father some time. He saw him taking off his shoes to rub his feet. Saw his big shadow cast against the wall of the room by the lamp on the table. Watched him getting into bed with his mother, taking his own place beside her, while he lay on a cushion on the floor, fully awake. In the middle of the night he got up and stood by the bed for a long time, listening to him breathing, his face only inches away from his own, until his father jumped awake with fright and told him to go back to sleep.

His father told them of his capture, how his leg was caught in a wire fence when he heard the wheels of a tank coming up like the sound of bells ringing right behind him, how he would have gone under those steel straps if he had not ripped himself away at the last moment, tearing into his calf. In a cloud of diesel fumes he received a blow to the chin that broke his jaw. But he was glad of being alive, almost glad of the pain, too, because it meant the war was over at last. His stories of endurance confirmed life, but they almost meant more to him than being alive itself, as though the living sometimes envied the dead. He would always remain more war veteran than father, more soldier than lover.

It was difficult to accept any warmth. It took weeks before she could hold his hand and stroke it. He felt the comfort of her presence in the bed beside him, but he had become so trained on deprivation that he could not surrender to the intimacy of her body or take possession of what he wanted most. They seemed to fear each other and threw themselves into their work instead, substituting material pleasures for the honesty of love. Between them lay the nightmare of war, the bombing, the horrors of the front which he had experienced. He woke up with those intruder memories every night. He felt only defeat, shame, the cramped, airless awareness of being wrong.

They were restored by the ordinary things. By shopping. By walking through furniture shops and car showrooms. By cake every Sunday. They stayed up late at night listening to live boxing on the American Army radio stations. They loved going out to the forests. The innocence of nature. The optimism of children. Gregor at the table doing his homework, writing with his head bent over the exercise book.

How could she tell him that this was not his own son? How could she destroy that fragile story of survival by telling him the truth?

Maybe there is no such thing as returning. It's impossible to go back to what was before, like undoing war, like repairing history. After the Berlin Wall came down, after the euphoria of instant love in the streets, it became clear for the first time how far both parts of the same country had drifted apart in the intervening years. The people in the East seemed more eager and more in love with new things, less cynical, less cool. They had their own ways of being frugal and stocking food, their own idea of bargains, their own kind of intelligence and their own damage. They spoke the same language but with different meaning.

When Thorsten first met Katia in Berlin amid the celebrations, they knew instantly without having to say very much that he was from the East and she was from the West. It was part of the attraction that when they spoke to each other in German, they still had to translate some of the expressions. There were different words for so many things, different concepts, different superlatives. As they fell in love and got married, they created a new family language of their own. Their work forced them to spend time apart. Long before they moved to the farm, Thorsten spent a year as an intern in Bremen while Katia continued teaching in her home town of Köln, so he often had to commute home in his spare time to see her and the baby Johannes. Life moved on in large sections of time and he could hardly catch up before he had to leave again.

When Juli recently had to go to Istanbul for a funeral, she was away for two days and it seemed to Daniel like an eternity. After a few hours it felt to him as though he might never see her again. Walking through the streets of a different city with thousands of other people around her, she seemed to belong to those who laid eyes on her at that very moment. That same evening he discovered he could not remember her face. He tried to visualise her smiling at him, but his imagination lacked the ability to recreate the features which had become so familiar. He could remember all kinds of vivid parts of her. The kinetic texture of her skin as she slid into her jeans, the imprint of her nipple in the palm of his hand, the curve of her neck, but not her face.

Perhaps the face is too much of a disguise. Something which is constantly in motion, a story unfinished, a mask, a representation full of incoherence and guessing, more in the realm of fiction than fact.

When Gregor returned to Berlin after his long time abroad, there was a familiar tension in the architecture, in the sound of the underground doors closing, in the echo of street names. The city was still full of excitement and confusion after the Wall had come down. He felt like a tourist and an inhabitant at the same time. Everything reminded him of Mara. He could see her face, like a portrait accompanying him around the streets. For years he had not had any dreams at night. He wondered if all that brain activity had stopped or if he had got out of the habit and suppressed them. Back in Berlin he found himself waking up once more with an overflow of illogical imagery in his head. Whole movies full of strange, half-material, time-travelling realities. He saw Mara vividly in his thoughts, in every crowd, on every platform. Merely walking down certain streets brought back random images of great inti-macy, highlights re-enacted with great precision in his memory. Insane, unrepeatable moments which seemed more real now than when they actually occurred. He recalled standing in the doorway of a bookshop with her one night on the way home from a concert, a hasty, insur-gent act. He even found himself going back to see if the bookshop still existed, to see where they had stood once in a different time and where he had almost left his trumpet behind. It was enough to push him beyond the boundaries of memory, back into the physical world. Never before had he felt so much alive in the present, with his feet on the ground, living in the real world of touch and taste. Her presence was everywhere. He could clearly recall the rounded shape of her lower lip and the sound of her breath beside his ear. He could recall inhaling the scent of her hair and the height of her head and the unique angle in which he had to lean down towards her face.

She had almost become too real. When they began to meet again, there was an awkward distance between them, as though memory could never catch up with reality. Painful reunions in which things would have to be said first and explained, apologies made before that gap could be closed. There was a duty to make up for lost time and to convert themselves back into living beings. After such a long time, he had to put the absence behind them before they could exist in the same place on earth, breathing the same air.

His solitude had become an obstacle. He was afraid of her forgiveness, afraid of her loyalty.

'I've left it very late,' he said to her on one of those occasions when he invited her to go for a walk with him. There were things he had to say to her which were difficult to say while she stared into his eyes across the table of some café, so it was better to walk with both of them looking ahead in the same direction at the path in the forest.

'I don't really deserve your company,' he said.

'We're here now, aren't we?'

He had expressed his regret before in letters. But these words needed to fall between them, out loud, in her presence.

'I'm sorry that I ruined everything for you,' he said.

'You made it up to your mother,' she said. 'That's important to me. You and Daniel are talking, that's what matters most.'

What really mattered was that he had come back, that they were walking side by side, that his physical presence was also a confirmation of her life.

'I still believe you,' she said to him with a great surge of emotion. 'I have always believed your story, Gregor. I never doubted it. Even though I never found the proof, I still believe that you're Jewish and that you were an orphan.'

He was shocked by that declaration. It was her way of saying that she still loved him, but instead it sounded as though she loved an effigy, a story, a version of Gregor that had existed in the imagination long ago. He could not get himself to say anything, and maybe he had gone beyond caring about those things. Her devotion to his story seemed to distance them, preventing them from being together without judgement, without that ancient duty to establish an identity, to explain, to say who you are. It was as if life was always merely some kind of confirmation of status rather than just a flow of air and words and time and careless love between people. Perhaps she had become more of an obstacle in the meantime, keeping them apart with her obsession with the past.

He started going to a late-night bar called the Pinguin. He could not get out of the habit of staying awake, spending time in this half-light, under the mirrored globe hanging from the ceiling. A big disco sun rotating continuously, sending yellow pennies of light circling around the walls and bottles and faces, sweeping across the floor and leaping onto the seats.

He has become part of this late-night shrine of rock himself now, the hall of has-beens, the place in which everything has gone by, eclipsed by cultural innovation accelerating into the future. The world has rushed on into a new set of obsessions. When Gregor was growing up, the planet seemed like an enormous place, full of sections all devoted to staying apart with their own culture and their own separate identities. North America was far away. Peru was unimaginably remote. The past was close behind, was the phrase from a song which described how everyone felt. Nowhere is far away now. Even the most distant places in Alaska are on everyone's doorstep, over-filmed, over-reported.

In the Pinguin bar, people still come here to pay homage to their era, listening to the sounds of their own time, recalling moments of great potential and adventure. For a few hours late at night, they can still imagine the world being a big arena, full of undiscovered places. They reimagine their own innocence and their own big-eyed wonder. A poster of Elvis in his tight, glittering white suit just inside the door. A reign of icons all along the walls. A black-and-white Telecaster guitar propped up at forty-five degrees on a ledge over the doorway like a musical anti-aircraft weapon. The decor has not been touched up since the high tide of punk in the eighties when people like Bowie and Depeche Mode came here regularly. The toilets are the same. Same plastic sofas. Same Formica bar, dotted with cigarette burns. In the corner, the same bumper car, rescued from some carnival, come to a halt for the night and turned into a table surrounded by bar stools.

It's not a live-performance venue, but once in a while when the mood strikes him, Gregor picks up a guitar and sings 'Should I Stay or Should I Go?'. A question they all ask themselves. One of the other patrons at the bar doing air drums on the counter with his hands. We are never more than the sum of our aspirations. Three-minute peaks of clarity in which everything seems possible. He has become a playlist of those temporary successes and failures, a man who has left no significant mark on the culture tree himself, but who has been a witness to a time in transformation. He has gone through all the self-searching profundity, wondering if anything was achieved in the end. He has been through the mental hall of mirrors and come out the other side. The man with no answers. The man with no explanations.

Since he has come back, he looked up some of his old friends in the music business, but most of them have moved on to other things. He still plays a few gigs around the city, but he gets most of his satisfaction from teaching now. He's happy to teach everything from Chopin to Cobain. The students love him because he gives them real gossip about the music scene, how they lived and how some of the most famous songs were constructed. He's got himself into trouble once or twice with such gossip and parents have phoned up the school in outraged tones, wondering if some of it is appropriate. He drifted into a conversation with his students one day about the cult of groupies and starlets around some of the great legends. Told them about one woman keeping a lock of hair from each one of her conquests. Another young woman who made a plaster cast of each rock star's penis. When they asked him who had the biggest, he told them it was Jimi Hendrix, by a mile, and then the principal started getting the heat from the parents. But in the end, he defended Gregor and said it was all part of the education of young people to be aware of what their forefathers did, not only in the Second World War, but also in the great madness of the post-war era of protest and cult worship.

One of the band members Gregor played with years ago in Berlin had taken up a job working in a school for disabled children. He goes there now and again to play the trumpet for them and he can see the music instantly taking shape in their reactions, maybe the best audience he's ever had. He has accompanied his friend taking one of the older children out around the city, shouting under bridges to hear the echo, sitting in a café with fizzy apple juice, listening to the profane joy of slurping sounds, when the straw reaches the end of the glass and there is nothing left only ice.

Mara surprised him late one afternoon at his apartment. Left her bike in the courtyard. Stood in front of his door carrying a basket with a bottle of wine and the ingredients for a salad. Heard music on the piano coming from inside and decided to wait there, listening until it came to an end. When she rang the bell, it turned out that he had a student with him.

'Just give me a few minutes,' he said.

So she waited in the kitchen until he was finished and ushered the student out. When he brought her into the living room, she put her arms around him and kissed his cheek, an embrace that was like an inverse measure of the distance between them. She gave him the news, the family gossip. She told him that she had brought a salad and some wine. Stood looking around, taking possession of his environment, examining the guitars he had standing in each corner, commenting on the brightness of the apart- ment. The tall balcony doors were open and the voices came in from the tables outside the bar in the street below, as though he still needed the protection of public spaces around him.

He explained to her that the student he had been teaching could hardly play music at all and was suicidal. It was clear that he would never become a musician, even though his heart was set on it.

'Terrible to see a young person like that,' Gregor said to her. 'He's unable to keep a beat. He tries his best, sticking his tongue out all the time as he plays, but even after an hour we've hardly got any further really. He's like somebody with a learning disability. I see him twice a week, but I can't charge any money for it. We're making some progress, I suppose. Slow progress, and maybe that's good.'

She listened to him talking and walked around picking up some of his belongings as if this was the highest, most intimate contact achievable between two people. She saw his passport, his medication, his diary lying open with all his meetings entered in. In her hands she examined the Russian icon. Then she picked up the souvenir harmonica. Even blew a childish note into it and reclaimed, with that one gesture, all the impetus of their former lives together.

And maybe this was the moment of immortality, the moment where they began to convert each other back into real people. Nothing is real in the end, not until it's reported. Nobody is real unless they have a witness to their lives. We exist only in the imagination. We may inhabit the physical world, we may be flesh-and-blood creatures in this material place, but it is along the axis of imagination that we come to life. We can only coexist, at most, reflected in the blur of human interaction and media events around us. Gregor Liedmann has been brought to life by Mara, by his family, by the external story created around him, existing only inside those experiences he has shared with others. These are the ingredients of his identity, his narrative, that strange human genius of belonging.

And maybe for the first time ever, with Mara in the same room, he was standing in the real world. While she walked back into the kitchen and took out plates and wine glasses he finally stopped being a ghost. While he watched her slicing radishes into minted white coins, while she smiled and lifted up her wine glass in both hands, both elbows on the table, he felt for the first time that he was at home.

Thirty-three

They're washing the dishes now. The remote clatter of pots comes down the hallway from the kitchen along with their voices. Bursts of laughter drifting through the house as they stack plates and slip cutlery into drawers. The doors of presses opening and closing, and glasses ringing. They are not laughing at anything in particular, nothing that might be remembered later on, only laughing for the sake of it.

At the other end of the house, Gregor, Mara and Daniel are going through the contents of the house in Nuremberg. She unties a green ribbon around a package of papers containing nothing but lists. Big childish handwriting, a series of words sloping down along the page. Another list saying thank you for the 'sweets, pencils, rubber, folder, Gregor'. A further list of things to do. 'Fold up my clothes, brush my teeth, say my prayers, go to sleep, dream about ships' – all ticked off. A list of names. 'Thilo, Gudrun, Marlies, Werner, Wilhelm', with Thilo and Marlies crossed out. Followed by another list of objects on a birthday wish list, such as 'mouth organ, a torch to see in the dark, a telescope, a book about outer space or stars, a book about bears, not any sad book about animals, not any book about losing a rowing race, thank you'.

Outside the window, the others are passing by now, carrying a small table and some folding chairs. Martin is singing to himself. Thorsten is heard telling the others to bring glasses. At the same moment, Johannes comes down the hallway, standing at the door.

'Papa says we're all going to look at the stars.'

'Tell them we're coming soon,' she replies. 'Just another few minutes, that's all.'

The boy answers with another bit of adult language.

'I can well believe that you want to be alone,' he says, full of innocence, then runs off happily.

Mara smiles. Daniel has become impatient again and tries to leave.

'Jesus, we'll never get out of the past now.'

'No, wait, Daniel. I want you to see this.'

She takes another box from the sideboard and places it on the table. The letter G is written on the side. One by one, she takes out the contents, each carefully folded and separated with a layer of thin blue paper, gone crisp with age now and smelling of mothballs. First, she takes out a jumper with three red buttons on one shoulder. Then a scarf and a sailor's cap. She holds them all up for Gregor to see.

'I never looked at these properly until yesterday,' she says. 'These must be the clothes you were found in.'

Daniel sighs.

'I don't fucking believe this,' he says, watching more items emerging from the box and being placed on the table. 'Here we go again. We're living in a museum.'

'There must be some reason why she kept them,' Mara says, ignoring him.

'It's just a box of clothes, Mama.'

A pair of trousers, socks and shoes. The shoes are polished and filled with pieces of newspaper to keep the shape, as though Gregor might come back and wear them again.

'There must have been so many displaced children at the end of the war,' Mara continues, taking out more things from the bottom of the box. A tin trumpet. A wooden truck. And some later items such as swimming certificates, music prizes and a picture of Gregor with his friends on a boating trip along the Rhine. She picks up the clothes again, examining each one of them carefully.

'Maybe she thought it was better for you not to know.'

Gregor's mother had come from a time when it was a custom to protect children and keep them safe from information. A generation of hope and mistakes, of religion and obedience and privacy, of diaries and secrets and love in the dark.

'She must have known that we would find them.'

'Please, Mara. Put them away,' Gregor says.

'Have a look at this,' she tries once again.

She turns the trousers inside out and points out a tiny stitch in blue thread, almost invisible, with the letters JB.

'Did your mother stitch this in?'

'My mother?' Gregor says. 'I have no idea. These trousers could have belonged to anyone. They may have been handed down.'

'Could this be some Jewish name?' Mara suggests.

Are these the limits of existence? A tiny, unsourced mark on the inside of a pair of trousers. A small signifier from the past still fighting against forgetting, still hoping to contain meaning, still clamouring for space in our memory. History is the question we keep trying to answer. It is the shape of our imagination, the accusation in our existence, the guesswork of our decisions, the measure of improvement and decline. We are the answer to history, this corridor of correction, full of intuition and invention and handed-down instruction. Our identity is our instability: the longing, the adjustment, the attempt to answer the question from which we have come, the trace of ourselves left behind.

Gregor takes the trousers out of Mara's hands and places them back in the box.

'Mara,' he says, 'Thank you for keeping these things.'

Here is the one vital piece of proof they needed. She has kept the memory of a survivor alive in this room, made him real again.

And maybe this is the greatest human achievement of all, to reconstruct the missing in our imagination. He has been brought back to life, this dead Jewish boy. He is standing right there among them, this living monument to the memory of those whose real identity has been erased.

They look at each other, all three of them, as if they have suddenly made a discovery about themselves which had eluded them so far. Daniel smiles. He places one arm around his father and then places the other around his mother.

'They're waiting for us,' he says.

He leads them both out of the room and closes the door. He takes them through the hallway back towards the kitchen where Thorsten stands with an expression of great enthusiasm, holding bottles of wine in both hands. He tells them that he has set up the small table outside in the field. Chairs and glasses for everyone. Beer mats to put over the glasses to stop the insects from falling in. He says the mosquitoes have lost all their aggression at this time of the year and they can sit there for a while, looking at the stars and the glow of light on the horizon coming from Berlin.

'Hang on,' Gregor says. 'Let me get the trumpet.'

The light is fading now. A monochrome blue that makes Gregor wonder if his mushroom allergy has come back. But then he steps out to discover that it is the moon. He returns carrying the trumpet and a guitar. They stand in the kitchen like schoolchildren, waiting for instructions. He hands the guitar to Daniel and tells him to play a simple progression of chords. He rushes around taking out pots, giving each person an instrument. They understand his plan. Johannes is holding the white enamel lid of a bread bin in one hand, a wooden spoon in the other, banging the lid so that the throbbing vibrations carry through his arm.

They are arranged in a line, a troop of eccentric country musicians, ready for the march. Everyone ranked in order of their height, with Martin at the very end carrying a drum fashioned from a bin, hastily strapped to his belly. Johannes in front and Thorsten somewhere in the middle with an old washboard that he has produced from the storeroom. Gregor takes his place at the top of the line and blows a stout note of departure. The first, brash note of an old Balkan wedding march, followed by the raucous band behind him, beating their wild accompaniment, scraping and banging on the way out towards the orchard.

They have gone to bless the trees. A protection march. A procession of pale blue faces, tramping through the orchard, past the ladders and the wheelbarrows. Juli knocking a spoon against a stainless-steel pot. Mara with a child's tambourine in one hand and jar of coffee beans in the other. Martin banging and sending ecstatic animal sounds into the sky. Daniel strumming wild punk rhythms and Katia, carrying the drum of her belly out in front, clacking two wooden boards together. The humming sound of the trumpet settling along the silvery branches. A fat, warm, bulging word in a brass language which is understood by all creatures, even the worms inside the apples. A long, living note spreading out across the flat landscape and floating away beyond the blue roofs of the farm buildings.

Acknowledgements

Special thanks to Hans Christian Oeser, Georg Reuchlein, Petra Eggers, Henning Ahrens, Rainer Milzkott, Christiane Wartenberg, Reinhard Förster, Moira Reilly, Peter Straus and Nicholas Pearson.

What's next?

Tell us the name of an author you love

and we'll find your next great book.

'A RARE BOOK …
ALMOST UNBEARABLY
MOVING, WONDERFULLY
UNDERSTATED, DAMN NEAR PERFECT'
Rachel Seiffert, *Financial Times*

1945. At the end of the Second World War, bombs rip through the
Berlin sky. A two-year-old boy drifts from dream into death; his mother
abandoned to the land of the living. She flees to the south, where her
father finds a young foundling among the refugee trains to replace the
boy. He makes her promise not to tell anyone – including her husband,
still fighting on the Russian Front. No one will ever know . . .

2008. Gregor Liedmann – revolutionary, runaway – is now a Jewish
man in his sixties. On a single day spent gathering fruit with family
and friends, Gregor retraces his life, sifting through fact and memory
to establish the truth. In the calm of the orchard, Gregor struggles to
unlock the secret of his past, in a compelling story of lost identity.

'Stirringly honest and engaging' *Scotsman*

'[A] novelist of great delicacy, originality and
thoughtfulness … oddly consoling'
Hermione Lee, *Guardian*

£7.99
ISBN 978-0-00-731470-6

9 780007 314706 >

FSC